The Shadow of
Nanteos

Best wishes,

Joe Black

I Sian Busby,
cyfaill dewr a haelionus

The Shadow of
Nanteos

JANE BLANK

yLolfa

With thanks to Jeremy, Cari, Catherine, Andrew,
Claire, Deborah, Norman, Ruth, Nia, Nigel, Eirian,
Eifion, Lefi, Robert, Hannah and Shane

First impression: 2015
© Jane Blank & Y Lolfa Cyf., 2015

Cover design: Tanwen Haf

ISBN: 978 1 78461 171 2

Published and printed in Wales
on paper from well-maintained forests by
Y Lolfa Cyf., Talybont, Ceredigion SY24 5HE
e-mail ylolfa@ylolfa.com
website www.ylolfa.com
tel 01970 832 304
fax 832 782

CHAPTER ONE

THE METAL CAGE squeaks and groans in the wind. Suspended from a pole at the crossroads, the highest point on the road from Devil's Bridge, it twists slowly on its chain. Through the bars a skull stares out. Eyes long gone, the fine teeth leer.

In the pass below, a coach with outriders and a laden wagon seems hardly to move against the dark bulk of the mountain. The wind is a constant moan that is by now hardly consciously heard by the travellers, but its presence is felt as a low, pernicious anxiety. The rain has failed to fall, but threatens still in the layers of grey sky. The land here is desecrated by the pits and lumps of lead mining, its contours misshapen by heaps of slag and winding gear, its natural colours blackened by the tear of a conduit, a deep shaft's mouth. Sometimes a long, grey structure disturbs the rough moorland, smoke rising feebly from each gable end. Here and there a small cottage has carved out a patch of sickly green, a circle of cultivation against the rust of bracken.

The cart's wheels make a deafening noise on the unmade road as it lumbers up hill. The faces of the people attending it are strained, the coach filthy. A powerfully built man mounted on a heavy horse shouts out, commands with his whip. The coach halts. He dismounts and helps to heave the door open against the wind as a woman, wrapped hard against the weather, climbs down. She turns to steady a boy of about eleven as he throws himself out. Last to leave is another woman, perhaps older than the first, her shape more defined, something more angular and stronger glimpsed in the side of her face beneath the heavy hat. This second woman is the only one of the party to look up and out from between the close walls of the pass. She lifts her hand to her brow, shielding her eyes as she focuses on the gibbet, high on the horizon. But the sun is gleaming, low and red behind it and she sees only the dark, crucified silhouette. The man leans inside before securing the door against the cold, lifting his whip as a signal to the driver. As they leave, two small, white faces, one above the other, press against the window. The coach moves on, the women walking to relieve the horses, the man by their side, leading his. The cloaks are heavy and dull-coloured, their boots strong, plain and dirty.

Meanwhile, in a sheltered valley near the coast, the grand, brand-new mansion of Nanteos prepares. Despite the chill, every door is propped open. In every room, it seems, figures are moving purposefully, just beneath haste. A man works down through the house, lighting the fires that have been made ready. As each is lit, he scans the room and then shuts the door on it, his gloved hand leaving no mark. In a room at the back of the house, two women dress the blue bed. As she smoothes the covers flat for the last time, the young girl's hand lingers. She can see her reflection in the heavy mirror on the far wall. She moves her head slowly, watching the late afternoon sunlight change the shadows of her face. A clanging of metal on metal from the kitchen breaks the spell. With the placing of lavender bags underneath the pillows, the women hurry downstairs.

Wine is brought into the front room to warm. Here the fire has been burning all afternoon and finally the shutters are closed, the drapes pulled across and the screens put in place. As cloths are laid over the food in the dining room, the servants gather in the outer hallway. There is not much noise, but much restless movement as hands smooth down clothes, fingers tuck straying hair into caps. All eyes focus on the main entrance, where the open door frames a section of the low ridge with its patch of sky glowing as the sun drops. Standing in the doorway, black against the sky, is the figure of a man. Cai is broad, better dressed than the others and perfectly still.

By now the coach party has moved down from the pass. The tough grass and grey of rock has given way to the damp, dead yellow of lowland autumn. In the distance is the sea, glimpsed as a ridge of blue grey between the hills over which the sun is going down. The heavy horses have no problem holding the vehicle on the gentle decline and the women and young boy have returned inside. The children chatter excitedly in Welsh. The coach stops outside a lodge which guards the fine gates of a mansion and the two older children clamber to open the window and lean out. The toddler pulls himself up on the stiff bodice of his mother's dress and stands, his feet slipping off her knee. She laughs. Staff from the main house and lodge greet the family and take them inside as a small trunk is unloaded and taken in with them. Both coach and wagon continue up the drive.

Mari, the younger woman, takes the children upstairs and, helped by a maid from the hall, has them quickly washed and changed into fresh clothes. Upstairs his manservant John, who has been sent up from London in advance, helps William Powell dress. William washes himself to the waist. His chest is lean and unmarked, the smooth lines hardly uninterrupted by hair. His servant shaves him, scrubs his nails and he puts on a fresh shirt, britches and coat; pulls on new boots. Finally he dampens down, scents and combs his hair and John fits a new wig to his head.

In another room a newly appointed lady's maid is washing the seated Elizabeth. Her soiled travelling clothes are in a pile by the door and her shift is pulled open as face, neck, breasts and under her arms are carefully sponged. The girl takes her mistress' feet from the warm bowl and washes each in turn, scented water trickling between the toes and back into the basin. Then Elizabeth crouches over the water, her petticoats lifted, and washes herself as the maid shakes out her fresh clothes. The towel is new and soft as she pats herself dry. With a great effort of will, she stands still as a tailor's dummy as the girl dresses her in a fresh shift, ties on her hooped petticoat and pulls on her stays. As the girl bends to tie the ribbon over her stockings, she lets out a gasp. Elizabeth looks down and laughs as the girl's head appears, red and flustered from under the layers of undergarments.

"The mark?" she asks, smiling. The maid nods, biting her lip. "All as God intended, I assure you – I had it from birth." But the girl stands, frozen to the spot. "Don't worry, Elin. I am no witch, I promise you." Still the girl has not moved. "Come now, we are keeping people waiting. Tend to your work!"

Impatiently she lifts up her own skirts and Elin bows down again, hiding her face beneath the clothes. Finally Elizabeth is laced into her bodice, stockings on, neatly tied with ribbon, and new shoes on her feet. As her hair is being dressed, William comes to stand in the doorway, watches her. She is quivering with excitement as she smiles at her husband from the mirror.

The two older children are running wildly down the stairs, pursued by Mari who is carrying the toddler and still trying to arrange her own hair. A smart, light chaise has pulled up outside the lodge. William waits by the door, his only movement the slap of gloves against boots. Watching him closely, the children quieten and when Elizabeth finally arrives they all stand for a moment. They are ready. No one moves, not even the servants. Suddenly Little William gives a screech of excitement and, like a gunshot in a rookery, everything happens at once: William helps

Elizabeth, Mari and his children into the vehicle and gets in after them, slamming the door; the staff from the house and lodge load the trunk onto a baggage wagon and the horses, never immune to tension, start to shift from leg to leg, tossing their heads and calling.

As the chaise moves beyond the gatehouse and workers from the estate gather to acknowledge them, Elizabeth is still fastening her gloves. William stops her hand, draws a glove off, and fits his fingers to hers. He clenches them rhythmically, absently; she feels his blunt, newly-cut nails in her palm. The coach moves down the long drive. Its windows are open now and the children lean out, the older two half-remembering the huge lake glimpsed again and again through the trees. Suddenly there is a gap in the woods and with a squeal, Thomas, the eldest, points to the mansion. It is lost again for a moment, the coach slows, then finally they see the candlelit house properly. It seems to glow, light in nearly every window, the huge door framed by elegant columns. Figures surge out from the yard and towards the drive. There is noise everywhere: dogs bark from the kennels; the horses, alarmed by so much activity and sensing food, whinny and snort; the coach man is calling out, trying to control them and inside the children finally give reign to their excitement. As William settles his new wig, Elizabeth takes back her hand and puts on her glove, fastening it tightly and flexing both her hands inside the new leather. She is ready.

As the coach pulls up with a flourish at the front of the house, the servants move forwards to form a formal tableau of welcome. All eyes follow Cai as he walks down the steps between them and approaches the coach, his boots crunching loudly on the gravel. As the door opens, Thomas tumbles out, stumbles. Cai helps him up, then extends a hand to Catherine, a girl of ten, who gives a small curtsey as she alights. Cai smiles and reaches in to steady the blushing nursemaid, Mari, and the toddler, who hides his face immediately in her shoulder when he sees the stranger. William appears from the other side.

Cai bows to him. "Welcome to Nanteos, Sir."

William inclines his head by way of reply. He straightens his clothes as his eyes move over the house.

Everywhere there are excited greetings and a burst of activity as the heavy wagon that has followed them across the mountains with their belongings is sighted, straining up the drive. But Cai is still with the chaise and finally it is Elizabeth who appears in the doorway, looks up at him as he reaches in to help her. He takes her hand and she holds his gaze: it is no longer a youth whose handsome face she sees, set against the brilliant new facade of Nanteos.

"Welcome, Mistress of Nanteos." His voice is deep as he grins at her; his face brown as a labourer's yet clean shaven, his hair thick and well cut. A gentleman.

She smiles back at him, managing to keep her hand firm, surprise at the change in him showing only slightly in her raised brows, and jumps to the ground. Quickly she looks away and arranges her dress. Cai steps back as William joins her, takes her arm and together, their children brought into line behind them, they ascend the steps to take possession of their new home.

In the inner hallway more servants gather and Elizabeth is able to greet some by name. She moves down the line – a brief greeting here, a small compliment or a smile for those she does not recognise. All the time William stands with his back to the main door, his valet waiting to collect his hat, gloves, cloak. When Elizabeth has reached the end of the line, William removes his hat and steps into the middle of the room.

"Good people of Nanteos, I thank you for your welcome. We

have all suffered a loss and indeed still smart from the grief of it. Inevitably any estate is inherited on the back of loss, but I wish to assure you that my brother's fine work will be continued here. Your previous Mistress has given a fine account of you all."

He stops for a moment. Elizabeth has joined him and speaks privately to him. He nods, then continues. "You will see some new faces, trusted staff come with us from England (though some were born as Welsh as yourselves). You need have no fear – these servants will not replace you here; they will complement you." He turns quickly to Elizabeth, then back. "Yes, that is all. May I wish you all prosperity."

There is a murmured return of this greeting from the staff and a shallow curtsey, passing as a wave down the line, eyes lowering as the family moves past them further into the house. Many though stare openly at Mari and John; despite what the master has said, they are aliens, surely come to replace them. The nurse maid is rescued by Catherine and excuses herself as she is dragged away by the hand.

William turns to his wife, whispers, "It is ours, my love!"

They move through the downstairs. There is activity in nearly every room, the distant sound of the children exploring, shouting; the dragging of trunks and heavy objects on the floor above.

Finally William and Elizabeth ascend the stairs with an unnatural slowness, moving in step. His hand runs along the graceful curve of the banister and she holds his arm, like a couple going towards their wedding chamber. Everything gleams or sparkles; it is all new, the house not even quite finished. The music room on the first floor is the most wonderful. Designed as an Italian salon, it is the depth of two rooms. Like all the main bedrooms, it looks out towards the front of the house, across the lawns, over the river and to the green ridge beyond. William closes the door and all other sounds are suddenly distant. He turns to Elizabeth, for a moment the two look intently at one another, holding hands tightly. They cross to the window and look out. His body is pressed up against her back, her hand reaching into his hair. He bends to kiss the nape of her neck as she keeps looking out of the window, watching Cai talking with one of the stable boys, his hands moving on the pregnant belly of a mare. The animal whinnies softly, her skin ripples, quivering in front of the hands as they search across her. He bends underneath her, and she shifts and lifts her leg to him. As he looks up he sees Elizabeth, her head tipped back slightly, resting on her husband's shoulder. He is the first to look away as she smiles down on him.

Thomas bursts in, "Come and see my rooms, Mummy. There's a rat's hole and… everything!"

Mari appears in the doorway.

"Is there food prepared for the children?"

"Yes, Ma'am."

"And the bedrooms?"

"Almost done, but they'll have to share for tonight. Yours are ready, Ma'am."

"Mine overlooking the stable yard? I like to hear the horses coming and going."

"As you asked."

"Thank you, Mari. And how is your room?"

"It's very comfortable. Thank you. Towards the back of the house, with the chimney running through it. So warm!"

It is night. The house is almost at rest, just the echo of servants still moving around; the fire shifting, a horse kicking at a stable door. Her new maid is unpacking in Elizabeth's bedroom as she is preparing for bed, but when the woman goes to help her undress, she dismisses her. She rubs lotion on her bare arms, her throat and behind her neck. Though richly furnished, the blue room is small, facing the side – not a room designed for the mistress of the house. The dim candlelight only serves to make more vivid the uncommon contrast between the paleness of her face and the darkness of her hair. There is a light tap at the door. Elizabeth does not turn round but watches in the mirror as William enters and closes the door softly. He crosses to her.

"You are not undressed!"

"That is a task I saved for you."

His laugh is deep as he stands behind her, his fingers brushing the back of her neck. "Close your eyes," he says softly. She laughs. "No, close them, Elizabeth. I have something for you." He takes her by the wrists and puts her hands deep inside a velvet bag. She brings out a polished box. "Open it."

He holds the candle for her. Compartment after compartment of jewels glint. Slowly she walks her fingers across them, as though their tips could count the gems' worth. "The Nanteos treasure?" she says at last. He nods, his eyes gleam with pleasure. "Beautiful! But why are they come to me? What about Mary?"

"They go with the house. Thomas is dead; the jewels don't leave with the widow. They belong to the new mistress now, to Elizabeth of Nanteos."

She laughs incredulously, holds up a handful to the light, separates the strings of pearls. "A field." She puts it back. "A mill. A farm." She opens a velvet box and a gasp escapes her. "Oh… surely a ton of dressed ore!" He stops her hand, closing his fist over hers. Inside the diamonds bite into her skin. She whispers, "A field, a cottage, a farm…"

He reaches for her hair and she bends over for him to undress her, unlacing and wrenching open her stays at the back. As he turns to see to himself, she kneels on the bed facing him, her clothes slipping from her shoulders, pulling the box towards her and hanging her body with treasure. One after another the gems come glinting or gleaming from the box. Whilst the diamonds are brash even in candlelight, the garnets and pearls glow against the shadowed hollows of her skin.

She moves back and settles herself against the deep pillows, slowly rolling up her shift, opening her legs. She watches his face as he bends forwards to look at her, forcing himself to take his time. The candle is unsteady in his hand as he pushes her knees apart.

"Don't set it alight!" she laughs as he moves the flame nearer.

Later he holds her head tight in his hands as he moves on her, his eyes thirsting for every flicker of expression in her face. A rope of pearls is caught, breaks under them – but it can be mended.

Afterwards, his elbows give way and he lies suddenly leaden, like a bullock she saw slaughtered, floored with a single blow from the blunt side of an axe. She looks to the window. The low bank behind the house looms dense and black. She will have wild flowers planted there, watch them spread year by year, watch the breeze dip their fragile, gawky heads. The sky is not completely dark – long tendrils of cloud are spun across the night through which the moon glows grey. William's weight pains her arm, but she does not move: nothing can spoil this moment.

CHAPTER TWO

IT IS MORNING at Nanteos, the sun bright, but at this time of the year no longer strong. Though the house martins are still here, the birdsong is already different: the individual voices cutting through are strident, more urgent. William and Cai are ready to ride. Both are mounted on well-bred horses, but William's is finer and less skittish. William is giving orders: to the outdoor servants; to the building manager, always gesturing with his crop. His son appears in riding gear; Jenkins, the groom by his side. Thomas' boots seem a little too big for him and he walks with straight legs, so they don't rub the back of his knees. The two men leave at a trot, William in front. Though the older man rises to the awkward gait, Cai sits his horse, the creature seeming to spring from leg to leg instead of clipping the ground. They are talking: a good sign.

Elizabeth watches them from the long window on the first landing, two figures becoming smaller against the backdrop of the fine parkland. Men and wagons are moving slowly up the drive towards them – workers coming to finish the house. Everywhere she looks there is activity, each person in her employ. Inside too is a constant restlessness. Though her back is turned, she is aware of soft footfalls on the carpet behind her as servants service the rooms for the day ahead. Though they access the first floor via their own stairs, they must still appear sometimes to do their work. Only one door separates the kitchen from the inner hallway and there is a constant noise from the copper which it appears must be banged and scraped as much as possible. A fat, late fly bangs and bangs itself against the glass. She chooses to set it free.

Two riders canter up the same stretch of isolated road that the family travelled down to take possession of Nanteos only days ago. The surface of the land here is lumpy with rock and pitted by mining. Even the trees look precarious, their colours not right, their lives disturbed at the root. The horses are heading towards the mines. The complex is spread over several acres: the ore processed further down the hillside from the winding gear, at a running stream. People can be seen at their work. From a distance they are moving detritus, part of the surface workings of the mine.

But close up they are ragged and drawn. Indistinct voices speak, shout or call out. Their hands are sorting the lumps of ore, bandaged for protection as they heave on ropes; their backs at strange angles as they struggle to break up rock with hammers for processing or to load the ore onto mules, their feet slipping on the wet tracks as they move across the hillside with the laden animals. Everyone is soaked through – not just with the processes but from the boggy terrain and the high rainfall of this place.

Some watch the riders approaching, glad of a chance to ease their backs and raise their eyes to the sky. William and Cai appear amongst them, their horses foaming with sweat. Cai jumps down and holds the reins for William to alight. Several men come towards them, showing only a slight deference in their manner to the new mine owner. The men have to shout above the noise of the work which continues even though many of the miners have now stopped to see the newcomer. From the still huddle, a warmly-dressed man steps forward. His riding boots are strong and well-made. Cai walks the horses forward a little and introduces him.

"The Reverend Powell. Trevelyan, Sir. Our engineer."

"Congratulations, man. You have improved the figures. The lode is yielding well."

"Yes, Sir, but I think the seam's going to turn. I think it'll cross the stream and go out toward Ystumtuen." William looks quickly at Cai.

"Common land."

"Damn it! How much silver's it yielding, Cai?"

"About seven hundred ounces to the ton."

Trevelyan moves closer, lowering his voice. "Your brother, Sir. He ordered a new survey, but it was suspended."

William turns again to Cai.

"Gogerddan's with us, Sir. It'll be found in our favour."

"It better!"

He stands for a moment in silence. "Do you speak Welsh? A Cornishman are you not?"

"I am. There are many of us in the industry. I understand much – but the speaking is slower to come."

William nods and moves away to look across the valley. He can see other workings in the distance, and far off, the sea of Cardigan Bay. Cai joins him.

"Do you want to see Nant yr Arian as well, before the weather comes in?"

"Yes. Thank you."

He turns back and, taking his hat off, shouts in Welsh to the men and women who have gathered.

"Many thanks to you on behalf of my dead brother for your work here at Goginan. We have a wonderful rich lode with silver in the ore at seven hundred ounces to the ton! I will carry on my brother's good work to protect what my father and grandfather built here; to protect the Nanteos estate. Despite the encroachment upon our land and our livelihood, we will do all we can to secure our rights to the wealth of these hills. The Crown will not take what is rightfully ours!"

There is not much of a reaction from the crowd, only a few mutterings and the occasional cynical smile. William continues.

"In honour of my brother, tomorrow will be a holiday for you all, with pay."

The men cheer heartily at this. Cai bends to speak privately to him; he nods and carries on. "Except that the flood engines need to be manned, and those men will receive double pay." He returns to English. "Mr Trevelyan, please see to it."

Trevelyan nods his assent. A man steps forward to hold William's horse as he mounts. For a moment the workers stand as if waiting for something more.

"Back to work!"

Trevelyan's gestures are clear to even the monoglots amongst them and, oh so slowly, the rhythms of the mine begin again: the rickety hand-pumped windlasses creak and groan; a horse trudges in circles lifting a full kibble of ore and water is driven hard over the undressed stone. Beyond the mine the hills are barren, punctuated occasionally by a smallholding. Rough tracks criss-cross the landscape, weaving between the random piles of stones and rocky hollows that mark centuries of mineral mining.

This time it is the younger man who leads as they follow the contour of the hillside, riding the rough mule track over into the next valley. William's horse is not used to this sort of work, its feet sore and unsteady.

"I should have listened to you!" he shouts.

Cai stops and turns around in the saddle. "Shall we exchange mounts? I find I would like to walk and build up some warmth."

"An honourable lie indeed, young man! No, but I believe that we'll leave Nant yr Arian to another day after all – dear God! What's that!?"

He points to a large gibbet at the crossroads just ahead of them. It is about eight feet in height and from it hangs what remains of a large man. His skeleton is suspended by the skull, held in an iron cage, which creaks and groans as it moves in the wind.

Cai laughs. "Let me introduce Sion y Gof, the blacksmith, from the Dylife mines. He murdered his wife and children and threw them down a disused shaft. Miners found the remains of his family and forced him to make his own 'head-dress'. They hung him in it."

William points to a variety of feathers, stones and animal bones suspended from the pole.

"And what's all this nonsense hanging off it?"

"Miners or their women. Charms to keep bad luck from the workings nearby."

"God alive! These people are backward!" Kicking his reluctant horse forward he brings the whole lot down with his stick. "They're like the negroes in the Indies! My wife's father used to tell us of their nonsensical ways. Stupid fool. I think he believed half of it himself by the end. Pick it up, will you. We'll take it back and burn it."

"Not I!"

William reddens for a moment at the seeming impertinence, then laughs. "I forget sometimes that you're one of them, of the common people. Leave it then, the wind and rain'll take it."

He turns his horse's head towards the sea and slowly they move down, hooves placed carefully for purchase, the riders jolted as the animals' haunches swing from side to side.

Meanwhile, under the ground, men hack at rock. They are nearly naked. Tallow candles fight the dark, lodged in cracks in the walls, wherever a dry spot can be found. Water drips incessantly – the miners' worst enemy; more feared even than fire underground. Though it is often deafening in the seams, during the quiet moments between activity, all ears strain, focusing on the sound of water, for when that drip turns to a trickle, to a torrent, there will be no time left. They heave and load the ore into kibbles for removal to the surface, the iron containers shudder and boom as each lump is thrown in; the winding gear groaning as it raises them. Driven by horse power at the surface, the lift is uneven and the containers lurch, sometimes scraping the sides of the shaft. It is unwise to stand underneath them for a moment longer than necessary. A primitive basket hangs from a rope in the same shaft, out of which Huw, a big man of about twenty, climbs. He is shouting before he even touches the ground.

"The new boss's been, boys. Doesn't look like a clergyman!"

The others laugh.

"Good news is… you want the good news do you?" He makes a dramatic pause. "We've a day off tomorrow to honour the dead!"

"What dead?" calls a voice from the shadows.

"Sir Thomas, of course! You want the bad news?" He pauses again, this time they oblige him with groans and cat-calls. "Someone's got to keep the pumps going!"

"That wouldn't be me, mind, or any of us. We're lode men," comes a voice from the tunnel. Away from the candles concentrated at the shaft entrance, the other men are only voices in the gloom.

Huw replies, "It isn't you, or me, for that matter – it's some lucky bastard who's having double pay for working on his holiday!" He hacks up, spitting the phlegm in disgust.

"There'll be trouble if we don't watch it. It's filling up." A small man, preparing the basket to go back up, joins in.

By now Huw is stripped to the waist, his torso reflecting the candle's dangerously steady light. "Bastards," he mutters. As he moves along the lode other men make way for him at the face, taking on the filling of the empty drum instead. A small man shouts out, pacing his words to find the relative quiet between the bone-quivering clangs of ore as it lands in the metal containers.

"He needs to get the money into the pumps and get that conduit flowing faster over the ore – not wasting time sinking shafts on land he doesn't even know's his. They'll find a seam and then it'll turn out to be Crown land."

"I'd go mad with thinking that!"

The other men are all involved now, throwing in their shilling's worth of wisdom, the words fitting the gaps in the work.

"Don't know how the gentry rest at night."

"I do, boys. On down mattresses next to women smelling of foreign scent! I could mull around a problem like that if I wasn't sleeping on a furze bed."

"Furze bed! You're on wool, man. Your wife spoils you!"

They laugh. As the full load is taken up, scraping the sides with a sound sickening to the ear, a canteen of water is passed around and they gather again in the meagre light at the bottom of the shaft. Even there they are hardly recognisable as individuals, so filthy are they from the mine.

"What'll you do tomorrow whilst the engine men're earning double pay?"

"Me? I'll work out the back. See if I can get manure down."

"Huw?"

"Thought I'd take a spade and do a few exploration

trenches for myself. Never know. Been lucky in a holiday. Might find something."

The others jeer.

In the main hall at the mansion Mari is with the youngest child, William. Mari is dark like Elizabeth, but it is different. Elizabeth's hair is thick and mostly straight, a slight kink perhaps to the right side as it falls across her face. It seems all of one colour and to absorb light, acting as a frame to the oval face, her dark grey eyes. But Mari's hair shines, strands of light brown mixing with the dark. It is wavy, never really neat, always escaping from the traces.

They cross the hall and ascend the stairs as she points out the stuffed faces of animals mounted on the wall. Apart from their eyes, they seem alive, as if the glossy whiskers would suddenly twitch, their teeth bite again. There is a hare, a fox, and she stops before a large otter. Both otters and foxes have their tails proudly mounted beside them and details of the hunt, including its length before their deaths. Mari reads these out to the child, speaking hesitantly in English.

"A dog otter (that's a boy one, William) raised by the Gogerddan pack on the Einion river. Total time, three hours and twenty minutes. That is a very long time to run for your life, I think." She frowns, continues in Welsh. "But it's so exciting to come across them wild, and then you can see their whiskers wet with the river when they look at you. But they can't see you. They smell you (she nuzzles into him and he screams in delight) and they hear you!" (She mimes gigantic ears.)

As they move up the stairs the sound of the pianoforte gets louder. Little William's cheeks are tight and shining as he bobs up and down in her arms, kicking his chubby legs to make her go faster, as if he were trotting a pony. She skips up the last few steps. On the first floor, a corridor runs the breadth of the house. It is broad and airy, lit by huge windows at both ends. Doors lead off to the main bedrooms and, opposite the stairs, to the music room.

They enter the room and stand silent. Elizabeth is expertly playing scales. Her body is animated, every part harnessed to the music's rhythm. Mari smiles as she notices her mistress' feet, bare again. William is wriggling to get down and runs towards his mother and she makes room for him on the stool, speaking loudly as he bashes at the keys.

"Now, what has put that look of glee on your face, Mari?"

"A servant has been from Trawscoed, Ma'am. There's a note."

Elizabeth reads and smiles. As she speaks, her left hand continues to run on the keys, repeating the same scale: sometimes loud, sometimes soft; some staccato, some legato.

"We are to call on them, just the ladies. Any morning this next week, the children too. What fun! I'll be able to try their wonderful instrument, and the children can play together." She takes hold of William's hand and repositions it on the keys. "Curly fingers, William, remember? Like a spider." She tickles him and he wriggles with delight. "I'm glad we're going without William the first time: he would turn it all to politics, and then get upset because he cannot stand for office."

"That is a good thing, though, Ma'am. That would take him away to London even more. Will he preach in Wales? Will he have a living somewhere close by?"

"No indeed! He will have enough to do as Master of Nanteos and with the mines. Cai says the situation grows worse all the time with Lewis Morris constantly finding new ways to claim the land for the Crown."

Mari blushes, which is not lost on Elizabeth. She pauses before speaking again.

"Do you know if Evans the harpist has been informed that I want to see him, Mari?"

"I know that Cook wants to see you, Ma'am!" she laughs.

"Oh yes, damn it. All the fuss… It'll be difficult to find time to practise with all the orders and decisions; the letters and questions. I suppose I now have a position to fill…"

She takes her son's hand and moves the fingers along the keys. He dribbles with concentration and the pleasure of his mother's touch.

"You are 'Mistress of Nanteos!'"

"Then you are 'Mari of Nanteos!'" They laugh, the little boy joining in.

The door bangs open and Thomas appears.

"Mam, the bay mare's in trouble and Gruffydd's here. Mam, he's got scary eyes and he speaks oddly. He's doing magic, Mam!"

"I think you mean the horse apothecary, Thomas. He's working on the mare? Is he using a poultice?"

"Yes! It's smelly and yellow under her tail and he's saying things. Jenkins the stable won't go near him, but I held Lady and she didn't seem to care, even though she doesn't know Gruffydd and he smells."

"Smells?"

"He does, Mari! A bit like bog water, and then like mint, but like smoke in a hovel, too."

"Peat smoke." Elizabeth's voice is quiet. She has stopped her climbing up and down the ladder of her scales; stopped the breathless arpeggios.

"Right," she says, tucking William onto her hip and stuffing her feet into her slippers. "I think it's time we went to see this wonderful Gruffydd!"

She races Thomas down the stairs.

Mari pursues them, leans over the banisters, "Mistress... What shall I tell Cook?" but Elizabeth has already gone.

In the old stables several men are hanging around, some move back when they see Elizabeth, but seem reluctant to leave. It is dark and cool there and oddly quiet. Elizabeth is led by Thomas to the last stall where the mare is on the ground. She's in labour, sweat pouring off her. Sometimes she makes a high, strangled whinny, but then groans from deep in her chest. A figure is bent over her, his strange, blond-bronze hair glows through the gloom. He is speaking in a low, rhythmic chant. The mare shudders. Elizabeth opens her mouth as if to speak, but does not. He moves behind the prostrate animal and puts his arm inside her. His face is strained. His voice is speeding up, the words, though still unintelligible, becoming more emphatic. The mare kicks uselessly. No one else moves. Suddenly all is activity and the horse is straining to rise. Gruffydd shouts instructions; men push unceremoniously past Elizabeth and the children to get to the mare. Some come behind her and push up and under the animal's rump; others pull on a wide leather cord around her middle, to encourage her to stand. Gruffydd moves to her head and continues talking to her, running both his hands hard under her belly, from head to tail. The bulk of her pregnancy moves alarmingly but she is standing without help. The men melt back.

Elizabeth's voice is a whisper. "It's coming! I think she's going to be all right. Look!"

The foal appears in its sack and slithers to the ground. There is immediately a strong new smell in the stable: sharp as blood, rich as meat. Thomas moves forward but Elizabeth holds him back.

"But is it all right, Mama?"

The mare bends to the foal and starts to clean it. The membrane comes away like the skin on milk, clings like phlegm to her. The foal is moving and soon struggles to its feet. Gruffydd sits quietly in the straw and watches.

"Oh look, it's alive! She's cleaning her baby, can you see, William. Look, Thomas."

"What's that smell? There's blood, Mam, everywhere. Urgh, she's licking it!"

"That's nothing to worry about, Thomas. She has to do it for him to breathe."

"But how can a grass animal do that! It's horrible; it came out of her behind!"

Elizabeth has no answer to that and Gruffydd indicates that they should move away.

When they come out of the stable, blinking at the sunlight, Mari is leaning on the water trough waiting for them. Elizabeth nuzzles her face in William's soft hair, pretending to be a horse munching hay. The little boy giggles. There is a clatter of hooves and Cai and his horse career around the corner. He jumps down before the animal has even stopped and shouts across at them.

"Lady?"

"She's well. A lovely foal," Elizabeth answers.

"Please, colt or filly?"

"Oh… I didn't ask."

Thomas pipe's up. "It's got blood on it and she licked it off and Gruffydd's there and he's doing spells and everything."

Gruffydd appears. In the light it is clear now that his

extraordinary copper hair is going grey. He puts on a dirty dress coat. Elizabeth laughs.

"Ah, Mistress Powell is amused… a present from Gogerddan!" He gestures down at his coat. "A surprise to you, I see!"

"Oh, I'm so sorry. I didn't mean to be rude. The excitement…"

"Colt or filly?"

Gruffydd turns to the younger man. "What is it you would like, Cai?"

"A filly foal."

"Then that you have!"

"And Lady?"

"She'll be with us a good while yet."

Elizabeth moves forward. "Thank you so much, Mr…"

"Gruffydd Gruffydd. Names are easy to remember in my family."

She laughs. "Will you take some refreshment, Mr Gruffydd? My husband will be back soon." She frowns and looks at Cai.

"Gone to Herbert Lloyd at Peterwell, Ma'am."

"Ah… I had forgot. Well, please, in that case, Mr Gruffydd, I must settle our debt to you myself."

"No need, Ma'am." He touches the brim of his greasy hat to her. "I'll catch up with the reverend soon enough, no doubt."

He smiles at Cai and crosses the yard to where he left his mule. Mounted, he turns his animal to leave then, stopping suddenly, seems to listen to something far off. Slowly, he turns back and his eyes fix on Thomas who is throwing gravel at the hens. He urges his animal over and leans down. Placing his palm flat on top of the boy's head, he speaks softly and privately to him.

"Take care of what you do, young Thomas; danger follows

you. Pick your friends well: even a youngster, given your power and position, could do much damage in the world."

He straightens up and without looking again at any of them, rides away. As he passes the lake he raises his arm and something splashes into the water.

When he is finally out of sight, Elizabeth exclaims, "A top hat and tails with an old sack on top. Extraordinary! Why would Pryse Gogerddan give him that, Cai? What could he possibly want from Gruffydd? He has his own horse physicians."

"Maybe it wasn't a horse that was sick, Ma'am. Do excuse me, I must…"

As he moves towards the stable, Thomas interrupts him. "Well I hate him, he's got funny eyes, and he hasn't even got a proper horse!"

"Don't be ignorant, Thomas. You know nothing of him… it seems he may have saved Lady's life, the foal's almost certainly." Elizabeth turns to Mari. "Please see about lunch for the children… and find Catherine, if you will; I haven't seen her since this morning. You too, Thomas, off you go, and find something useful to do: and if those hens stop laying it will be you to blame!"

They go back to the house, Thomas scuffing at the gravel with the toe of his boot.

Elizabeth makes her way back into the stable. Jenkins is settling Cai's horse and looks at her sharply for a moment, then pinches the brim of his hat in greeting. She acknowledges him and makes her way to the far stall. She stops in the gloom. Cai is with the mare, his voice soft. His back is turned to her, thin light from the high window falling on the side of his face. There are no words that she can make out but, through the open half-door, she can see him urging the foal to feed. He holds the spindly body between his knees, supporting the head and neck with one hand. With the other he pulls gently on the mare's teats, wetting the filly's mouth with milk. The mother seems unconcerned, delicately pulling strands of hay from the net on the wall. It seems the moment has passed for her to call out casually and make her presence felt. The foal is sucking now, clumsily, milk dribbling down her face. Cai laughs and straightens. He is about to turn and then he will see her seeming to spy on him and it will be too late to call out. She acts quickly.

"Cai? How are they both?"

The man wheels round. Alarmed, the mare stamps her foot and turns, the hairy velvet lips pulled back over her gums, her yellow teeth bared, testing the woman's scent.

"Ah, Mistress Powell! They are very well, as you see." He pulls a rug quickly over the animal and leaves the stable, pulling the door shut behind him. He looks at her, his face questioning.

"I... just wanted to say how pleased I am about the outcome today."

He nods and gestures for her to lead the way outside into the yard. She saves her speech until they are back in the sunshine.

"My husband, you say he has gone to Peterwell? He mentioned nothing of it this morning. When will he be back?"

"A rider came for him when we were on our way down from the mine. It seems Lloyd has called a meeting of the landholders to discuss developments –"

"But when will he be back, Cai? The works manager needs to speak to him and we need to pay the quarry."

"That can be done. I can issue funds for the estate."

"Perhaps we should see the manager together. Where are the plans for the stable clock tower?"

"Everything's in the library. I have all the keys –"

"Well, we'll look at it together after luncheon." She looks

him up and down and smiles. "You've had a very busy day, I see, and I'm keeping you from washing yourself, forgive me. Til this afternoon, then."

She returns to the house, picking her way tentatively across the small, sharp stones. Cai watches her for a moment before he moves to the pump. Her head is down and her left hand makes a poor attempt to lift her hem off the ground. With her right hand she holds her lace cap in place and he notices her thin-soled slippers. He smiles to himself: she is dressed for the parlour, not the stable; a slight, lithe figure interested in everything – one would hardly know she was mother to three.

CHAPTER THREE

A<small>T</small> P<small>ETERWELL</small>, <small>NEAR</small> Llanbedr Pont Steffan, most of the mansion is in darkness. Light from the service rooms at the back stains the courtyard cobbles, but only from the library is there any sign of life from the owner. No one has drawn the curtains and the fire drives moving shapes and shadows up the walls. The large room holds seven men; burn from their cigars pin-pointing their mouths as they draw deep. Lord Lisburne is on his feet, gesticulating with a glass of Madeira.

"They've started to dig already. They're going into Bryn Eithin with a trench, Johnes!"

"There's nothing more we can do. A deputation has gone to London. Powis has been petitioned. You yourself drafted the letters."

Evans, a compact man, not as richly dressed as the others, gets to his feet.

"It's all right for you: MPs, JPs; but I've got no protection. What are we supposed to do – lock 'em up! See sense, will you not. Will you bring the law on our heads?"

Red glows from a big chair in the corner as Lloyd breathes in a fine cigar, exhales slowly. "We are the law."

A low rumble of laughter passes through the room. The candles, their weak light magnified by the burnished silver set behind them, seem to steady and burn brighter. It is William who breaks the silence.

"There'll be fighting before long if we can't resolve this."

"Resolve it! The bastards are digging on my land!" This time the rich wine spills out from Lisburne's glass.

Again it is Johnes who answers him. "They've already cut a trench into Henllan and ruined my conduit."

Another voice joins them, Pryse of Gogerddan, the biggest landowner in the district. "We need to get a militia together and drive them out. That bloody Corbett and his deputy need cracking over the head and teaching a lesson. He's got armed men on the look-out up there. Well, if he wants trouble –"

"But what'll we do? It's said that some of our men are helping him. That they want the land to be found for the Crown, Johnes –"

"Course they do, Powell! They'll have grazing if it's found as common land – and licences for cheap to try their own hand at a bit of prospecting. Morris is no fool, either. He'll make himself popular in London and get first offer on developing anything promising."

Evans is pacing the room by now. "What can we do about it? We can't exactly lock him up!"

Into the silence again comes Lloyd's voice, low but perfectly clear, his face hidden by the gloom. "That's exactly what we'll do." He pauses; no one speaks. Then he gets to his feet and turns to William. "Right, Powell, you will…"

It is a clear, bright morning at Nanteos. The building work to the far side of the house is progressing well, filling the sharp air with noise and dust. There is not yet any service road for the mansion, and wagons pulled by mules or oxen from the quarry have to use the main drive and pass in front of the house.

Elizabeth has set herself up on the front lawn, sketching designs for the new stables. Dead brother Thomas' designs were satisfactory, and will have to be followed up to a point (given that the foundations are already dug and the undressed stone paid for), yet she can do better. Catherine joins her, leaning on her mother's chair, her weight shifting from foot to foot. She is a tall girl of ten, her hair pale like her father's.

"Mama?"

"Mm?"

"What are you doing?"

Elizabeth laughs: surely it is obvious. "Sketching," she says.

"What?"

"A design for the new stables."

"Mama?"

"What now, Catherine?"

"May we go into town? Or will we visit the Lisburnes at Trawscoed, perhaps?"

"Not today, my darling. Have you nothing to do? What about your new music? Have you mastered it yet?"

"It masters me!"

She watches her mother's hands, bold strokes then the delicate shading.

"Mama?"

"For pity's sake... What?"

"Nothing."

Elizabeth puts her sketchbook down and looks directly at her daughter.

"Well?" The child does not answer. She relents. "Here, you may help me. You make fine drawings of trees and flowers at least. Now, what should we choose to balance the straight lines and ugly corners of the building? A horse-chestnut, perhaps? A row of elms leading to the coach entrance?"

She takes the rug from her lap and settles the girl at her feet. Soon Catherine's paper fills with the shapes and colours of summer trees, not to scale, but full of grace and movement. Elizabeth looks at the work.

"Lovely. It would be a fine sight indeed. We must engage a

drawing master for you while we try and find another governess or something… oh dear, yet another thing to do!"

Down by the lake, Cai is giving Thomas a riding lesson. He holds the long rein as the horse is schooled in a circle, covering the same arc time after time, wearing a path through the long grass. Cai, at the hub of this wheel, turns a small, tight circle with every full sweep of the pony and rider. At first there is a rhythm to it, an elegance even, in the creature's gait. The pony holds his head up and seems confident, the small rider erect and relaxed. Several men from the estate, breaking from their work to lean on the gate, watch the curious, hypnotic scene. Working on the child's balance, Cai starts to vary the pace.

"Good, Thomas. We'll work without stirrups now. Put them across your saddle." He brings the pony down to a walk for Thomas to get used to the new feeling. "Stretch your legs and feet and sit deep in the saddle."

The men grin at each other. "He's got big ideas," one of the grooms smirks but is silenced by Jenkins' irritated glance. This is new to the older man certainly, but he can see what it will do for the boy's balance.

"Just ride the bugger!" a stable boy scoffs.

Jenkins turns on him. "Hold your tongue and get those stalls mucked out! Go on, get out of it!"

Reluctantly the boy moves away. As the pony is brought up to a trot again Thomas begins to panic, used to leaning on the stirrups for balance, he keels dangerously in the saddle.

"Just stay relaxed, Thomas. Sit deep and move with him." Cai's voice is calm.

"More he panics, more he slips about," Jenkins observes, the others having decided silence is the best option if they don't want to be sent back to work. It is uncomfortable for them to watch the young master flail around on the saddle. Cai brings the pony back to a walk.

"Why do I have to do without the stirrups anyway, it's stupid! Only gypos ride like that!" Thomas cries.

"And they're the best horsemen around… you need to be able to stay on your horse without stirrups, saddle or bridle. A real rider only needs a head collar – the rest is just a bonus. You shouldn't try and cling on to the tack. Work with the horse."

"He must work with me!"

Thomas takes his stirrups back and, gathering up the reins, jerks on the pony's mouth. As Cai picks up the long rein again, Thomas gets the animal into a canter.

"Not so much of the whip! Control him with your seat! Don't pull his mouth: tell him what to do with your legs. For God's sake, Thomas, how many times do I have to tell you! You'll have his mouth like leather!"

The pony is moving unevenly, no sense of a regular rhythm as he arches his neck and tosses his head in protest.

"Keep him out! Get that inside leg on him and keep him out. God damn it!"

But Thomas' face is set hard. He shouts and kicks at his pony to go faster but the animal has had enough, shaking his head and bucking. The boy starts on him again with the crop.

"That's it! That's enough. Get down. You're not fit to be in charge of an animal!" He reins the pony in and grabs the bridle. Thomas is crying in humiliation.

"You can't tell me, you're only a servant! It's my pony!" He throws himself down and trips over. Cai goes to help him. "Get off me! I'll tell my father what you did!" Still sobbing he stamps out of the field, ignoring the men who silently open the gate for him.

Jenkins watches him leave and turns quietly to his

companion. "The Reverend Powell could do with being at home more, I reckon."

The other man nods and they take the sweating pony off Cai as he passes, careful not to catch his eye.

Thomas approaches his mother, stamping across the drive towards the house and swiping the tears away with the back of his hand.

"Just a moment, young man." He ignores her. "I said, wait!"

She looks at him for a moment as he kicks his feet at the gravel, his face hidden by the hair that is surely growing too long. "I see that your lesson has finished rather prematurely, Thomas. What is the explanation?" She pauses. "Well? I'm waiting!"

"It's that Cai. Who is he to tell me what to do! I'm Thomas Powell of Nanteos!"

Elizabeth laughs. "You're certainly proud and stubborn enough to have a big title."

"And he's only a servant."

"Cai Gruffydd is no servant. He's run the estate and mines since your uncle's death and we need him still. No one knows this land as he does. He grew up in Nanteos."

"But he tells me what to do, and with my own mount!"

"You are not a horseman, Thomas; not yet, at least. When a horse does not go well it is nearly always the rider's fault. The horse must be your friend. After all, you'll be trusting him with your life!" But Thomas, flicking his riding boots with his crop is not listening. "And next time you ride, leave that whip at home!"

"May I go now?"

"No, I…" She sees Cai approaching. "Yes, off you go."

But he has already gone. She calls after him. "And wash yourself! Ah, Cai, I… must apologise for my son." Cai acknowledges her but makes to move on. "He has not yet realised that the whip is the last resort for any good horseman."

"Indeed."

"He does not find correction easy… it was a recurring theme of his teachers at school."

She shields her eyes as she looks up at him. Though his body blocks the majority of the sun's light, it still bleeds out around him, dazzling her. She manages to keep down a smile as she notices that he too frets at the gravel, impatient to be gone.

"He must find the life here very strange, very… lonely for a young boy grown up in London," he says at last.

She smiles at his attempt at graciousness. "He doesn't like to take orders from anyone except his father."

"I can see it. And now you must excuse me." With a small bow he leaves.

Elizabeth watches him disappear around the back of the house, stopping briefly to answer a query from one of the builders. Lightly she taps the pencil on her front teeth.

"He never uses the front door, do you notice, Catherine?"

"Why would he, Mama? He's a servant."

She looks quickly at her daughter, whose expression is hidden by her hair. As she watches, Catherine, silent again besides her, bends to her drawing. Seemingly effortlessly, with clean sweeps and loops of her fine hand, she adds two young girls on a swing and three cavorting spaniels to the lawn under the trees. Only then does she look up at her mother.

"There we are, Mama – Nanteos as it should be, with fun and company enough for everyone!"

Inside, the cook, Martha, and two other servants are preparing the lunchtime meal of steak pie. Mari is feeding William, her eyes returning time and again to the window and to Cai who is now chopping wood in the back yard.

"He shouldn't have to do that."

"He doesn't. I'd leave him alone, girl, if I were you."

"What's happened? Something must have happened."

"What do I know? He's got a temper on him. He's used to having his own way about Nanteos. Things were different when the reverend's brother was in charge."

"How?" Martha doesn't answer. "How different, Martha?"

"There weren't any children, was one thing – and no lazy nursemaids to bother me! Did you ask the mistress when she wants this dinner?"

"I did, but… I can't remember what she said."

"You mean she didn't bother to say! She should have been a man, that one. Show her a horse or an account book and she's happy. Where is she now?"

"Doing the designs for the new stables, she said."

"Stables! She should put her own house and family in order."

"What do you mean?"

Martha purses her lips, lays in harder to tenderising the meat. Mari repeats the question, but she isn't to be drawn. "Where's the young mistress then, Mari?"

"Catherine? I'm not certain. She would return to London, I think."

Cai slams in, still wet from his wash at the pump. Buttoning his shirt, he takes a long swig of milk from the pitcher, nods at Mari and leaves. Martha slaps the battered meat down on the marble and starts to tear through it, dividing the muscle into neat cubes.

"I thought so. As soon as you climbed out of that coach I could tell. You girls all like him."

Mari smiles and looks down. "Does he have a sweetheart?"

"He used to go out to Tregaron to the big horse fairs, when

Sir Thomas was building up his stables. They say there was a woman there, a horse trader. But they travel the country."

"A horse trader!" William has finished his food and she takes him on her lap and cleans up his face. "How old was she? What did she look like?"

"I've no idea. Well, I tell a lie; I heard the men say she was a lovely woman. A woman, mind you, not a girl; a widow I believe, tall by all accounts."

"Well he didn't go with her. He couldn't have loved her that much!"

"Love is a small word, Mari. Ambition is a bigger one."

"Oh well. He doesn't like me. Not enough, anyway."

"You have to make a man like you."

"What do you mean?"

Martha smiles, bends low with the brush, glazing the pastry crust with long, firm strokes.

"Tell me! Please! He sees me looking at him, I know that."

"Everyone sees you looking at him…"

"But I can't help myself!"

"He's a good-looking man. Restless, though. Cai is never still – neither his mind nor his body… you're blushing, girl!"

Mari's laugh is caught by William and even by Annie the scullery maid, who turns from her work at the sink.

"I wouldn't say no, neither!"

"You concentrate on getting that ewer clean!" Martha snaps. A figure appears in the doorway. "Oh… back again, Cai. And what can we kitchen slaves do for you now?"

Mari and Annie try not to look at one another, stifling the giggles. He looks from one to the other, a slight smile passing across his face.

"I wondered, Martha, when you will be serving dinner? I have to get up to the quarry and back before dark."

"Depending on the mistress, and that's always, it seems, a risky thing to do, I would imagine about two hours – when this is cooked, I reckon."

"Thank you. I think I'll take something now…"

He reaches for one of the cooked pigeons but she slaps him away. "Oh no you don't! Get off with you. I'll send you something in on a tray."

He smiles and backs off. "Thank you, Martha. I'll be in the study."

As soon as he is out of earshot, Mari and Annie explode in giggles.

"And you can take it in to him, you silly girl!" Martha laughs, pointing with her knife at Annie who flushes and turns hurriedly to her work.

William picks up on the atmosphere and chuckles, banging a spoon on the table but Mari expertly distracts him with a piece of discarded pastry and moves it away.

"I wonder… I've heard tell –"

"What do you 'wonder', girl?"

"About Cai, that he's somehow… there are rumours."

"Rumours! A fart on rumours! You shouldn't listen, and if I hear you spreading them, you'll see the back of this spoon in my hand, even though you are a maid above stairs!"

CHAPTER FOUR

T HE FOLLOWING MORNING, Cai sits in the small office off the library, working on accounts. The room is ideally placed, as the occupant can see both down the main drive and into the service yard towards the back of the house. Here, between the kitchens and the main house, just beyond the stairs off the inner hall, nothing inside the house escapes his notice either. He is wearing riding clothes but his shirt collar is open, his sleeves rolled up. His longish, dark hair is dishevelled. There is a light tap at the door and Mari comes in, but he doesn't turn around straight away.

"Cai? I'm not disturbing you, am I?"

He smiles and sits back in his chair, stretching his arms up behind his head.

"Could you take us to Aberystwyth? Please, Cai. We want to see the fair."

"We?"

"Me and the children. There are jugglers there and dancing, they say!"

"Who says?"

"Oh, John… and Elin and –"

"Oh, well, you don't want to believe a word they say, Mari. I'd stay at home, if I were you."

"You're teasing me!"

Cai sits up to the table again and glances down at the ledger. "What's your mistress doing?"

"I think she rides out."

"What, alone?"

He is already rolling down his sleeves, doing up the button on his shirt.

"Please, Cai. The children would so love to go and we've been at home for weeks now. It's difficult after London."

"I can't let her go on her own." The girl sinks onto a chair, flicking listlessly at the edge of the papers. He watches her for a moment. "All right, Mari, I'll speak to her, see what can be done. Maybe she'll put it off until tomorrow. The master'll be back then. He can take her, perhaps."

"Oh thank you, Cai! What do I tell the children?"

"What have you told them already?"

"Nothing yet… I'm not that stupid!"

They laugh. Cai stands and reaches for his coat.

"But if she must go today, maybe Jenkins could take you and the children? Mari?"

"I wish it would be you… um, Elizabeth says most assuredly, it must be you!"

Cai laughs and helps her to her feet. He holds the door open and she passes under his arm.

"Cai? I…" But she breaks off as she sees her mistress in the hallway, dressed to ride. Elizabeth acknowledges the pair with a smile but keeps walking.

"Madam!" Cai calls her, she stops. "You would ride out?"

"Yes indeed! What a lovely morning. I thought I would."

"Alone, Ma'am?"

"Of course… or do the brigands range this far south now!"

"If you wait a moment, I'll accompany you."

Elizabeth smiles and looks at Mari. "I thought you had more pressing, duties!"

"Tomorrow, Ma'am. Tomorrow we will go to the fair at Aberystwyth."

"And I will go with you! Please excuse us then, Mari. It seems we are to ride out together."

Mari tends to Catherine's hair, watching from the nursery window as Cai and Elizabeth mount up. He cups his hands for her to use. She is agile and has soon settled herself in the saddle and gathered up the reins. Cai's horse is a youngster who can't stand still. Elizabeth laughs to see the horse turn circles, its rider still firmly stuck on the ground. Her head is thrown right back and her eyes closed with mirth.

Mari suspends her brushing, rests her chin on the young girl's head. "I would like to learn to ride," she murmurs.

"Not me. Mama tries to make me. She used to ride with Grandpapa in north Wales."

"Yes, she tells me stories of it."

Mari silently resumes her slow brushing. Cai is mounted at last, his horse, all the weight thrown on his back legs, dancing on the spot. They set off at a canter down the drive, Elizabeth's horse at an easy pace, Cai's prancing sideways, then they are lost to the trees.

"What will we do today, Mari? Elin says the fair is at Aberystwyth."

"Oh, you have heard it too. Well, your mama says that we may all go tomorrow."

"That will be truly wonderful! I'll go and tell Thomas!"

Mari stays at the window, tidying the dressing table. Soon she sees the two horses galloping along the ridge beyond the river. Elizabeth is in front and her hair has come loose, flying behind her like seaweed in a strong current. They come to a halt under a huge oak tree that Sir Thomas left as a picturesque feature on the skyline when he created his new mansion's park. The deep green of Elizabeth's habit only accentuates the creeping brown and rust of the autumn tree.

Like a whirlwind Thomas rushes in shouting, "The fair! Devilish!" and hurtles out again.

When Mari turns back to the window, the riders have disappeared.

The ground rumbles under the galloping hooves. The oak in sight, Elizabeth, laughing, her hair wild, fights to slow her horse. Cai's horse follows a couple of seconds later, it bucks in excitement as he sits deep into the saddle, attempting to calm it.

"It appears I win the wager!" she shouts, breathless.

"I was not aware of a wager!"

She laughs. "I took the liberty of betting for you."

"I see! A London habit, surely, Ma'am!" He pauses for breath. "I don't know how women can remain mounted in such a position!"

"And we do not see how you men can do without permanent injury to your progeny, riding as you do." She puts her hand to her mouth. "Oh dear, I hope I haven't embarrassed you!"

He laughs and shakes his head. As the horses cool, they look across the shallow valley towards Nanteos. In the cold sun, her lines are harsh and new, but it is easy to see how beautiful she will become in a couple of generations, the symmetry and balance of the building maintained on all sides. She is a new feature in the landscape, but the grounds, created for the previous house, are mellow and established and they will soon tame and draw her in.

"Oh, I have such plans for us…" Elizabeth breathes.

"Beg your pardon, Ma'am?"

"Not Ma'am, please. 'Elizabeth.'" She pauses a minute. "I remember you as a youth, home from school for the holidays."

"You were newly married…"

"And much lighter for my mare!" She laughs. "Didn't you live at the gatehouse, then?"

"Yes. They asked me to take you riding."

"I remember! William and Thomas had gone into Aberystwyth to sell some land – by the castle, I think."

"You wore a red riding habit. We…" He looks down, embarrassed.

"Well… remembered. But I'm surprised you remember anything! Your horse spent all the time turning circles! A youngster you were training. It appears things haven't changed!" They laugh. "What happened to her? It was a mare, was it not?" He nods but remains silent. "Did Thomas sell her? I would have thought that she'd have developed into a beautiful animal."

"She had to be destroyed. They were out hunting and she broke her leg at the knee. It took three shots to finish her."

"A clumsy marksman indeed!"

"My… Sir Thomas was on the floor, unconscious because of the fall – so it was my job –"

"Oh, I'm sorry, Cai –"

"Lady's her daughter."

Elizabeth is silent for a moment, her gloved fingers gently twisting in the horse's mane. Cai tightens his girth.

"Cai, your mother, I've heard said –"

He doesn't answer. Instead he gathers his reins and turns his horse away from the house.

"A wager, Elizabeth!"

"What wager?"

As his horse lunges forwards he shouts over his shoulder. "That the one who makes the wager wins it!"

An hour later and the riders are still, dismounted and standing at the top of a steep gorge, looking down at the activities of a group of about twenty men. Several seem to be standing guard, facing out of the pass, and are armed. Others are clearly measuring and surveying. The remainder, apart from two, are engaged in deepening a trench and widening what seems to be a conduit. One man, short and corpulent but better dressed than the rest, is bent over a makeshift table poring over some papers. He has a fair-haired youth with him who is sketching. Elizabeth speaks first.

"So, there he is – the famous Lewis Morris."

"The very man!"

"He doesn't look very dangerous – only perhaps to mutton chops!" Cai doesn't laugh. She looks at him quizzically. "Surely it cannot make that much difference to the estate? Cai?"

"Nanteos is in trouble, Elizabeth. Sir Thomas spent much. Political office is expensive. The house, a pit of money –"

"Of course. But the mines, the land, the farms?"

"The mines are nearly played out. Well, not the lead, but the silver. We have to go deeper and deeper and the yield is thin. The costs are great and to get it out, in these hills, along these roads…" He gestures hopelessly.

"And I suppose the land is poor and the farms quite hand-to-mouth. I see."

The surveying party has noticed them, the sentries alert, but not alarmed. Cai acknowledges them with a wave of his crop and they begin the descent into the gorge, leading the horses for safety. Elizabeth turns around. "I am eager to meet this Lewis Morris!"

Work stops as they approach and a quiet not even punctuated by birdsong descends on the desolate place. Morris has not taken his eyes off them during their descent, but greets them politely, gesturing for the younger Davies to hold Elizabeth's horse. There is a very slight acknowledgement of familiarity between Cai and Davies which is not lost on her, though Morris does not see it. He calls out, hearty and confident.

"Cai, Nanteos! Good afternoon."

Cai nods his greeting. Morris turns to Elizabeth, addressing her in English.

"You are happy with your new home, I trust, Mistress Powell?"

"Indeed, Mr Morris. But let us not stand on ceremony."

She gestures for the men to continue their work. Morris nods and barks an order. The men reluctantly resume. Elizabeth turns to him in Welsh.

"I am pleased to see you out enjoying the ample fresh air and exercise that Cardiganshire affords, Mr Morris."

He smiles and pats his belly, enjoying her inference.

"Would you mind if we spoke in English – I do find my English grows a trifle rusty if I do not use it? And to have the privilege of talking to someone fresh from London town – well! But to answer your question. I am indeed enjoying Cardiganshire and I find that I make many friends here." He gestures expansively to the workmen who are trying to look inconspicuous. "As for exercise…" he prods his fat thigh in amusement, "luckily for myself and my trusty pony, the hills are not so steep as those in north Wales! I find, therefore, that my strength is not at all diminished!"

Elizabeth humours him, answering in English. "Indeed, I am sure they are not! The wolves, I believe to be just as fierce however. Do be on your guard – especially if you stray from the path onto private property."

"Indeed! I find in Cardiganshire there is a woeful ignorance of where the paths might be, Mistress Powell. It is indeed lucky that wolves have been extinct these two hundred years and that I am well armed and well protected."

He holds up a pencil. Elizabeth can't resist a smile. Even Cai is enjoying the banter. She moves nearer to look at Morris' work.

"You are a very fine draughtsman, Mr Morris."

"Oh, merely field sketches – but the finished maps are beautiful things. This young boy here has a fine eye, but fancies himself a bit of a poet– not able to resist the odd gliding bird or blasted tree!"

The indignant Davies is about to protest but the three are laughing. There is a pause in the conversation in which the party watches the men at their work. Cai frowns. His eyes are drawn to some figures digging at the edge of the group, their heads turned away, hats pulled down low. He turns suddenly to Morris.

"I hope you do not intend to waste much more of your time in this area?"

"On the contrary. I find it most agreeable and interesting. There is clearly much need of maps in these parts, and much confusion about boundaries."

Elizabeth steps back to her horse. "I could not disagree with you more, Mr Morris. We and our neighbours, Gogerddan and Trawsgoed, are very confident of the boundaries and always very careful not to trespass, or indeed to tolerate any trespass by others."

"Indeed, indeed, Madam!" He can barely suppress a smile. "Such… errors, such trespasses even, will not be possible when the area has been properly surveyed and an authorised map made. You see then, of course, why His Majesty wishes *me* to clarify matters."

Elizabeth takes back her horse's reins. "So I understand, Mr Morris. May I wish you good afternoon."

She mounts up unaided, much to the admiration of some

of the watching men who are taking the opportunity to rest, leaning on their spades. Cai still seems distracted, looking hard again at the group working the far trench. They seem keen to keep their heads down. He turns abruptly to Morris, speaking in Welsh.

"Your workers, Mr Morris. Are they imported? Cornish, perhaps?"

"No indeed: good, local men – all more than happy to take part in the progress being made."

Cai makes no reply but mounts up, his expression grim and, with a small tilt of his hat at Morris and Davies, rides after Elizabeth. Morris and his men's soft laughter is distorted by the bare walls of the canyon as they watch the riders out of sight.

The cool, white sun is low now and Elizabeth and Cai have reached the river where it passes through a steep gorge. The water runs fast here, forming small falls that can drown a voice. Fed by the spray, the sheer banks are rich with green: vigorous ferns, bushy as hair from an old man's ears; bulbous, emerald mosses. Between the waterfalls the river passes shallow over slabs of rock or is held for a while in deep pools. Cai stands holding the horses on a small gravel spit by one of these pools. Rock has been cut away, formed into a shelf by the water as it becomes trapped into a small whirlpool.

Elizabeth picks her way across a sheet of rock at the entrance to the pool. Above is the dark slit of a narrow cave, its entrance dressed with a different sort of moss – elongated, dripping like matted hair. As she gets nearer she sees that there are wild, late flowers and clumps of berries slotted into every vertical nook and cranny. Facing outwards, just within the cave's darkness and not visible from a distance, is the complete skull of a goat. Not a domestic goat: the horns, bevelled like a unicorn's, show it to be a wild goat skull. Leading away on both sides, making the shape of an arrow head with the goat as apex, are the skulls of other creatures, diminishing in size as they pass beyond the reach of sight back into the cave. Elizabeth backs away fast, shouting above the noise.

"Lord help us! What is practised here? Let us get away from this place!"

Led by Elizabeth, they scramble up the path and away from the chasm. The slate shale crumbles under their feet and the horses' hooves lurch and slide as they leave the deadly cold of the river behind. Soon the water's tyrannical voice is replaced by the trees. The turning autumn leaves make a dry sound as they move in the slight breeze that reaches this far down, but there is real power in the sound of the wind in the canopy above. As they push up onto the open moorland, the wind tears into them. Elizabeth sits on a boulder to catch her breath.

"But why?" she shouts above the wind. Cai shrugs. "No, Cai – someone must feel, must *be* very desperate to go to those lengths… or are there witches here? Who would do such a thing?"

"Miners. It keeps the underground spirits quiet. They believe that the mines are inhabited – small men from ages past, the *cnocwyr*."

"Good heavens! Who are they?"

"They're miners themselves. They often warn those underground just before there's a roof-fall, or if a level's going to flood. Men underground can hear them at their work sometimes. They have sometimes been seen."

Elizabeth looks quickly at him but his face is hidden beneath the horse's belly as he adjusts the girth.

He stands up and puts his hat back on. "As I said, what else can they do?"

She searches his face again and is reassured: though his voice lacks the irony of a truly sceptical man, she can at least see the objectivity of his compassion for them in his face.

"But what is the need? There are always prayers in church for the safety and profit of the mines."

"We must go deeper and deeper for profit. It gets more dangerous with every fathom we go and the men know it. Damn it! That is why I speak myself hoarse to the master about investment: we cannot carry on digging with hand-worked windlasses and horse gins! We must get mechanical pumps for the air, get a proper system for pumping out the water."

"A priority."

"Just so."

She waits for him to say more but he is looking away, far off, where the sea is a dirty line on the horizon.

"Turn for home, Mr Gruffydd?"

He nods. She stands on her rock to mount up and leads on. The horses pick their way through the coarse grass and heather along sheep tracks. Faded bilberry stalks hide underneath the pale copper of the dying bracken, scratching at the animals' legs.

"Stop a minute, Elizabeth. Walk on in front again, will you –"

"She's lame again, isn't she?"

Cai is off his horse and lifts the mare's foreleg as Elizabeth slides to the ground.

"She's just not used to this sort of ground. I'm sorry. I should have insisted you took one of the Nanteos horses."

"You'd have been lucky – she's my favourite and I'm stubborn, you know."

"Probably just a bruised frog, but you can't ride her. Please, take Tal."

She knows there is no use arguing with him. He helps her into the man's saddle and she laughs as she tries to hold her skirt up enough to swing her leg across, but not too much to embarrass her companion. In a moment she has settled herself and collected up the reins.

"You've ridden like this before."

"I have to admit it. As I told you, my father had no sons and I was something of a ruffian… I did have some light britches under my dress, though, in those days."

Cai turns quickly away hiding a smile, and grasps her horse's bridle.

"We'll have to stop somewhere. We can't walk her all the way back in this state."

The sun is low when they reach a hovel by the road – little more than a bender covered in sods with gorse, bracken and furze, held down by boulders, on the roof. Smoke leaks through the very walls of the structure. Cai calls out, "Myfanwy!"

There's no answer.

"No matter, Cai. Come, we will take turns walking."

"No. She shouldn't be moved anymore tonight. I'll come back in the morning when the light's better and look after the foot. It will be safe to walk her home in a couple of days."

"Oh, William will be pleased to have you hiking about the hills all day!"

A woman comes out of the 'cottage'. Apart from her skirt she looks just like a man – pipe and hat. She is bundled so thick in rags that she's totally shapeless. Her face, like an apple stored all winter, lights up to see Cai and they embrace, she retaining hold of his hand. She ignores Elizabeth.

"*Cariad bach*. What a dear face for me to see on this mountain! You're getting so like your grandfather! But are you blessed yet?"

He laughs. "I think not, sadly!"

"He is blessed with a charm over horses – I can attest to that," Elizabeth laughs.

Myfanwy at last looks hard at Elizabeth, her high, tight cheeks vivid with broken capillaries. "Ah, Mrs Elizabeth Powell."

The two women acknowledge one another with a nod of the head. Elizabeth breaks to speak first.

"We return from a meeting with Lewis Morris at Bwlch Gwyn."

"Ah, Mr Lewis Morris. A great scholar and poet, they say. I cannot read, of course." She gestures towards her threadbare home. "No book could survive the damp. I have not learned it, anyway."

"I could read to you. I will come by," Cai says quickly. She laughs and strokes his cheek. Standing on her toes she whispers at him.

"You are too busy deciding whether you are horse or donkey!"

Cai says quickly, "Myfanwy, may I leave the mare here, she goes lame? I'll tether her under the lean-to."

"Son of Eira, you do what you please!" She kisses his cheek.

Cai sees to the horse, tending to the foot and fetching water. He gets a muzzle feed sack from the saddle bag as Myfanwy shouts across at Elizabeth.

"You want to warm yourself, Mistress Powell? Have a drink of flummery; some warm birch wine?"

"Thank you kindly, but we will be at home in an hour or so and I will be expected to eat a hearty dinner. Please, let me give you something for your trouble…"

Cai cuts across her. "Please don't involve yourself. I'll take care of it when I collect the horse."

"Of course. I'm sorry to interfere." Hastily she puts her purse away.

Cai kisses the old woman and goes to take Elizabeth's reins.

"No, jump up with me," she says.

He shakes his head, goes to take the reins to lead her horse again.

"In front, or behind? What's your poison, Mr Gruffydd?"

He laughs and dismisses her.

"Look. If we go at your walking pace, Cai, we do not get home by nightfall…"

"Please ride on ahead, then!"

Myfanwy sucks on her cold pipe, watching the exchange keenly from under her bowler hat.

"And I should not be riding alone. Your plan does not make sense. As I said before, Cai, fore or aft!"

He concedes and jumps up behind her, not knowing quite where to hold on as she is determined to keep charge of the reins. In the end she forces one of his arms around her waist. He is embarrassed, pulls away.

"Nonsense. It will remain where I put it." She holds his arm in place.

As they make their descent, locked together in the rhythm of the young horse, they talk, furiously swapping plans that have long been frustrated. As it is Elizabeth in front who controls the animal, Cai's hands are free to create his fabulous water-powered wheels and winches in the air, his hands now settling back comfortably on Elizabeth's waist as they move together. From time to time she looks up at his animated face, smiling up at him over her shoulder. As they come down from the pass and onto the Nanteos road, Cai's energy seems once again to turn to frustration.

"We must invest to make profit. We cannot afford to stand back. There were men from our mines with Morris. We could lose everything!"

But Elizabeth is determined not to let the day end badly. "It can be done, I'm sure of it. Investing in the mines now, looking after the land and building up the people will lift us all. I will speak to William myself."

Cai does not reply and before they reach the lodge gates he dismounts and leads Elizabeth up the drive. With one quick shuffle she is back side-saddle, socially acceptable again, though precarious with only the one stirrup. As they reach the house Thomas and Catherine run out to meet them.

"You went without me, Mama! You said you'd take me!"

"And indeed I will, Thomas, but you must improve your riding first. In fact, I believe you must have a new pony, especially if you are going to study horsemanship so keenly with Cai."

Thomas opens his mouth to speak, but decides against it. He cannot wipe the glee from his face. Catherine looks her sternly up and down. "Mama, you look a fright! And where is your horse?"

Elizabeth's hand moves to her hair. Her cap is lost, her shoes and the bottom of her skirt are drenched and her hair hangs, sodden and matted as a cockle-picker's. Cai smiles and reaches up to lift her from the saddle.

"That is the last time I will agree to being looked after on a ride by you, Cai Gruffydd!" She leans forwards so that only he can hear. "But what a wonderful day – so full of plans, and so exciting. I have learned more in a day of your company than in all the weeks I spent as my brother-in-law's guest!" As she slides down the horse's wet flank she is caught for a moment against Cai's chest. It is warm under his jacket, the smell of him both a surprise after years of marriage to William, his valet trained to mask his body's scent with perfume, but also familiar. She is at home again, her father helping her dismount after they have ridden out all day on some adventure, telling her, "You will be my son, 'Lizabeth; you will be 'master' at Rhiw Saeson when I'm no longer here…" As her feet reach the ground, she finds his arms slip around her back, her cheek against his chest. It is only a moment, but long enough for her to realise she does not want to pull away.

"Mama! Will you not catch a chill?" Catherine is at the horse's head and he sneezes as Cai steps back and catches him under the bridle. He leads the gelding around to the stables, hands him to Jenkins and then enters Nanteos at the back.

Elizabeth puts her arm around her daughter's shoulder and they go towards the front steps.

"Mama, you stink!" Catherine giggles.

"Oh dear! Do I really?" As Elizabeth goes quickly through the front hallway on her way to change she sees Mari coming out of the kitchen. The girl looks pale. "Are you well, Mari?"

"You two have been out so long, Mistress!"

"And what of it! No need for such a fuss, surely! A horse went lame; nothing to provoke so long a face. Please ask Elin to have some water sent up and to attend on me immediately – what a sight I must be! And please let Cook know we're back, you must all be famished."

CHAPTER FIVE

THE FOLLOWING MORNING the family is up early, breakfasted, dressed and ready. There has been no hint of sulkiness as Mari dragged the brush through Catherine's hair; no irritating last-minute search for the missing Thomas when everyone is in the hallway ready to go. Not even little William made much of a fuss when he was squeezed into his embroidered waistcoat. Though the light coach only really needs the driver, it seems the full Nanteos staff is about today, ready and volunteering to accompany them to town. It is a chill but clear morning on top of a week without rain and the rutted road is passable. All sorts of people, animals and vehicles are making their way to the small town. There is even a woman with a pig on a lead. Some women carry their babies held against their breast in large shawls and many are knitting as they walk. They stand aside to let the coach pass, removing their hats or touching their brows in respect. Mari, Elizabeth and the youngest two children are in the carriage, Thomas and Cai mounted beside them. As they approach Aberystwyth, the crowd thickens, no longer taking much notice of the coach, and they are forced to crawl along with everyone else. As they draw nearer to the town walls, the noise increases with drums, whistles and Welsh bagpipes blasting out.

Once through the gates, the women and children are unloaded and wait whilst Cai and the coachman take the horses and vehicle to livery. Catherine and Thomas are hopping with excitement and even William has picked up on the atmosphere and bounces around in Mari's arms. Dancers pass by in colourful costume, women carrying large handkerchiefs and slip-stepping. Cai joins the family just in front of a man leading a young bull. Though clearly afraid, his eyes white in his head, the bull walks in an orderly fashion and seems quite tame. Men clear the way with sticks, constantly having to restrain groups of small boys who try and hit the animal. Elizabeth frowns.

"Let us go a different way, Cai."

"Come, have they seen the castle?"

"No indeed!"

Elizabeth and Cai walk side by side, absorbed in their plans for the estate, Thomas skipping between them.

"We should make back the money spent in five years, ten at the most depending on the weight of silver."

"It's so exciting! But you have yet to convince my husband… and I have yet to convince him to make changes on the surface! We will persuade him together!" Playfully she reaches across Thomas to shake Cai's hand.

On the castle green, the fair dancers are performing. Both performers and crowd are whooping and shouting, the brown-faced dancing women picked up and spun by the men, their skirts flying up to expose their legs. Mari, Cai and Elizabeth laugh and join in the clapping, pushing the dancers and fiddlers always faster. Catherine frowns, looking with distaste at the sweating women, but Thomas is thrilled, bending down to get a better look up the skirts until he receives a cuff from Mari. A hat is being passed around. Mari goes to contribute but Elizabeth stops her, putting in extra from her own purse. The clapping still in the background and the dancers organising bystanders into a *twmpath dawns,* the party walk through the castle grounds. There, Mari, Cai and the children play hide and seek in the ruins. Other children join in as Elizabeth crosses to the seaward side of the headland and looks out. As the noise of people fades away it is replaced by the steady suck and sigh of the waves on the rocky shore. Cai approaches, carrying William asleep in his arms and stands quietly beside her. There are many vessels on the sea: fishing boats, some leisure craft and out towards Aberdyfi, several ocean-going ships.

"Likely to be carrying some of our dressed ore and bark, Elizabeth, out from Glandyfi via Aberdyfi on the last tide."

She blows a kiss to the ships. "I used to watch them with my father. We had the land and mines then, when I married William. But we borrowed against them for our plantations."

"Sugar and lead."

"Slaves and silver."

"A vicious combination," Cai says quietly.

Elizabeth pulls her wrap more firmly around her as she watches the hunched, tatty figures foraging in the rock pools below the headland. Small carts are gathered on the gravel shore, ragged people with billhooks cutting and dragging loads of glistening seaweed up the beach.

"The woman in the hut, Myfanwy?" she says, suddenly.

"What of her?" He doesn't look at her.

"Who is she, Cai? She loves you, I believe." She puts her hand on his arm and he stiffens. "Who is she to you?"

After a pause he answers. "She cared for my mother as her mother had died in childbirth. It's something of a family tradition." He looks away.

"What do you mean? What tradition?"

"To die giving birth. My mother died days after having me; I was her only child."

A small group of oyster catchers, startled from the rocks, flies low in formation over the sea, they call to each other.

"That sound," Elizabeth sighs. "There's nothing more mournful than the sound of sea birds." She is silent for a moment.

"A tragedy to have to leave your child alone in the world." He doesn't reply and they follow the birds as they disappear across the bay. "What does a woman on her own like that do for her living?"

"Myfanwy?"

She nods.

"Well, she used to work at the mine but now she joins the women to gather sheep's wool on the mountains. They come up from the coast, bringing enough food for a week or so and walk, gathering discarded wool and sleeping wherever they can. Villagers send their children to her and she organises them to gather lichen –"

"Lichen? Who on earth would want that?"

"It's quite valuable. It's used as a dye."

"What a living," Elizabeth murmurs. "Her home, Cai... a hovel, and in this climate. My father used to say that slave quarters are sometimes better!"

"You should see how they are in the mines, Elizabeth. It is ugly lives the people live."

"But can't you do something for her? For pity's sake, you are not without means!"

"I can give things, Elizabeth – but she is proud, superstitious too. She will not move down, neither will she take the 'tainted things' I buy."

Again Elizabeth touches his arm. "You are not happy." He makes no answer. "I realise now how... awkward it must be in your situation. Oh, but Cai, you have such gifts!" Failing to make him turn to face her she moves to look directly up at him.

At last he smiles. "You are the most extraordinary woman. Though you can ride like a devil, music pours from you; you are dainty as any duchess yet seem happiest in a stable or talking tonnage of building stone or draining mines..." He pauses, looking intently at her. "And... I forget what I was saying... Your eyes, they change colour, Elizabeth. Mostly they are grey, but sometimes blue and even green. I noticed it on the mountain yesterday. They seem to shift – like looking into the sea."

Elizabeth stands amazed, unable to find a reply. She still has her hand on his arm. He looks down at it, his smile teasing her. "Oh, I beg your pardon – I forget myself." She takes her hand back and tidies her gloves down, pressing them into the joints of her fingers. She's laughing. "I'm sorry, Mr Gruffydd – I do not find myself speaking sensibly around you."

Before he can answer, Mari and the children arrive, breathless with excitement.

"There're travelling players, they say, Ma'am!"

"Who says?" asks Cai, jiggling the groggy William in his arms.

They laugh, Mari remembering his teasing from before. But Elizabeth is not part of the joke.

"Well, I say... let's go and find them, then!" she says, gathering her elder son and daughter by the hand.

They push through people and past casual vendors and stalls, stopping where a small crowd has formed. Drums, quite expertly played, thunder out. Nothing can be seen of what is happening in the centre of the circle. Suddenly there is a cheer and applause; the drums roll. The crowd parts a little and a man staggers away, blood on his shirt.

"An extraction!" Cai shouts and grabs Thomas. "Come, young man, you were complaining of a loose tooth!" Thomas, shrieking in excitement, wrestles to escape, putting his laughing mother between himself and his tormentor. They move on.

Reaching a small square where the crowd is suddenly quiet, they see that a play is on. The players have wigs and colourful costumes and perform from a temporary stage. It is in Welsh with the odd mocking word or phrase in English. Cai still has William on his shoulders, Mari holds Catherine's hand and Elizabeth stands with Thomas, a hand resting on his shoulder. At a particularly quiet passage of the play, they hear the terrified bellow of a bull and the excited response of an unseen crowd. The actor breaks off and imitates the animal's cry, then picks up his lines again and everyone laughs. Thomas pulls to be allowed to go and see what's happening but Elizabeth is irritated, shaking him to stand still. A woman comes on dressed as the late Queen Caroline and carrying a large marrow which she scolds mercilessly. Then, placing it ceremoniously on a three-legged stool, she lifts up her skirts, sits astride and rides with great enthusiasm. The crowd go wild with laughter. Thomas meanwhile has disappeared from his mother's side, dodging away through the crowd. Elizabeth, though laughing herself, looks at Cai and grimaces, but when she glances down to see what Thomas is making of it all, she finds him gone. No one saw him leave.

"Please track him down, Cai," Elizabeth says, calmly. "He won't have gone far. We'll go into this tavern and wait for you there. He will be found soon, I am in no doubt. Where would a boy of eleven seek to go rather than watching bawdy political satire, I wonder?"

At that point there is a shout of delight from the bull crowd, Cai, his face dark with anger, now knows exactly where to look for Thomas.

He is in the crowd in the main square as the bull, now tethered to a specially designated ring, is being baited by dogs. The dogs are short, the better to dodge the animal's sideways kicks, and heavy at the jaw, trained to fasten down low onto the tendons. One jumps up, snapping at the bull's testicles and he screams, eyes rolling in his head. Men with sticks are beating him, dodging out of the way, to the great delight of the crowd. The frightened animal's dung is everywhere and one of his tormentors slips in it and is almost struck, but, despite his fine horns, the bull's head is tethered so tightly, pulled so low, no one is in any real danger. Men in the crowd are shouting or groaning, shaking money in their fists.

"I'll bet my dog can have him!"

"There'll be four dogs down before he's dead."

"He won't last another ten minutes at the stake – who'll take me on it?"

Thomas wriggles his way to the front and is transfixed. His ravaged leg muscles now unable to support him, the bull is down and the dogs can get at his neck whilst young boys are allowed free rein to beat the last out of him. Thomas is with them, but no child will let him have a go with their stick.

Suddenly a gentleman appears from the crowd. He is putting a considerable amount of money into his purse. He offers Thomas a smart cane.

"Thank you, Sir!"

"Not at all, young man."

Thomas beats the bull across the thin skin on his shoulders. The thuds are gratifying and the boy soon breaks into a sweat. Suddenly Cai appears, pushing through the crowd. He shoves aside a clutch of disgruntled gamblers to get to the front, grabs Thomas by the collar and drags him away, snatching the cane off him. He is about to snap it.

"Get off me! Get off, you bully!" Thomas shouts.

"Hold, Sir. Mine, I believe." The betting man steps forward, holding out a gloved hand. "Oh, Cai! How pleasant to see you!"

Reluctantly, Cai returns the battered cane which the man wipes with an embroidered handkerchief.

"You know us, Sir?" asks Thomas, delighted.

"This is Sir Herbert Lloyd, Thomas."

"Indeed, I am a close business associate or, you could argue, even a dear friend of your father's."

They move away from the bullring as the animal is dragged off by a brace of heavy horses to a round of applause, leaving a trail of gore and excrement in its wake.

"Where is the Reverend?" Cai asks.

"Oh, here somewhere. We came into town together. I decided to see him back to Nanteos. I am glad to see you. As you know, we have business to discuss. Where do you go now?"

"I must take Thomas back to his mother."

The boy pulls a face.

"How diverting!" smiles Lloyd. "I'll join you."

He goes with them to join Elizabeth and her party at the Gogerddan Arms, Cai walking ahead with Thomas jogging at his side, looking back regularly to grin at his glamorous new friend.

"Ah! The beautiful Mistress Powell," Lloyd exclaims as they enter the dining room, removing his hat and bowing graciously. "I am so pleased to be able to congratulate you on your inheritance of Nanteos – oh, and, of course, commiserate with you on the sad loss of your brother-in-law!"

"Thank you kindly," Elizabeth says, proffering her hand for him to kiss but looking angrily at Thomas. He is dirty, having stepped in the animal's dung, dishevelled and clearly over-excited.

"Mari, please be so kind as to take Thomas and have him cleaned up. You, young man, I will speak to later!" Turning, she smiles tightly. "And how did we come across you, Sir Herbert?"

"Well, it was your spirited son who caught my eye, Mistress Powell. It seemed he was lacking a stick with which to beat a bull, so I lent him mine. I fear it is a little the worse for wear from the experience."

Nobody but Lloyd laughs. By now they are all seated and have been served drinks.

"You seem stern, Mistress Powell. Has something perhaps offended you?"

She puts down her glass and takes a deep breath. Then she looks up and straight at him.

"The baiting and beating of bulls, calves and other livestock I understand to be an important part of the tenderising process, Sir Herbert. Whether it is indeed necessary, or should be allowed at all, I propose is a matter for debate. It is, however, clear to me that the practice is an ugly one and, if truly essential, should take place out of the public eye. It is certainly not an entertainment to which I would like my son to subscribe!"

"I see you have a refined taste, Mistress Powell, and have long been out of Wales and in rarefied London society."

"There is no lack of bull baiting, cock and dog fighting in London, I assure you. In fact I find that it is in these pursuits that the capital excels. Have you read Descartes, or John Locke, Sir Herbert?"

He raises his eyebrows and pulls a face of mock surprise.

"No? Well they have most interesting and enlightening theories on the humane treatment both of animals and human beings."

Mari is returning with the sulky Thomas.

"Oh dear! Let us change the subject, for fear of exciting young sensibilities again! Mistress Powell, may I borrow the ever-trusty Cai to run an errand for me?"

She turns to Cai. "Would that be convenient for you, Cai?"

"Certainly," he replies.

"Very well then," Lloyd says. "Go to the Bull's Head…" he

makes a smirking gesture of apology towards Elizabeth, "Where I believe you will find the master of Nanteos, waiting for his loyal servant Sir Herbert Lloyd of Peterwell. Please invite him to dine, at the latter's expense, with his old friend and his own family at the Gogerddan Arms." He laughs and claps Cai on the shoulder. "You see, Mistress Powell, how I am all contrition and most anxious to make amends for leading the innocent astray!" He makes a low aside to Thomas, "though you were doing very well on your own, young man, only in want of the proper tools! Ah, a serving man, how convenient! Do let us order!"

Cai slips through the back streets and down past the harbour where a newly-landed boat is selling fish from the deck. Outside the Bull's Head a woman of about fifty stands in the pillory, chin resting on the wood, her eyes closed. A near-silent crowd is starting to form around her, their faces sullen.

Inside, William is seated with several other well-dressed men, a couple of whom were at the Peterwell meeting. Lisburne and Pryse are not there, but their representatives are. William is holding forth at a doughy-faced man of Pryse's.

"Very well! A militia it shall be – but tell your master that he'll have his seat to lose if it comes to the courts!"

"When'll it be, Sir?"

"I can't tell you – soon; well, we need to speak to Lloyd, he –"

Another of the men pipes up, "Where is Sir Herbert?"

"He should be here –" William replies.

"Will you be there yourself?" Johnes asks. "Or will you give command to your... to Cai Gruffydd?"

"What is it to you?"

Pryse's man speaks again. "My master wants to know. How far are the gentlemen to be associated?"

"Tell Sir Pryse he'll be up to his arse, like the rest of us!"

They smirk: it's a rare treat to hear obscene language from the Reverend. Cai comes in and is greeted politely by the men but they make no move to have him seated with them. Amongst the general noise of the tavern, Cai gives his message privately to William who announces to all.

"It seems our gallant Sir Herbert is installed with my dear wife in the Gogerddan Arms in front of a dish of beef, gentlemen! Please excuse me. I will get word to you of how many of your men we will need and when."

Johnes stops him. "Will it go all the way to the courts, do you believe?"

"It must. Morris must be stopped."

William takes his leave. Outside, the woman is being released and a sizeable crowd is starting to form. Two officers take hold of her and strip her to the waist, the rotten fabric of her dress is easily ripped. The crowd is jeering now, cat-calling and throwing detritus at the officials. William and Cai move quickly away.

When they arrive at the tavern, the party is eating. Lloyd stands to greet William who says, "There you are, you rake! Dining in style whilst you leave your poor minions to make all the unpleasant arrangements for you!" He sits down.

"A thousand apologies, my dear Reverend! What will it be?"

"Nothing for me, my thanks to you, Lloyd – I have already dined."

"Very well, Powell, but I fear to tell you how your wife has suffered, being forced to tolerate my vulgar company in your absence. She is all good taste and learning since residing in the capital."

"No indeed, Sir Herbert. But this is a subject I thought had been exhausted in favour of more pleasant table talk," objects Elizabeth.

"Quite so. I do beg your pardon. Let us talk of pleasant things… so, young Thomas, do you hunt?"

"I do, Sir."

"And what creature, pray tell me, do you hunt?"

"Why Sir, them all!

There is general laughter here. Lloyd, feigning surprise answers him. "Good heavens! Are there wolves and bears now in Cardiganshire?"

"No, alas Sir; but we make do with our devilish foxes, crows and badgers."

"I wish someone would kill that wretched dog otter of mine," grumbles William. "He gets into the nets and the fish he doesn't eat he mauls – like some fox in a chicken coop!"

"We'll have to see what we can do about him for Papa, then, won't we, Thomas?"

As Lloyd ruffles his hair the child's eyes light up. For several minutes now there has been an increasing sense of commotion outside the pub. A couple of members of staff are drawn to the window with expressions partly of glee, partly of horror.

"What's happening, I wonder?" says William, half-rising from his chair.

Thomas tries to go and see but is restrained by his mother. William turns to Cai.

"Would you mind, please?"

"I will lend you my own eyes, young man," says Lloyd, restraining Thomas as he gets to his feet.

Lloyd stands with Cai in the doorway. A procession passes in which the woman from the pillory, her torso exposed, has been tied by her hands to the back of a cart. She staggers, moaning, as an official whips her listlessly. Behind her, a crier intones her crime.

"By order of Justice Sir Herbert Lloyd, this same Ann

Morgan, guilty of the crime of vagrancy, formerly carted in Lampeter, is to be similarly stripped and whipped through the streets of the good town of Aberystwyth 'til she be bloody. Let this be a lesson to all!"

The crowd boo him and he has to dodge their clumsy missiles. The procession passes by.

"Ah, I thought she looked familiar!" exclaims Lloyd.

Cai does not answer.

"A poor show indeed. Those men need sacking, no wonder the crowd was peevish."

Cai turns away and Lloyd follows him indoors.

"Well?" asks William. "What was all the excitement? Some distasteful practice one can be sure. No cultured entertainment would draw such a crowd."

"Some miscreant whipped through the streets as a lesson to others," Lloyd replies.

"For what crime? Do we know who charges her? Who condemns her to the carting?" Neither man answers Elizabeth. "Cai?" she asks.

"She was a pauper woman, punished for vagrancy, as I understand it. She was stripped to the waist."

"Stripped?" Thomas cries.

"Thank you, that's enough Cai," William says, hastily. "Go and make ready the horses… if you will, young man."

Cai picks up his coat and leaves.

"You manage him with a very light touch, William, if I may say so. How long will you keep him on?"

"It is not at all a matter of 'keeping on', Sir Herbert," retorts Elizabeth, preparing to depart. "Nanteos is Cai's home."

As she turns her back, Lloyd looks archly at William who drops his head, embarrassed. When Elizabeth, Mari and the children leave, Lloyd turns again to William.

"Perhaps I will ask once more: How long will you tolerate him?"

"I have need of him, Lloyd. The estate, well the mining certainly, cannot be run without him. And… I find he reminds me of my brother."

Lloyd's laugh is hollow. "His grandfather is a conjuror, is he not? Beware the boy does not share some of that charm. I understand that the ladies are particularly susceptible to such as he."

CHAPTER SIX

A T FIRST IT is almost impossible to see anything inside Myfanwy's hut: there are no windows and no proper chimney. The fire burns straight from the middle of the floor, smoke doing its best to escape through the scanty reeds of the roof and through the few holes in the mud walls that, covered with sacking, serve as windows. But it's windy outside and most of it is blown back inside. A free-standing iron prong holds a black pot over the peat. From this vessel comes a comforting steam and a pleasant, herby smell.

Myfanwy's face, as she sits on her three-legged stool by the fire, is animated and she punctuates the story with vigorous gestures. "And he rubbed the herb-soaked stone hard against the *dafad* –"

"By *dafad* you mean the cancer, the tumour?"

"Yes, yes. The *dafad* that grows on the face. It eats a way through the face –"

"But surely his learning can't do that! Cancer, Myfanwy. Even the best London doctors –"

"And the *dafad* grew smooth. Week by week it melted back into the face, like a rough lump of lard on a low heat."

Her final gesture is one of triumph, her palms outspread, empty, demonstrating the disappearance both of the tumour and the hypothetical lard. She rises stiffly to stir the pot with a stick. Cai is silent, staring into the fire.

"Miracles, Cai, as in the Bible – but there is no need of a book. Are you sure, you can't? That there's nothing in you?"

"Look, I have said. I would know, would I not?"

For a while the two sit quietly. Myfanwy ladles stew into rough wooden bowls. It is so thick with chopped and mashed wild herbs that it resembles a pond filled with weed.

Cai breaks their silence. "This is good. Rabbit?"

"From your grandfather."

They eat in a comfortable silence, even the peat fire almost silent, lacking the crackle and spit of wood. Cai rises from the low settle he's been honoured with. "I must go back."

Her shoulders hunch a little lower and she puts down her bowl. "Will you have some berry cider to warm you on your way?"

Cai smiles but shakes his head. "Myfanwy, will you not move down to the valley? Will you not let me find you somewhere more comfortable to live? I have money, I am paid well –"

"Your mother did not leave you with him to be a servant! She could have left you with your grandfather, with me. Any one of us would have cared for you, Cai."

"I'm surprised he acknowledged me at all."

"He was afraid of Gruffydd!"

"Still… A bastard is a bastard!"

"I know who's the bastard…" she mumbles. "You would have been easier in your mind if you'd been raised by us!"

"But I wouldn't have had my schooling."

"He had to get rid of you somewhere!"

Cai doesn't answer and she gets to her feet. "Do you have a sweetheart? There is a lovely girl at the house, is there not?"

"No. I –"

"They say she has eyes for you. You're a handsome boy, Cai. You said you had the gift of charm, when I asked you –"

"I was only jesting –"

"When you were there with Mistress Powell you seemed not short of charm, nor short of a sweat when she put your arm about her waist!"

He goes to protest, but it would be a lie. He is silent, looking into the fire.

"I said, boy, and I say again, horse or donkey? You do not know. The local girls aren't good enough, are they Cai? The gentry…" She pokes the embers viciously, then, lifting her skirts slightly to let the warmth in, notices him embarrassed and smiles gently. "Don't go like your mother. Don't run after gentry –"

"I'm not; I wouldn't."

"You need a girl who is half and half. Or better still to go away from here. Go and start fresh where the stain is invisible."

"I'm not running away. I won't be driven out."

"Well, Cai. If you want to get on, perhaps you better be gamekeeper turned poacher, then." He does not answer but moves nearer the gap in the wall that serves as a door. She starts on him again. "Why are you not working for Lewis Morris? He's an independent man. For what you know, he would pay dear."

Cai smiles and lets out a low whistle of admiration. "For an old woman living in a hovel, you're an excellent politician!"

They laugh. Before he leaves, he picks up the big hamper of food and clothes in the entrance, putting it carefully down on the settle. She mouths, '*Diolch*' and they embrace. Though her many layers made her look sturdy, Cai feels alarmed at how light she is, though there's still some strength in the bony hands that clutch his arm.

"Don't betray yourself, *cariad*. Don't let them make you betray yourself."

Gently he pulls free and kisses her on the head. As he fastens the lead rein to Elizabeth's horse her eyes never leave him, though they narrow against the smoke from her pipe. "Don't leave it so long next time!" she calls to him as he rides the road made of slate slag out of sight.

William and Elizabeth are dining alone, William sitting with his back to the long window, Elizabeth at right angles to him. Elin waits on them, her shoes making a light slapping sound as she crosses and re-crosses the polished boards. A big fire burns, but neither the shutters nor the drapes are closed and the black mesh of the trees outside the window tosses and groans in the wind. Elizabeth has worn the big moonstone. It does not glint like a true gemstone, rather it glows on the skin, not the same colour, but the same quality as liquid lead. Her dress too is pale grey, the silk gleaming now and then as it catches the candle's light. She eats quickly: like everything she does, there is the feeling that she is not quite wholly present, that her quick mind has left the table and is running on.

"I thought him a very talented gentleman. His English is excellent and his drawing exquisite!"

"Don't tease, Elizabeth."

He pauses to pour the sauce, taking care to cover the game, but not letting it bleed onto his potatoes. "What did he say?"

"He was witty, very witty, and 'much concerned that we ignorant landowners of Cardiganshire should be disabused as to our unfortunate confusion over private and common boundaries!'"

He doesn't laugh at her attempt at an Anglesey accent.

"I said, do not tease. You do not seem to realise that things are not what they seemed. My brother lived like a lord – but it was borrowing. Everything is mortgaged. Even the mines – they are finished, Elizabeth!"

He slams down his cutlery. Elin glides in but is dismissed by Elizabeth with a wave of her knife. Quietly she answers him.

"I cannot believe it, but they need direction, I think. Thomas was too busy with his politics, but you have the time to give them. Cai says –"

"Cai says! Why does everything seem to centre on Thomas' bastard?"

She looks at him, then places her cutlery tidily on the plate and pushes back her chair. William leans forwards and puts his hand on her arm. She freezes.

"I'm sorry."

For a moment it seems that it is not enough, but then she nods slightly and settles herself again on her chair. William resumes eating, but Elizabeth cannot remain silent for long.

"Cai reads the mining journals, William. He talks to the men in all the mines. He is able to go to the taverns and lodgings of the Cornishmen who oversee the mines. He knows the Gogerddan engineers. On our ride he was telling me of a Derbyshire engineer, recently come to Trawscoed, who talks of a powered engine to clear water –"

"Lisburne told me none of this!"

"There are new machines. We can clear the water better, go deeper, we –"

They are disturbed by Elin coming to clear the course. Elizabeth gestures impatiently for her to be gone, but how excruciatingly slowly she moves, returning again and again. "Fetch a tray please, Elin – or at least get someone from the kitchen to help you!" she exclaims. At last the door closes behind the girl.

William can hold his tongue no longer. "I was told none of this! These men are my allies. We are working together to defend our interests!" He opens his mouth to speak again but fails to find the words. Slowly he gets to his feet and crosses to the fire. His back to the flames he looks out at the night, the wind a rumble high in the chimney.

"They're in competition with us. Yes, they are our friends socially, but it's business, William." She pauses a moment, pushing her chair back from the table a little. "Cai says we could go deeper more safely, double our output in less than ten years –"

"'Cai says' again! Woman, are you bewitched!"

She smiles and looks archly at him. He holds up his palms in submission, forcing himself to speak more calmly.

"I intend to find out what Morris knows and sabotage his plans. We will blacken his name with Lord Powis. The gentry of Cardiganshire have powerful friends; we can make it worth someone's while to withdraw this fox forever."

Elizabeth snorts, "More pig than fox!" She crosses to the fire to join him. "I just think that all these Machiavellian games are not becoming; Cai…" She breaks off, smiles, and makes the same gesture of submission that her husband's just shown. "Sorry; *I* think that you should dig out the old deeds, interview the tenants, seek statements of established use and custom. Most of the people would be better off with things as they are. We can build new cottages for them, a school. We can make them *want* to work for us."

But William raises a hand to silence her. "Enough! We have neither the time nor the funds. Lloyd is for raising a militia and storming the site, arresting Morris and flinging the traitor in gaol –"

"I wasn't advocating that we do everything at once, I –"

"Enough, Elizabeth. You used to try and write my sermons, now you manage the mines. Is there anything you cannot do?"

She smiles ironically at him. He fetches their glasses and raises a silent toast to her. They drink deep, their eyes locked.

They are distracted by a great din as Herbert Lloyd, Thomas and sundry men and dogs return from the hunt. Elizabeth and

William hurry through the inner and outer halls as servants run after them with his coat, her wrap. Outside, torchlight makes the scene even more chaotic as the filthy dogs are collected up for the kennels.

Thomas, wet and feverish with excitement, is shouting. "Look, Father, look what we took!"

There are rabbits and various dead birds draped over several of the men's arms. He proudly holds up the body of a snipe, its head lolling on its long, dead neck.

William gestures to the carnage. "Well, I see our friend, Sir Otter, has evaded us again."

Thomas makes a stabbing motion with his mini trident. "I would have stuck him, Papa – right in the head, right between the eyes before he could get in his den!"

Lloyd stays his hand, firmly pushing the prongs out of the way of his own eyes. "Unfortunately, Sir, the objectionable gentleman was not at home to receive our call." They laugh. Lloyd continues as they move towards the house, indicating the departing dogs. "And, though I sent your trusty servants to call on him, sadly, he was nowhere to be seen."

William turns again to his son. "I see that you, Thomas, have led a very active part in these investigations."

"Indeed, Papa, I –" Again the otter spear seems to have a life of its own. Lloyd intervenes, taking it off him completely this time.

"As you can see, William, your son thinks of himself as amphibious." He gestures at Thomas' sodden clothes. "In fact, the only use to which this prong was put today was to prick your young heir from the water. He was making very good speed towards the weir before we could apprehend him."

"But that's where the otter lives! That's why we cannot get him – he has a whirlpool for an entrance gate." As his parents move up the steps into the house and out of earshot, Lloyd turns on the boy.

"I told you never to interrupt me, did I not?" Thomas nods and gulps.

Cai looms out of the darkness of the drive. He is leading two horses which he hands to Jenkins. Lloyd calls out.

"Ah, the elusive Cai! You were not with us for our sport this afternoon. Poor show, young man."

"I had business to attend to."

"Of course – you are an important man, I see. Could I trouble you to organise these…" He throws a couple of dead game birds at Cai. "And, oh," he makes an expansive gesture with his hand, "all the rest of it?"

He stalks inside after William. Cai, his face dark, calls a couple of the Nanteos men to put away the remaining weapons and game. He stands looking across the valley where the sky still seems bluish above the dark ridge. Elizabeth appears beside him.

"Since Sir Herbert came, Thomas has been all hunting and killing."

But Cai only grunts by way of an answer. She pulls William's coat further around her.

"I see you are not the model of gracious parlour talk tonight, Mr Gruffydd."

"I'm sorry."

Somewhere across the river a rabbit screams. She continues. "Will the conflict with Morris be soon?"

Cai looks quizzically at her.

"Come, Cai. I am not as stupid as some would like me to be."

"There's a lot to organise, but it will be only a matter of months."

They look out at the night. With every moment, more and more detail emerges to them, grey and visible to the eye. Finally Elizabeth breaks their silence.

"I see. Well, that will be the end of the upright country squire! We must bid good day to peace of mind and let ambition –"

"And lawyers."

"And lawyers, in by the front door."

An owl screeches. Far away, a dog barks in protest.

"Do you know, I have never heard a nightingale, Cai?"

"You'll not hear one here. It's just a name."

He is buttoning his coat, releasing the tension in his neck by stretching his head back. She senses he is about to leave.

"Will you stay with us?"

Abruptly he straightens: she cannot resist a smile at his surprise.

"I can't tell."

"I would like that more than anything," she says softly, brushing her fingers lightly across his cheek. "Pardon me – a spider's web, from Myfanwy's doorway, perhaps."

He rubs his cheek where she'd touched him. "I'm sorry. I should perhaps make time to shave twice a day. Stubble is unbecoming."

She shakes her head, just once, before turning to go in.

The next morning is clear and still. Though there is still no glaze of frost on the ground, even the blades of grass are stiff and brittle with cold. Herbert Lloyd however is not a man to dally. Although it is not yet nine o'clock, he and his valet are already mounted and ready to leave. As the family gather on the steps to see him go, William moves forward to shake his hand.

"Will you not stay 'til St Nicholas' Day and join us for our musical soirée? We will be putting on quite a show for the county."

"No indeed. But thank you."

"I'm sure Sir Herbert must return home sometime!" Elizabeth exclaims.

"Oh… please stay, Sir!" Thomas' earnest face is level with Lloyd's stirrup.

"Never fear, young man. I will return to help you wreak your revenge on that elusive watery fiend. I bid good day to all."

With a flourish of his hat, he wheels about and canters off, making ample use of the whip. Thomas imitates him.

Elizabeth turns grimly to her son. "Come on, 'young man', we have a lot of practising to do before we'll be fit to entertain our guests next week."

CHAPTER SEVEN

F ROM HER WINDOW Elizabeth watches a party of men who have gathered in the service yard. Though a few of the small spaniels and terriers are with them, the hounds are nowhere to be seen. Jenkins stands in the middle of the yard distributing billhooks, scythes, shears and other evil-looking implements. Snow has fallen overnight, freshening the soggy valley and there is a light-hearted atmosphere, with Jenkins giving instructions, pointing into the wood and making sawing, chopping and clipping gestures as he hands out the tools. Behind his back a young lad imitates him and one of the grooms gets a cuff around the head off the older man as he practises with his scythe instead of listening.

Elizabeth rushes to her bedroom door and calls, "Mari! Thomas! Come quick!" There is no answer and no answering stampede of feet. "Mari!" she repeats. "Catherine?" She runs back inside and heaves the sash open. "Jenkins!"

The men turn as one to look up at her.

"Do you go to gather boughs for the party?" she calls.

"Yes, Ma'am."

Suddenly Thomas skids round the corner of the house, dressed for action and brandishing a short scythe. "Mama!" he shouts up, and waves.

"Do wait, Jenkins, if you will," she calls and ducks back inside, slamming the window behind her. The men stand easy, some lighting up, some having a shifty pull on their flasks. Thomas practises his moves.

Elizabeth rushes downstairs and into the kitchen. "Elin, please try and find Mari and my daughter."

The girl goes immediately. She turns to the scullery maid who is busy scouring a pan.

"Um… I wonder?"

"Yes, M'am," the girl bobs a curtsey.

"Annie, I wonder if you would be so good as to lend me your boots?"

"Beg your pardon, Ma'am?" the girl answers.

Martha looks round from the fire, her fat-ladle suspended in mid-air.

"Well," says Elizabeth, "I wish to join in the hunt for greenery to decorate the hall. I find I do not have suitable footwear. I will recompense you, of course. Here, we may swap." She has already eased off her kid house-shoes and is standing in her stockings.

Annie looks in panic towards Martha.

"Well, go on, girl. Change with your mistress!"

She does so. Elizabeth sits and pulls on the boots.

"Go on then – get those slippers on, you'll catch your death on these flags!" Martha waves her ladle at Annie who carefully picks up the slippers and puts them on. She hardly dares move. "Get on with you! You can still do your work even if you are wearing lady's shoes."

"These boots are a little big. I fear my shoes may hurt you, Annie." The girl shakes her head and smiles. "Are you sure? I could try and borrow someone else's."

"No, Mistress. I like them."

Elizabeth laughs and pulls on her gloves as Mari and Catherine join them.

"Ah, ladies! Will you come with me to the wild wood?"

"Why, Mama?"

"For sport, of course. Come, let's help the men gather the festive greenery – the first job of Christmas and my favourite!"

"I better stay here with William. It's too cold for him outside," says Mari, hastily.

"Oh. Of course. Yes, you must stay warm." She looks around as if she might spy a pair of boots hiding somewhere. "What will you wear on your feet, Catherine?"

"Pardon me, but could she not wear an old pair of Master Thomas'?" Martha turns to Mari. "Did you not throw some out from the trunks you brought from London? I was going to give them to the farm lads."

"Oh yes," Mari replies.

Elizabeth claps her hands. "The very thing! Catherine, go with Cook and put them on. Mari, please get Catherine's outdoor clothes. Be quick please: we keep the men waiting."

She goes outside. "Good morning to you all!" she calls.

"Morning, Mistress Powell... Ma'am," the workers answer, standing to attention.

As she crosses to the stables there are a few titters and raised eyebrows – the previous Lady of Nanteos would never have shouted out of a window or gone out with them to the woods.

Luckily Thomas is too busy and too young to be embarrassed by his mother: having got hold of a billhook, he now brandishes a weapon in both hands. "Gladiator! Look, Jenkins: I'm a dimachaerus!"

Elizabeth reappears, shoving the last of the straw down into her boots.

"Footwear a little big," she mumbles, suddenly conscious of the men's amusement.

The warmly-bundled Catherine is delivered by Mari and they set off along the drive. The snow creaks to their boots and the dogs, even the veterans, act as though delirious, cavorting like puppies and barking and nipping at the fresh snow. Though most of the younger men stride out and pass them, Jenkins stays by their side.

"I've told young Master Thomas he must stay by me," he says, earnestly.

Thomas looks ruefully at his boots. His heavy billhook is trailing in the snow by now but he's too proud to admit he's struggling to carry it.

"Thomas, may I borrow that, please? If Catherine and I find some mistletoe, we'll have nothing to harvest it with."

Eagerly he hands the heavy tool to his mother and puts both hands to work on his aerial scythe-chopping.

"Jenkins, we really mustn't detain you. I'm sure you'll want to keep an eye on the men. There's no need for Thomas to be always at your side, either. I'm sure he would enjoy the company of some of the younger lads."

Though the man is reluctant, Thomas can see an opportunity. "Please, Jenkins. Let's catch them up!"

The man smiles at Thomas and tips his cap to Elizabeth. "Take care then, Ma'am. I won't be far away if you should need me."

He lengthens his stride, the boy skipping at his side as they enter the wood. Though at first there is still some noise from the dogs as they crash through the undergrowth, silence seems to rush in with every moment. Elizabeth puts her hand on Catherine's arm and they stand still. Even the birds are silent. The extreme white has only served to emphasise the darkness of the damp, bare trees.

"The snow rests on the upper parts of the branches so delicately, Mama; it's as though someone had painted it on to highlight the shape."

"Oh, yes. I had never seen that! I love to see the shapes of the trees revealed. Somehow, without their leaves, they look so much more like creatures."

"I like to see the nests that you would never know are there."

They walk on together, their arms linked. Now and then snow falls lightly over them, dislodged from the trees that reach across the drive.

"Where are Papa and Cai?"

"Well, your father is at another one of his meetings, and Cai I believe has gone to see the quarry manager. We are pleased neither with the quality or the prices he gives us."

"I did wonder why building seemed to have stopped."

Elizabeth bends to retie a boot as Catherine remarks. "Those lumps of snow hanging off the branches look like flesh hanging off a carcass!"

"When have you ever seen flesh hanging off a carcass?"

"Well, I haven't. But it would drip and hang in globules like that, particularly if it was being cooked on a spit."

"Good heavens, children are so strange sometimes. Whatever will you say next!"

"My boots hurt!"

They laugh and continue on, their boots creaking in the clean snow. Catherine slows and looks up at her mother.

"Is Cai very handsome?"

"Whatever makes you say that?" Elizabeth exclaims, the comment stopping her in her tracks.

"But is he?"

"Well, he has a very broad and symmetrical face and is well built. Why do you ask?"

"I like his hair."

"Yes; darkness is becoming in a man."

"And I like his smile."

"Yes, so do I – but he doesn't smile very often."

"No. But he smiles at you."

Elizabeth feels her cheeks grow hot. Catherine is looking earnestly at her. She is clearly expecting some reaction, but a question has not been asked, she doesn't have to reply – doesn't even have to return the girl's intent gaze. They are at the lodge by now, and she is reluctant to draw the attention of the family inside; reluctant to disturb their rare privacy.

"Come, let's dodge through here," she says quickly. They take a narrow path off the drive through the woods. Men and dogs are long gone now. "Why do you ask about Cai? Do Mari and the other girls speak immodestly of him?" Catherine doesn't answer. "Well, they shouldn't; not in front of you, anyway."

Catherine still doesn't speak. Elizabeth, uncomfortable now, loosens her scarf and tips her hat back off her face, grateful that the narrowing path forces them to walk in single file. There are birds in the wood, but they make no noise. A male blackbird freezes, hunching down as they pass; a robin streaks towards them, perches on the snow for a moment and then disappears.

"I think it's time we settled down to finding you a tutor. Or there are many fine girls' schools being established in London." The child says nothing. They have to concentrate not to trip on branches and stones hidden under the snow.

"I think this path goes to the lake, Catherine."

"Why are you whispering?" whispers her daughter.

"I don't know," she whispers back. They giggle.

At the edge of the wood a vast expanse of white hurts their eyes. The unbroken snow sparkles here and there, looking so clean against the pale, greyish mustard of the sky.

"I think it will snow again."

"Why?"

"Why do I think it'll snow?"

Catherine nods.

"Well, the sky always seems to look dirty before it snows."

Catherine's brow tightens as she concentrates. "I like that – I'll remember it," she says, gravely. Elizabeth turns away, hiding a smile at her daughter's earnestness.

The lake stretches away to their right, snow reaching right down to the water, obscuring the edges.

"Look," Elizabeth points to an incongruous clump of yew trees by the far side of the lake. "That's where Llechwedd Dyrys used to be. That's where the Powells used to live before Uncle Thomas married Martha Frederick and we became rich. Then the family could start to build Nanteos up – though it seems it is not easy to maintain so large a holding."

Suddenly she sees a fox. She puts her hand on Catherine's arm and they both freeze. The animal has seen them and holds itself suspended, its sharp face turned towards them. It keeps its nerve as they hold their breath, tail and front paw poised; then it moves away – a streak of air, a sigh, a stroke of red sable.

"Mama!"

"You've never seen one before?"

Catherine shakes her head.

"We should have shouted out to scare it away. Shouted for the dogs, I suppose."

"The way it moved... much more graceful even than a cat!"

"One can hardly see it move at all: it just appears. One's eyes can hardly register, so lithe is the creature. Come, Catherine, we better be getting back."

"Or you'll be in trouble again for being late."

"I'll be in trouble?" Elizabeth laughs.

"Yes – it usually *is* you."

Arms linked again, the redundant billhook swinging, they make their way across the perfect snow, back to the house.

As they pass through the inner hall, Elizabeth can't resist the happy commotion coming from the kitchen. She kisses her daughter and leaves her to go upstairs and change, making her own way to the back. The men have returned, unseen by herself and Catherine, coming back via the walled gardens to the east of the house. Martha is in her element with a table full of men in their stockings, even their britches soaking from the snowy wood. She controls the scene with her back to the range, a giant wooden spoon in her hand whilst Annie, still wearing the slippers, serves bowls full of pottage. Elin sets some steaming jugs of gin on the table.

"You won't feel the cold on your walk home tonight, boys!" shouts Martha, just as Elizabeth pushes open the door. Every face seems to turn her way.

"Mistress Powell! What are you doing in here? For goodness sake get yourself out of those damp clothes! Elin, stop that and get your mistress upstairs and into a warm tub!"

"Oh really, I'm not cold in the least, and only our feet are even slightly wet. Please don't trouble yourself, I'll find Mari."

She backs out hastily and quickly closes the door on the warm fug of the kitchen; the loud banter, having stopped during her exchange with the cook, resumes again. Catherine has already gone upstairs to the nursery. She is alone.

She goes into the library and shuts the door. The horrible feeling of opening the door and, like an icy wind, driving out the camaraderie and freezing everyone in the kitchen, won't leave her. She warms herself for a moment at the fire, then crosses to the window where she watches Jenkins and a few other stalwarts stashing the greenery in the stable hay barn. They have done a wonderful job and have brought from the drying barn the great log that will see them through right to Twelfth Night. The bay shire is even now being unharnessed from his chains and led away from the saw pit to his stall at the farm. A small figure trots at Jenkins' heels. Elizabeth chuckles to herself as she sees the man give him a billhook and point to the Yule log. "That's right, keep him busy," she murmurs as she watches her son attacking the smaller branches. "What energy!"

No one has come to find her and she stays watching until the yard is still, Thomas going in the back way to the kitchen with the others. She lowers herself onto the window seat and draws up her legs, as is her way. In some respects it will be a shame to move the stables and the other work building to their new site behind the house to the east. It'll be impossible then for her to see the animals and all the people of the estate going about their business. The snow makes the night light and she can still see individual branches, even small twigs, black against the sky. But they don't seem tangled; it seems more that they have been arranged, their structure teased out and spread carefully, as the roots of a rose grown crowded and trapped in a tub, now freed and planted in open soil.

She can't remember if William will be back tonight. It's possible that neither he nor Cai will be able to get home through the snow. Then she smiles; it would not stop Cai. She has a vision of him leading his horse, his long legs punching through the snow. The vision mutates and inexplicably becomes Cai leading, with herself riding the horse, a blue caul, like Mary's, over her head. She shakes her head sharply, gets up and rings the bell by the fireplace. She is more tired than she had realised. She will drink a bowl of frumenty, soak her feet in warm water and get herself straight between the sheets!

CHAPTER EIGHT

S OME DAYS LATER, Elizabeth, wearing a gown of deep violet, is in William's room as he finishes his toilet. She has a small pot which she dips into, taking the white grease a little at a time and rubbing it, slowly and carefully, into her skin. As he bends to fasten his boots she looks at his shapely back through the new coat then, dropping the pot into a pouch on her wrist, pours two large glasses of port. As he straightens up she hands one to him.

"Opening night!" he says as he raises the glass to her.

She laughs. "Do you know your lines yet?"

"Do you know yours, Elizabeth?"

"Oh yes." They drink. She holds out her wrist and he pulls it to him and inhales, letting out a low whistle of admiration. "I know," she murmurs. "Who would think it? In the pot it is nothing – worse than that, really rather unpleasant; inert lard! But on the skin –"

"On *your* skin," he says, kissing her arm.

She leans with her shoulder against the wall, careful not to crease the silk of her dress. "Will they receive Cai do you think? William?"

He shrugs and, downing the drink, sits in front of the mirror to check his wig. She crosses to him and pokes a sliver of escaped hair back in.

"He's like a nephew to us; is a nephew to us."

"He's a steward, Elizabeth. Oh, and mines manager –"

"Oh don't start that again; and estate manager, and companion to me when you're not here."

"And bailiff," he laughs.

Elizabeth crosses to the window. She adjusts her hair and gown, then freezes.

"I think they're here!"

There's a hasty knock at the door. Elin's face appears. "Sir, Madam, the Gogerddan carriage has just turned onto the drive."

"Thank you, Elin."

William goes to close the abandoned door. They embrace and she steps back to appraise him.

"It's time for the show," she whispers.

Three long windows make up the fourth wall of the beautiful first-floor music room that looks out across the river to the ridge beyond. It is gilt, marble and mirrors, the wood of the harpsichord mottled and veined like the marble, though the wood's sheen is deep and rich. Unlike many houses, Nanteos' instrument is no ornament.

The room is full of the Cardiganshire gentry tonight. Many of the women are seated facing the window and the music, the men tending to lounge – against the fine pillars, the mantelpiece, the back wall. Some guests are walking in the gallery between the stairs and the music room, testing the depth of the carpet, looking closely at the portraits. Behind William and Elizabeth's backs the conversations are whispered but animated; there is no one, having received an invitation, who has not come to view the house and its new owners. Everything at the mansion seems modern and that can mean one of only two things: a job lot by some obscure, cheap provincial artisan of whom nobody's heard, or that there is some real money here – the items the latest thing from the metropolis. No one likes to be heard lecturing too much on the subject just in case they are caught out, shown as ignorant. Is it Elizabeth who brings the money? Her father was a strange one by all accounts (was sent down from Oxford too early and came from the small estate near Llanbrynmair, Plas Rhiw Saeson, really too far from civilisation). Her mother perhaps, heiress of the big Ynys y Maen Gwyn estate near Tywyn who brought the money? Maybe there are plantations in the West Indies?

Nobody knows quite how much these new neighbours are worth. Though the acreage can be counted, now a private man can own invisible treasure underground and overseas. One Powell brother died in South Africa. Perhaps Elizabeth wears his short life's work sparkling around her neck and pushed down over her fingers?

A clutch of people have stopped to examine the new japanned cupboard.

"Extraordinary!"

"Green! How… unusual."

It is green, instead of the usual black and gold. Is this an example of bad taste? Or is this the very latest London trend? No one is sure whether to mock or admire it. The exotic leaves and flowers caper out of context in the Cardiganshire mansion. A bird, a little like a water rail, bends to peck at the bottom of a reed; a swan is about to take flight.

Elizabeth moves quickly from guest to guest, lingering only for pleasantries, to assure herself of their comfort. The house servants are cleaned and changed into a uniform of sorts. Elin, clearing the spent glasses, cannot help but glance down at herself: at her feet, dainty in the new serving shoes; at her legs that swish faintly as she moves in the new layers of petticoat.

Catherine shadows her mother. She speaks when she is spoken to, lifting up her arm from which the new lace hangs and wobbles, mesmerising her. Thomas finds with delight that he is amusing. He stands with his legs apart, his tails a little too long for him, at the edge of a group of six men at the top of the stairs. He regales them with his hunting adventures and the exploits of the bad boys at school. Several of the men rest against the banisters, the new wood gleaming. One man cannot resist, his hand returning again and again to stroke the perfect varnish. When he stops, he wraps his hand around it, absent-mindedly pinches the wood between his thumb and third finger, as if it would yield its secrets to his touch.

A professional singer performs in Italian over the keyboard accompaniment. There is a huge wine vat in one corner and Lord Lisburne has had his chair put in a perfect position – both in the path of the servants with the wine and of those coming up from the kitchens. He speaks loudly in English to Elizabeth.

"Of course it must have been so hard for you to leave London."

"Not at all. We welcome the air and I, certainly, the chance to see William more."

"How is that? One would have thought him to be much more busy now as a gentleman with so much to manage?"

"Compared to a clergyman's days, the life of an estate owner, even a mine owner, is easy. And of course we have excellent support in Cai." Lisburne doesn't answer her. She continues, "William's nephew."

John, William's valet, dressed as a waiter for the evening, brings refreshments and Lisburne piles up his plate.

"One's... retainers... can be a great boon. I would imagine your husband's duties to be much less than mine, however; as a clergyman he is not allowed to play a real role in politics, of course."

"The satisfactions and advantages of politics I'm sure are highly over-rated." She looks him boldly in the eye.

"If one wants to get on… or indeed get *into* any circle, one must pick and cultivate one's friends with care."

"Indeed. Do excuse me, Sir – I feel I must press on with the cultivation of my friends."

He laughs at this and raises his glass to her, admiring her slim figure as she works the room. She gestures to John to follow her as she approaches a group of women playing at cards.

"Something to refresh you, ladies? I do hope that you have everything you need?"

The lighting is very low with the occasional flare of colour as a face, jewels or cutlery catch a candle's light. The singer is replaced by a harpist and gradually the room quietens. Mari is sitting quietly by the window with William on her lap, watching Cai as he stands in front of the house. He is talking to a young blond man she hasn't seen before. They are obviously in dispute. Flushed, she hides her face in the child's hair, kissing him.

There is a burst of applause and calls for more. Expressionless, the harpist stands for his praise. Then the keyboard player gets to his feet and asks the party for volunteers. Sent by William, John collects Thomas who holds his chin high as he walks the length of the room with stiff, straight legs. A silver flute glints in his hand. There are low titters in the audience as he plants his legs unnecessarily widely, and there are giggles each time he counts himself in loudly, but he plays well: nothing breathy or feeble about the sound; the phrases structured musically and the rhythm impressive; only the rather too flamboyant circular flourishes with the flute at the end of each piece spoiling the performance.

The applause is spontaneous. Lisburne calls out. "A perfect young Frederick of Prussia you've got there, Powell!"

There is general laughter at this, some of the audience

turning to applaud William. Instead of acknowledging it himself, he gestures to Elizabeth who smiles proudly. After bowing perhaps a little too enthusiastically, Thomas strides down the aisle and joins his mother where she's been hovering by the door. She pulls him into her side and squeezes him whispering, "Excellent, young man. You really have worked on your tone!" As the harpist plays again Thomas polishes the instrument on the hem of his waistcoat and taps his foot to the music, a big grin on his shining face.

William is engaged in conversation with John Rhys, a small landowner from near Aberaeron. "And that damned otter's losing me money again!"

"Never mind the bloody otters – what about that pig of a Lewis Morris?"

Lisburne, ever alert to the mention of that name, joins in. "That wretched little man. Who does he think he is, to come down here? Where's the cur from?"

"Anglesey, I believe, and he 'talks like this'." Rhys puts on a comedy north Wales accent. Both William and Lisburne laugh heartily. After a pause, he resumes. "Something needs to be done however – and fast I've got shares, you know. They don't like the uncertainty."

Lisburne takes a big gulp of his drink before replying. "Something will be done; *is* being done." He taps his cane on the side of his nose and lifts his glass to them. "*Iechyd da*... as they say north of the Dyfi!"

Another piece comes to an end and the harpist stands again, this time greeting the applause with a very slight incline of the head. He continues to stand as the clapping falters. He is staring at Elizabeth. Those in front of her turn around. She declines. He stretches out his hand. There is a slight murmur of disapproval and a woman's voice, much above a whisper, hisses behind her.

"Only a servant! Who does he think he is, demanding she play like that!?"

Lisburne's wife talks over the music as Elizabeth sings an English song. "And of course she was from the North herself and really, I do believe, almost certainly very overwhelmed by the capital. What a shock it must have been for her after growing up so very far from civilisation."

Her companion answers her, hardly bothering to keep her hand over her mouth. "But where, exactly?"

"In the hills above Tywyn, I believe. Really, with the roads as they are, she might as well have been in Scotland for all the society she must have enjoyed as a child. She has a servant with her from her father's estate; I hear the girl can hardly speak English and in charge of the children too! That's her."

"Good Lord! What's she doing sneaking about with the child here? How very irresponsible! Have you seen that huge cauldron for the wine? How vulgar…"

The song comes to an end. Quite vigorous clapping ensues. Before it ends, Elizabeth begins a song in Welsh, *cerdd dant* style. She has a strong and characterful mezzo soprano voice, her tuning impressive, but there are many eyebrows raised to hear Welsh at a supposedly fine gathering. Though Elizabeth herself turns to congratulate the harpist, who again stands like a statue, the applause this time is distinctly lukewarm.

Lisburne's voice, deep with drinking and still sporting the mockery of a north Wales accent, calls out. "And '*Iechyd da, Iechyd da*' to you all."

William gets to his feet, calling abruptly to the harpist, "Play again, man. What are you waiting for?!"

As William and Elizabeth are saying farewell to their guests in the beautiful front hall, Lord Lisburne stumbles on the stairs.

Everyone moves towards him but it is Cai, standing under the far shadow of the steps, who actually catches him as he pitches forward. Not seeming much shaken, Lisburne reaches for his purse.

"Well done, young man. Well fielded. You won't take it? What's the matter with you?" His wife has a word in his ear, he nods and frowns. Then, suddenly seeming not to be drunk any more, he addresses the company. "Well good night to you. Fine singing… if a little parochial." They sweep through the hall and are gone.

William turns quietly to Cai, "Well fielded."

The younger man acknowledges the compliment with a curt nod of the head.

As the last guest departs William stands, warming his hands at the grand fireplace in which the Yule log smoulders and spits. He watches as Cai secures the front door.

"Come and have a nightcap," he says and makes his way to the study.

As he follows, Cai glances over his shoulder at Elizabeth who stands alone on the stairs. There are distant sounds of preparations for the night – the party detritus will wait until the morning. She looks up at one of the more jaunty fox's heads.

"Not entirely successful, I fear. No matter… Good night. Dream about the dew and the dawn and good, fat rabbits. Do not dwell on the hounds!"

She ascends the stairs without looking down as Cai taps quickly at the study door and goes in.

William gestures for him to make himself comfortable and pours two large brandies. "Well? What came of your meeting with Morris' man – what is he called?"

"Davies."

"Did you take care of it?"

"He wanted to be paid off!"

"Of course he did. Really, you are naive… so like my poor brother." He looks into the fire, feels his lower back slump to fit the chair, the thick liquor and the peace beginning to work on him after the strain of the party.

Cai, sitting on the edge of his seat, twists the heavy glass round one way and then the other between the fingers of both hands. He blurts out, "I still believe that we should put our funds into developing what we have instead of wrangling over new land we don't know has any profit in it. This fight with Morris could cost us everything."

For a moment there is no answer. Then, without looking up William speaks. "We?"

Cai's answer is perfectly controlled. "I'm sorry for the presumption." He puts his glass down. "Bad decisions were made back in… your brother's time."

"I know all this, Cai."

"Please, just listen. Land we sold to Gogerddan –"

"There was ore there! Yes, I know! No one was to know –"

"No. People did know."

Finally William looks straight at him. His voice when it comes is quiet but full of menace. "Be careful what you say."

Cai gets to his feet. "Some of the men knew, and they sold what they knew."

"These are serious allegations you make – and against your betters. What was your part in this?"

"I learned later… too late."

"How? How did you learn this? Thomas never spoke of it."

"He didn't know. I didn't know how to tell him." William drains his glass and slams it down on the table, but Cai is not prepared to stop now. "I thought he'd blame me. I was going to make sure it never happened again."

"You!" He looks at the younger man in scorn. Then continues, "How did you learn of this?"

"People talk to me. Not a servant, not one of the family –"

"Quite. I see."

Again he seems to release himself into his chair, searching the flame's random patterns. Cai watches him for a while, but it seems that there will be no more response. He moves to stand by the fire, putting himself in the older man's line of sight.

"William, it will do no good to petition Lord Powis. Everything has been tried before. They all turn to one another, pass money under the table. You have no political office. You are even more powerless than your brother –"

"I told them it can't be done! I'm a clergyman, I can't just raise a militia and arrest a Crown representative! Are they all insane?"

"They say we have no choice."

William bangs his fist down on the chair arm. "Enough! You will know your place!" Then, breathing deeply, he continues. "You are bailiff for Nanteos. You are even manager of the mines. That Cai, is enough – even for such as you."

Cai doesn't reply.

"This meeting is ended."

"William –"

"The meeting of the Reverend William Powell with his steward is terminated."

"Please –"

He jumps to his feet and punches down on the table. "I said 'Doctor William Powell of Nanteos dismisses his bailiff!'"

Cai looks at him as if about to speak. Then, with a small bow, he departs. He closes the door behind him and pauses a moment to gain control of himself. Mari, standing in the shadows under the stairs is watching out for him. She moves forward as if to speak but he only nods briefly to her and leaves.

The big job of tidying up after the party is underway but Cai and William are both in the yard and dressed to ride, with Thomas haunting the younger man like a border collie his master.

"And I'll hold the bags on the way back."

"As we agreed," replies Cai.

"And if there will be brigands, I'll have the first chance to stick them?"

"As agreed." Cai smiles at the boy.

Their horses are waiting for them and Cai flicks Thomas up onto his. He has clearly matriculated and now rides a mature cob.

William nudges his grey abreast Cai's mare. "They can have until the eve of the New Year if they make a fuss, as is the custom. No quarter after that. I'm not taking old debts into a New Year. If you need to explain matters, do so. I'll be singing the same tune with the major creditors – except for the fact that there'll be no explanations."

"I will do so." Cai pulls on his gloves and gathers up the reins. "What about in kind? Do we accept work for rent still?"

"Use your discretion. If they seem hardy, accept." He wheels about. "And look after that young squire of mine."

Cai cocks his hat; Thomas flourishes his whip.

"The last job before Christmas, and the worst," William mutters to himself and he pulls away at a canter.

Thomas' pony is eager to follow and the boy wrestles valiantly with him, dropping his whip on the floor as he loses a stirrup.

"Ah. What did I say about this contraption?" Cai bends low from his horse, sweeping the crop up and tossing it to a stable boy.

"Sorry, Cai."

The man smiles and manoeuvres his horse in front of Thomas'.

"Right, we'll lead the way and you can guard our backs against the brigands."

They trot on down the drive.

That night Elizabeth is sitting on William's bed, her legs raised, arms wrapped around her knees as she rocks on her bottom. William finishes changing from his riding clothes and dismisses John.

"At last I may find myself settled for Christmas-tide!"

"I hope it. It seems you are always riding away down the drive, or arriving in a flurry of spleen, only to gallop away down the drive again."

He laughs. "You seem merry enough, Elizabeth."

"I am. I know I should be worried about the coming conflict… but really, I cannot be! The children are well; every morning I wake to birds, not the grind of wheels on cobbles; I can gallop all day if I wish; oh, and the harpsichord is in tune!"

"I wish you wouldn't do that." He gestures to her shoes, kicked off at the doorway.

"You wish that I would wear them to trample on your bed, my darling?"

He smiles tightly. "What if someone was to call on us, and you with stockinged feet?"

"As soon as I hear the dogs bark, the servants shout and wheels on the gravel I promise, without a second glance I will run immediately to the nearest pair of shoes and squeeze them on. I will not appear at all until they are firmly on. Anyway, no one will call on us."

"I know."

"Which reminds me… I wish to see Jane. I thought of inviting her to stay."

William comes to slump beside her. She reaches for him and settles his head in her lap, twisting her fingers in his pale hair.

"I think we must address ourselves to the question of finding tutors, schools, or governesses for Thomas and Catherine."

"Yes. I have it on my list."

"Well then, if it is on the list that means, 'Wife, I do not want to speak of it further'. Then I will not."

They sit quietly for a while, the noises of the house far away behind the oak door.

"I have a mind to send for Jane in the spring."

"You should be mixing with the local women more, Elizabeth."

"I know. But Jane is the only one who will talk to me of books and new ideas –"

"And she has endless patience when you inflict some strange continental composer upon her."

"True," she laughs. "And you liked Richard."

"Yes; an intelligent man, a knowledgeable man, but we are gentry now. I don't have time enough to cultivate those I must know, let alone to talk philosophy and discuss the *Gentleman's Gazette* with a London physician."

"Well, I will keep up with Jane."

"I suppose she can bring you all the news from the capital. It might make you fret to be back in town, however."

Elizabeth lets out a snort of derision. "The season will come upon us soon enough and we'll have to be back on the endless round."

"Much more so now," he sighs. They sit companionably for a moment.

"Why did you ask me to come to your room, William?"

"Oh, yes!" He shoots up and goes to his bureau, fetches out a package. "*Voilà*," he bows, presenting it with a flourish.

She opens the crude leather covering to reveal a sturdy box made of yew. "Very curious," she murmurs as she opens it. "Last time you brought me a present it was the Nanteos jewels. This is a little more humble I fear." She lifts an ancient piece of crumbling wood from the felt-lined box. "Humble indeed!" she exclaims.

"Humble, woman! It may well be Christ's Holy Grail!"

"Heavens! I have heard of it. But how do we come by it?"

"The Steadmans. They had nothing but a handful of dried beans to pay their blasted debt to us."

She examines it carefully, even smelling it. "Do you believe in it, William?"

"I?" He takes it from her, holding it carefully as one would a fragile shell. "Do I believe it is the Grail? Possibly, and for that reason I honour it of course. Can the relic heal as they say? Do I believe in miracles? No, I am not a papist. Neither am I an old woman in a hovel or a peasant conjuror."

CHAPTER NINE

CHRISTMAS EVE AND the house is filled with light. Gilt everywhere magnifies the candles' effect and a monstrous fire burns in every grate. Yet it is not too stuffy tonight, in fact it is almost cold as nearly every door is open. The family have put themselves in the library in the middle of the house, ostensibly to avoid the chill, but really to be part of the hustle and bustle of the occasion. Fresh greenery loading every shelf, suspended from every corner, cheers the room and the hot wine flows. Thomas comes in from the kitchen, holding his hands out in front of him like a murderer, his long hair sticking to his face on the left side.

"Dear God – save us from the ghoul!" shouts William from his sofa seat, Elizabeth tucked up under his armpit. She laughs, having to sit up smartly to avoid spilling her wine.

"What on earth have you been doing?"

"Toffee!" shouts Thomas, licking his hands.

"Oh, can I do some?" Catherine is on her feet.

"No good – all finished. Cook sent me to ask if you want some."

"Of course. Send in the toffee – my teeth are awaiting the challenge!" William snaps his jaws together like a horse.

"Oh, don't! You're like the *Mari Lwyd*!" Catherine squeals.

He drops onto his knees and snaps at her, shuffling after his delighted daughter. Thomas joins in, acting the fool and chasing after the pair. A lustreware vase wobbles dangerously.

"All right, calm down please. William; will you please calm down!"

He laughs and resumes his seat, panting, but as is the case, the children, once wound up, don't know when to stop. He takes a big swig from the goblet as Thomas, now chasing Catherine with a poker, nearly trips over the rug.

"Woa; woa there, young stallion," he warns. But Thomas won't hear. "I said, stop!" William shouts, making as if to get to his feet.

Thomas collapses in a heap on the carpet as though shot. They laugh.

Mari comes in carrying William. He's damp from his bath and rubbing both eyes with his fists. "Someone wants to say goodnight." Mari smiles and passes the little boy to his mother.

"Oh you are so gorgeous, I could *eat* you!" she cries, nuzzling him hard and sitting him sideways across her lap, playing absent-mindedly with his bare feet as he snuggles up to her and sucks his thumb. "Have you decided between you who stays behind tonight?"

"We were to draw lots, but Cai volunteered. I think I'll stay behind too. If William wakes he'll be much happier to see me there."

Elizabeth can't hide her smile. "And who is to chaperone you two?"

"There's no need! Really, Mistress... is that what you think?"

"What?" Thomas pipes up. "Anyway; who wants toffee?"

He doesn't wait for an answer but tears off across the hall, pursued by Catherine.

"I can answer that question." William drains his glass. "Jenkins and his wife are staying. He's becoming quite a Dissenter, apparently (though he knows better than to say anything about that nonsense to me)."

"But I thought that even Dissenters joined us for *Plygain*? What a joyless lot they are!"

"Exactly. But I think our Jenkins is something of a recent convert and still feeling his way. Maybe he won't always be such a zealot."

"Toffee!" shout Catherine and Thomas from the doorway, bowing low and proffering what is left of the tray to their parents.

"Stand back!" William warns, as he lays into the block with a hammer and chisel. The toffee ricochets off everywhere, much to the delight of the children, who swoop on the pieces as soon as they hit the floor.

Sweets eaten, wine drunk and Little William taken upstairs, Catherine and Thomas are at last persuaded to go to bed.

"But only because we're allowed to get up at five and go with you, yes, Mama?"

His mother's voice is firm. "Of course. But only if you *do* go to sleep, you two!"

Alone at last, the door closed on the rest of the house, Elizabeth and William doze together on the sofa. The long-case clock in the inner hall keeps the quarter hour which William registers, although Elizabeth is sleeping more deeply. He sees, from under his half-closed lids, John check on them at about eleven o'clock with a fresh jug of hot wine; sees him leave, returning again on the balls of his feet with a quilt which he puts over them. Every time the kitchen door opens, singing and raucous laughter can be heard – the sound of a healthy house and its staff on the verge of the festive season. At about two a.m., the door clicks open again and John returns, this time to build up the fire. William has been fully awake for a while, but the pleasure of his wife – for once still and quiet, asleep on his chest and the prospect of at least twelve days respite from worrisome meetings, cannot move his warm, heavy limbs. He smiles at the man and gestures for refreshment. John grins and leaves.

He kisses Elizabeth awake: her forehead, her head, her eyes. She lifts a hand to brush him away as though she's trying to keep birds from her hair. He can't resist tormenting her more and she moans and complains as she unglues herself from sleep. By the time that John, accompanied by Elin, return with trays of food and drink, she is fully composed: her hair and cap tidy, dress shaken out and her eyes sparkling.

"*Nadolig Llawen!*" William wishes them. Elin bobs a curtsey and John mimes an imaginary glass clinking in a toast.

"Have you all you need back there?"

"Yes indeed, Sir. Cook does us proud."

"When will the coach be ready? I can't recall…"

"You said for five, Sir."

"Good. Many thanks, John. Go now you two and have some fun."

By five the house is ablaze, the drive and yard full of estate workers with torches. A couple of the young men practise on their horns to the frenetic bark of the caged hounds. A puffy-faced Thomas and a very white, pinched-looking Catherine, are bundled up warm and already installed in the coach when Elizabeth comes out. Before she climbs in she turns back and looks up at the nursery window where a distant Mari is waving enthusiastically. She looks around for Cai but he is nowhere to be seen. She shakes off the faint echo of anxiety as she gets into the coach. Tonight everyone is too busy to fuss over her – there is no one trying to hand her in to the coach or cover her in furs. She cuddles up between the children under layers of quilts and eiderdowns. "Good heavens, you're warm!"

"Jenkins gave them to us, Mama," says Catherine, and, imitating his nasal voice, giggles. "You'll be freezing to your death in there!"

They laugh and feel the coach rock as the staff climb aboard and shriek at the cold as their father stands talking with the door open before he gets in. Then they're off. Elizabeth takes a last look at the glowing house as they round the corner but is soon caught up in the magic.

It's a jerky ride, the horses on a tight rein, excited by all the people, wary of the flaming torches. The coach is hemmed in by the increasing crowd. Thomas, now oblivious to the cold, hangs from the window.

"Oh Papa, can we not get out and join them – just for a little way, just until we reach the big road?"

"Certainly not. You're in your best winter clothes, Thomas. Anyway, knowing you, young squire, you'll be lost. Remember the time we went to Bath?"

"I wasn't lost – I was just having an adventure."

"Well, you were the only one in England who *didn't* know you were lost that day! Just enjoy what you *are* doing instead of always wanting more… and *Nadolig Llawen*!"

The horns blast out and the crowd thickens as the Nanteos party meet the main road to Llanbadarn Church. Thankfully, though it's a dry night, low cloud is keeping some of the cold at bay. There are other coaches, chaises and carts on the road; some are just farm vehicles come down from the remote homesteads and mines, full of people. The singing has started already and the regular throb of drums starts to make the people move together. Some pass dangerously close to the coach's wheels and the coachman shouts at the Nanteos men accompanying on foot to take more care of business. By the time they reach the church, even the delicate Catherine is half out of the window in excitement. The graveyard is full to bursting, some dancing to a fiddler at the north end, the odd note heard between the tolling of the bell. As the gentry are greeted by the clergy, the people wait their turn. Some will have to wait outside the packed church until dawn brings the service to an end. The old building is filled with the candles people have brought, quietly depositing them with the sexton before turning to go back outside.

A short address and prayers, in which the vicar has to stop and look pointedly at some members of the restless congregation, end the formal part of the Christmas morning service. Now is what they've been waiting for. The mole-catcher and his wife come down from the loft, stand in front of the altar and sing. The people join in when their voices reach the loved and remembered tunes and continue with a low hum, or snatches of harmony as the two extemporise. The sexton is next, the warm hush complete as he sings the new carol he's written for today. Then come small groups from the farms; ten men from the mine at Ystumtuen and a woman with a club foot who sings to the folk harp. All these are interspersed with communal singing, begun either by the sexton, or informally by someone in the crowd starting up and being joined by their friends and neighbours.

At about eight, hunger forces the meeting to a close. The Powells follow Lord Lisburne and Sir Pryse's party from the church. On his way out, William turns to the sexton and shakes his hand.

"Excellent work today – a beautiful hymn… and I have not forgotten that interlude you wrote against the Methodists: first class. *Nadolig Llawen* to you!" He presses something into the man's hand.

The sun is nothing but a faint, white disc through low cloud as they get into the coach. There is no warmth left in the blankets which seem clammy, only the eiderdown gives relief as they huddle together. Catherine climbs onto her father's knee as she used to and even Thomas concedes to having the quilt tucked under and around him like a cocoon. Elizabeth does the same for herself, then pulls a rug over them both.

The children and William doze as they make the thirty-minute journey home but Elizabeth looks out of the lurching window. They themselves might be cold and tired, but the people have to walk home, some to far-off farms. Others are loaded onto their open-topped bone-shakers, the mist-drenched air surely creeping right through their thin clothes. But, though the drums and fiddles are silent and the road has emptied somewhat, there is still tired laughter, the groups standing back to let them pass usually smiling, calling a *Nadolig Llawen* and raising their caps or bobbing a quick curtsey. Once they reach the private road to Nanteos the coachman can go faster, the horses showing no objection as they anticipate their hot mash. The lake steams grey and the candles from the house cast a sulphurous glow as they approach, but Jenkins and his wife are there to greet them and the fire under the Yule log snarls and spits. Just behind them, other vehicles carrying Nanteos servants are pulling up and unloading, staff tramping over the gravel to get to the service wing or the stables.

Sarah Jenkins settles them in the parlour where breakfast is laid for them. Thomas tucks in, but Catherine is visibly wilting, her head heavy as a lily's as she droops forward on the edge of her chair.

"Bed for you, young lady!"

For a moment she looks as if she's going to object, but then smiles wanly at her father.

"I'll ring for Mari. Actually, where is she? She's usually the first to come running to greet us when we get home from anywhere?"

"Probably fallen asleep with William, Papa."

"Leave her," Elizabeth says, quickly. "I'll take Catherine up, and you won't be far behind either, Thomas. Straight up for a rest when I come back —" She holds up her hand to silence her objecting son. "That is, if you *want* to be allowed out with the men before lunch."

He shuts up. She takes her daughter up through the house. It seems that everyone is on duty this morning; all the doors are open, even those to the service rooms, the staff unafraid to laugh and call out to each other. To everyone she passes she gives *Nadolig Llawen*, finally arriving at the nursery, the door of which is open. William's fluffy head can be seen poking from his blankets and the fire has been freshly made up. They tiptoe past the sleeping Mari's room and Catherine quickly uses the pot and washes her hands and face.

"Don't bother to undress properly, my love, just get into bed. You'll be up and about in a few hours' time anyway."

She tucks her in and hovers for a moment over William, inhaling his damp, cheesy scent. Gently she kisses his warm head and leaves. Just before she goes, she puts her head around Mari's door. The girl has fallen asleep fully dressed and lies on her front across the bed, as though she has flung herself down in a fit of pique. Someone it seems has covered her with a sheepskin from which her boots poke out. Elizabeth smiles and tiptoes out, not risking shutting the door. As she comes down the stairs, Thomas is coming up.

"Papa says, the sooner I go to bed, the sooner he'll wake me up!"

"An excellent plan!" Elizabeth kisses him on the cheek. "But be very quiet; everyone's fast asleep. Can you manage on your own?"

"Of course. I'm not a baby!"

He trudges upstairs as she makes her way to the kitchens. Martha, still wearing her outdoor cloak, is supervising several men as they wrestle with the meat spits. The spit-dog seems less than willing to oblige on his wheel and Annie is poking him with a stick.

"*Nadolig Llawen i bawb!*" Elizabeth calls through the chaos.

Everything stops for a moment as they greet her and Martha comes over to her.

"Have you everything you need, Mistress Powell? I sent Elin with some hot flummery for you a moment ago... was there anything else you wanted?"

"No, no indeed, we are very well served. I just wanted to wish the company *Nadolig Llawen*."

"And the like to you, Mistress."

"You must be tired, Martha. Coming back from *Plygain* and straight to work. How do you manage it?"

The older woman smiles wryly and turns to pick an open bottle of homemade gin from the table.

"I can do anything on a bottle of this!"

Elizabeth laughs. "Well, I'll leave you to get on. Good day to you all!"

She opens the door to the parlour and slides in. William is asleep, a plate of untouched food by his side. She folds herself a pancake from a slice of cold meat and whispers, "Come on, my darling – to bed," squeezing him gently on the shoulder.

Groggily he comes to and they make their way upstairs.

"Yours or mine?" she asks.

He smiles and opens the door to her room. Her Christmas Day clothes have already been laid out but there is no sign of Elin, though the fire here is bright. They undress, William helping his wife with the back fastenings and the corsetry and they get into bed. The linen is icy and William starts to thrash around, kicking his legs and trying to warm the sheets, something he'd done on their wedding night to break the ice, and a tradition ever since. Elizabeth laughs and he does it more, then hunts her with his freezing hands, trying to get at any bit of warm, bare flesh he can. She squeals and he torments her mercilessly as she bats him away. For once it doesn't seem to matter what the servants hear. Soon the bed is warm and the two are sinking into sleep, his palm closed around a breast, his warm breath on her neck, his diminishing erection tucked cosily between her buttocks. She murmurs drowsily, "Fancy being up all night and coming back to make Christmas lunch. I feel rather guilty sometimes, you know."

"Don't be. We pay the wages."

Later, as the indoor servants are preparing the dining room for the Christmas feast, the estate men gather outside. A few lucky terriers run mad at their feet and a couple of pottery flagons do the rounds. Thomas, kneeling on the window seat in the library, is transfixed.

"Oh please, Papa – can I? I won't get lost. I'll stay with Cai… or I'll stay with Jenkins."

"Where is Cai? The man's been absent since last night!"

There's a tap at the door and Jenkins appears. "Rev. Powell, Sir."

"Jenkins?"

"I come requesting a favour from you, yourself a man of God."

William smiles at the man – all earnest and pompous. "What can I do for you?"

"They're gathering for the squirrel hunt. It'll be rough sport, Sir, and is not the spirit. It's not a seemly practice. Many parishes are stamping it out – all the gross pursuits of the common people are being cleansed away."

"Who's doing this 'cleansing away', Jenkins?"

"Well the new preachers and the enlightened landowners, Sir."

"Ah. You mean the ranters and their lackeys! No Jenkins – the hunt is a Christmas tradition that will continue to be observed at Nanteos. In fact, I was about to entrust this young man to your safe-keeping." He points to the delighted Thomas.

Jenkins stands stiffly and says quietly, "Other arrangements will need to be made, Sir. I'm afraid I will not be accompanying him."

William studies him a moment. His defiance, though unattractive, is not really serious insolence… anyway, it's Christmas Day and he will let it go.

"As you please. Find Cai for me, however. I need a nursemaid for this young blood."

Jenkins gives a small bow and leaves.

"Go and change then, Thomas," William says.

The boy hurtles off with a whoop of triumph.

But Cai cannot be found and it is the reluctant John, bundled into another man's heavy coat and boots, who has to be Thomas' minder. As they leave the yard, rain comes spitting on the wind. The leaves, all fallen now, do not swish and whisper as the boots kick through them. The piles have lost their charm, the oldest leaves now turned to black slime; the younger ones on the surface bleached and grey, curling up like strands from a cheap rag rug.

Small flocks of long-tailed tits flit through the canopy, whistling and hiccupping. The men have muzzled the dogs and creep through the bare trees, the twigs jagged like the crazed glaze on old pottery against the leaden sky. Suddenly a squirrel is spotted and they hurtle after it, dogs released from their constraints and croaking for blood. The small, red creature flings itself from branch to branch until it runs out of tree and hovers on an out-crop of thin twigs. There is nowhere left for it to jump, even the nearest neighbouring tree too far away. Its body quivers and its tail flails as the men hurl their weighted sticks into the canopy, dodging and laughing as they come crashing back down. Thomas, frustrated by his puny throwing, makes up for it by shouting at the top of his lungs. One of the stable boys starts to climb the tree, a sack over his shoulder, a rope coiled ready. Suddenly there is a shout of glee as the animal makes a desperate jump and falls – right into the jaws of one of the dogs.

"After she's shaken that, the skin won't be worth having!" grumbles John as the men laugh and applaud the hound.

The keeper, Roberts, is in charge today, whipping the dogs out of the way and pinching the bitch's mouth for her to give up the body.

"Will he chop off the tail, like they do with a fox?" Thomas whispers.

"No. Only use for that thing is a whole skin." John takes a swig from his flask and grimaces.

"May I?" Thomas holds out his hand.

"Don't see why not."

The boy gingerly takes a swig.

John is impressed. "You've tried it before, haven't you! You're not going to give us all a laugh by spluttering it all over your trousers. Well done."

With the body draped over his forearm the keeper comes towards them. "Yours, Young Master," he says quietly, flicking the dead animal's head into his big hand. Though there has been some damage to the face, the tufted ears still look perky.

Thomas shakes his head and points.

"No. Give it to him – the one who climbed the tree."

Roberts smiles beneath his hat and nods, the moment broken by another sighting.

"Maybe its mate!" shouts Thomas.

John grunts and they stumble after the party.

"Just tell me when you've had enough!" John shouts to the boy's back.

"I'll never have enough!"

But the wood is becoming denser, the increasingly thick undergrowth of holly acting as an advantage to the tree-dwellers. No one is bothering to muzzle the dogs any more and, although they persist for another twenty minutes, not even a bird is to be seen. The keeper shouts for the party to stop and counts the men. He laughs when he gets to the boy, proudly wearing the squirrel around his neck.

"Who said we can't keep up with London fashions here in Cardiganshire!? That's right isn't it, Master Thomas – what the fine ladies wear in town?"

"Oh no indeed – I have never seen a lady in all London as finely dressed as this boy here!"

The men love this and cat-call and whistle the boy, who doesn't seem to care, holding up the animal's head and front paws as if to acknowledge the applause.

Roberts leads them out of the wood and they return home along the drive. The dogs no longer run ahead but cling to the men's heels or sniff away and return in constant loops, their tails low, their undersides black and scraggy with mud. As they reach home, the men disperse – some to see to the dogs, others to their quarters above the stables from where there is already the sound of a fiddler. As John and Thomas make their way to the back door Cai is unloading two big wicker panniers from his mare.

"Oh aye – he's here now, is he, when all the work's been done already!"

Cai had turned with a smile that dies on his face at John's bitter tone. He touches his hat to Thomas and turns back to his task.

"I'm talking to you, Mr High and Mighty!"

"Cai!" trills Thomas.

The young man turns in answer to the boy and waits. John walks up to him and pushes his face at him.

"Because of you I'm in this bloody garb! I'll have it all to do now when I get in." Cai doesn't answer.

"Well?"

"What's the question?" he says, quietly.

"You cheeky…"

He shoves Cai in the chest. Thomas is looking from one man to another in shock. Cai turns away but John grabs his coat at the shoulder.

"Where the hell've you been, anyway?"

Cai pulls his coat from the man's hands.

"It's best you go in now, Thomas," he says. To John's surprise, the boy immediately does as he's told. "What is it you want, Bradfield?"

John doesn't answer and Cai goes to gather the reins.

"Don't you turn your back on me. You think you're better than us – you're nought but a bastard, and I bet that's where you've been, out with the gipsies making more bastards!"

He grabs at the horse's head and Cai trips him up. He sprawls in the grey mud of the gravelled yard. Cai looks down at him.

"You better clean yourself up. You've got your valet's livery to put on and a Christmas dinner to serve!" He walks his horse to the stable.

As he struggles to his feet, John throws a parting shot. "They'll see through you – and I'll bloody well help them!"

As he stands, looking at his wrecked coat, the keeper comes from the shadows.

"There's not much of a brain on you, is there?" John doesn't answer. "I wouldn't get on the wrong side of him."

"What – that stuck-up shit!"

"Is Cai Gruffydd! I'd get on inside and get cleaned up, if I were you, before the finery misses your smart London arse," and he laughs as he walks away behind the house.

CHAPTER TEN

IT IS MORNING and Elizabeth, Mari and Catherine are sitting in the parlour. Elizabeth has the Grail on a cloth on her knee and is oiling it, taking broad slow sweeps across the wood. The other two are pretending to sew, constantly distracted by the chaos outside as the Nanteos men prepare to rout Morris and his workers from their new dig. Mari glances at Elizabeth from time to time but the latter does not look up.

"Should you really be rubbing things into the wood, Mistress? The Rev. Powell says…"

"I know what my husband says, thank you, Mari." She continues with her task.

Mari gets up and crosses to Elizabeth. "Is it really the Grail?" She bends to peer at the cup but her eyes slide to the window.

Elizabeth smiles. "Who's to know? It is extremely old, that is certain. We know two other things too – that it has been precious to people for centuries, for some reason, and that pilgrims have believed in it. Look at the edges – eaten away!"

The girl backs off fast. "Rats! How could they have been allowed to get to it! I would have kept it safe, locked –"

"No, people. The Nibbling Pilgrims!"

"*O Duw*! How could they be so stupid?"

"Desperate, more likely."

The girl returns to perch on the edge of her seat.

"Have you ever been desperate, Mari? What do you do when you don't know where to turn?"

"Well, I pray, and…"

"And?"

"She does charms! I know because I've seen her!"

Mari blushes. "Catherine!"

"Charms?" Elizabeth laughs.

"Yes. To make things happen."

"Spells, you mean?"

"Well, not spells exactly…"

Elizabeth teases her. "You are a witch, I see!"

"No indeed, never!"

"I'm only jesting with you! Sit down. These charms… where would you get them? Gruffydd, perhaps? I hear he's… special."

"Gruffydd! No, Ma'am, he would never agree to give a girl a love charm, he only works sickness spells… what?"

Elizabeth is laughing openly now, as she puts the goblet away. "Ah, a love charm, I see."

Mari laughs herself and, unable to resist any longer, goes to the window. "Shouldn't you be supervising the preparations, Mistress?"

"Ah that! Let them play soldiers! The whole thing is ridiculous!"

Cai enters, bringing with him a blast of cold air from the hall.

"Elizabeth, William asks for you. It seems there's a coach load of ladies coming from Gogerddan. They're bringing maids and a change of clothes. It seems that they're expecting to be entertained here for the duration of the fight up at the mines!"

"Oh, for goodness sake! I've not agreed to this – have I? Damn it!" She gets up.

"Mama, can I come?"

They leave and Cai crosses to the window, watches amused as an ornate coach pulls up and Elizabeth talks to the occupants through the open window.

Outside, despite William's look of reproach, Elizabeth is

doing her best to put the visitors off, leaning in through the opened carriage door. "So you see I'm afraid we aren't prepared for you, ladies. I'm terribly sorry. Please do come in and take some tea and rest a little, but then I must ask you to return home. We really can't accommodate you all."

Most of the men are mounted now, the horses restless to be gone. Thomas is busy holding their saddlebags, weapons and whips for them until they're properly settled in the saddle. At the head of the band is Herbert Lloyd, his horse already foaming at the mouth under the tight bit. Elizabeth seems to have had some success in that the luggage remains tied to the roof as the coach is driven off to the carriage house. The Pryse women and their maids are disembarking, being led into the house by a flustered Mari. Cai is leaving as the women enter the house, standing aside to let them pass. He is hardly out of earshot when one turns to the other.

"I should think so too! It's a wonder he's allowed to use the front door, at all!"

"Handsome, though," giggles her companion.

"They say he's allowed to sleep in the house – on the first floor, if you please!"

"Maybe William Powell wants to keep his eye on him?"

"Maybe it's *Elizabeth* Powell who wants to keep her eye on him!"

"Oh, you're wicked!" she howls, having to stifle the laughter with a gloved hand.

As Mari settles the women in the morning room, Elizabeth is giving hurried instructions to Elin and Annie. Even as she speaks they are pulling off their work caps and heavy aprons, tidying their neckerchiefs. A makeshift butler, doing up the last buttons on his liveried waistcoat but with the air of the stable still clinging to his hair, enters with refreshments. Sir Pryse's wife emerges from behind the screen where she's been making use of the chamber pot. She positions herself close to her friend, Johnes' wife, on the window seat and whispers in her ear.

"I cannot believe her arrogance! I could buy and sell her five times over!"

"And that Cai – I'm told that they have him at table…"

"Oh to have a, um, nephew like that. I'd be a thorough Messalina!"

The youngest woman, Pryse's niece, pipes up, "What's a Messalina?"

"Ssssh! I'll tell you later!" her mother hisses.

But Lady Pryse is enjoying herself and not afraid of sensitive questions – as long as they are about other people's families.

"Well, gentry bastards are often fine looking, I hear. Similar apparently to the mulatto in the West Indies. My husband says that it's the vigour of cross-breeding, breeding out of one's proper race, so to speak."

Outside, the party of men is ready to leave. Elizabeth stands by William's horse, one hand resting on his thigh.

"Be careful, William – and not just of your safety. We have long lives still to live in Cardiganshire."

He gestures in frustration towards the house. "Let you address yourself to the comfort of our guests inside! I've told you before, Elizabeth. You could make me –"

"Or help to break you. I know."

"Why did you not prepare properly for them coming? It's an honour to be hosting them. They do us a great service."

"I'm sorry – I've been so busy with the designs for the new cottages, it slipped my mind. They're only here as we're the nearest estate to the mines, William – they're only here to be nosy. Anyway…" she reaches up and kisses him passionately, the nearby men looking away amused. "You shouldn't be thinking about women – you've got a war to win!"

Thomas comes running to his father. "Cai says I can't, but he can't say that to me. Papa, I'm coming, aren't I? That damned Morris, I –"

"Get inside Thomas – and mind your tongue!" William snaps in answer, wheeling his horse around and joining Lloyd at the front of the group. The men get into formation behind them. The boy stands, scowling and bashing his crop against his boots. Cai pulls up next to Elizabeth. As usual he seems to be riding a nervous youngster which scrapes at the gravel with its front hooves.

Back in the parlour the women are watching. Again, it is Lady Pryse who leads the conversation.

"Look at her out there now, directing operations! And the sooner the better that boy goes away to school somewhere, he's almost feral!"

"And so Welshy. Oh…" The older women exchange glances as they see Elizabeth with Cai.

In the yard Elizabeth holds Cai's horse's reins and slowly strokes its cheek.

"I'll send runners back to keep you informed, Elizabeth."

"Watch out for William… and come back safe yourself, of course." She kisses the horse's nose.

"Good luck with your own battles." His gesture takes in both the distraught Thomas, sobbing now against one of the pillars by the front door, and the parlour window in which several women can clearly be seen.

Elizabeth laughs, "Nothing a seasoned campaigner like myself can't manage." She takes his hand. "Take care, Cai. Don't be *too* much of a hero."

He nods and, jamming his hat hard onto his head, lets his horse join the others. She follows him with her eyes as they canter down the drive, round the bend by the lake and out of sight. Thomas is still howling into his sleeve. As she passes into the house she ruffles his hair.

"Come on, young man. Let's go in for something to eat – I hear Martha is making griddle scones."

Back in the parlour the visitors, show over, are seated, waited upon by Elin and Catherine, who's very much enjoying setting up the special tea table with her mother's best set. When Annie enters with a delighted William, Mari excuses herself and goes to find the grieving Thomas.

Lady Pryse holds forth, a cup of warm wine in one hand, a fresh scone in the other. "Of course, she has far exceeded any expectations she might have had on marrying the Reverend Powell all those years ago. A second son! Only think of the good fortune she's had – an older brother to die childless, well, without any legitimate heir. What is the likelihood of that? And so here she is, mistress of Nanteos and we with a clergyman leading the troops!"

Always one to affirm her friend's assertions and, if possible, to push each point a little further, Johnes' wife joins in. "They say her father failed to matriculate, probably due to lack of funds – scandalous. He was a poet, apparently."

Lady Pryse shakes her head. "Oh well, that explains it. What can you do with a man like –"

Elizabeth joins them, her face fresh and strands of damp hair trailing out from under her clean cap. "Pardon me, ladies. I've just been finalising the arrangements for battle. I do feel this is all rather unnecessary!" This meets with silence and a few pointed looks. "I do hope that you are comfortable and have everything you need?"

Pryse's sister speaks up. "Indeed. Thank you." She looks at her companions.

"We were just wondering," says Mistress Johnes. "Is that the famous Grail Cup we see there on the sideboard?"

"Yes. I was just trying to oil the wood a little. Would you care to hold it?"

"How diverting! What does one do?"

"It's supposed to heal, is it not?" asserts Lady Pryse, putting down her wine.

Elizabeth crosses to the cabinet and gently lifts the object. "Supposedly," she answers as she passes it to Mistress Johnes.

"I expect one prays over it?" says the woman, peering short-sightedly at the piece of semi-fossilised wood.

"Or perhaps rub it on the ailing part!" laughs Lady Pryse as she mimes rubbing it on her breast. There is general hilarity at this as the cup is passed from hand to hand.

Elizabeth frowns. "Well, in the past it's said that the pilgrims nibbled at the edges, bit pieces off."

Pryse's sister, whose turn it is to hold the Grail, hastily puts it down beside her. "Heavens!"

"Oh, let me try!" cries her daughter.

"Certainly not!" Her mother pushes it away from her, across the couch.

"No!" Elizabeth firmly recovers the cup and replaces it on its cushion inside the case.

For a while there's silence from the party as the tea table is replenished.

Mistress Johnes is the first to break cover. "I had heard it came to pay part of a debt owed to Nanteos by the family who were its custodians."

"Yes. It came from the Steadman estate at Strata Florida. I understand it was kept hidden from Henry VIII's soldiers when they ruined the monastery. Possibly brought previously by monks from Glastonbury and before that… well, perhaps it even came from the Holy Land!"

Lady Pryse looks across her tea cup and says drily, "What a veritable scholar you are, Mistress Powell!"

"Perhaps it could even be the Grail itself!" Mistress Johnes chuckles.

They laugh. Elizabeth smiles a tight smile. Taking her key and opening the tortoiseshell caddy on the table, she scans the company. "Some more tea before you depart, ladies?"

Morris is looking out of the window of his rented rooms in Capel Bangor as Davies arranges various files, pasting in receipts, testimonials and letters.

"I still think that we should have been out and about today. The storm you promised never came."

"Oh but it will, Sir."

"Where do you get these quaint predictions from anyway, Davies? Some local soothsayer? Some sibyl? Or a convenient tavern maid perhaps. We should have been there today, to check on the exploratory work. These," he gestures to the maps and plans laid out on the long table, "are almost ready. The Cardiganshire gentry are going to get rather a surprise are they not?"

"And what happens when you present your findings?"

"Ah, that is when the real work begins. Licences, Davies, licences will be up for auction and you and I will be most ideally placed!" He returns again to his detailed study of the sky. "Did you talk to the Powell men about the direction in which the lode is going?"

"It comes our way, Sir."

"Excellent! You will find that your prospects have not suffered from your association with me, Davies. No, indeed. Now, let us hear no more about this storm." He reaches for his coat and shouts in English, "Let's to horse!"

An hour later, Lloyd, Powell, Cai and others of the gentry's private posse arrive outside Morris' lodgings. As the men surround the building, Lloyd, Powell and Cai enter the house, ignoring an alarmed maid who attempts to check them.

Lloyd flings open the door to the small parlour. No sign of the two men.

"Where are they, woman?" he shouts in the maid's face.

"Gone, Sir. Just now. You've only missed them these last minutes."

"Gone where?"

"I don't know, Sir… the mines perhaps?"

She is close to tears. Cai turns to her, "Have they taken their goods? Did they pack up and leave, or was it as if they were just going as usual." She shakes her head. "No, they didn't pack up?"

"No, Sir. Mr Morris ordered his dinner for tonight. He's to have mutton chops and currant suet pudding with a veal pie."

"That has a ring of truth about it," mutters Powell.

Lloyd goes back into the parlour intent on destroying the maps and charts, carefully labelled and laid out on a trestle table by the far wall. "Blasted man! He should be whipped through the streets!"

But Powell holds his arm. "No Lloyd, he has powerful friends."

"And so do I." He shoves Powell away and, adjusting his coat,

shouts to Cai, "Get these stashed away! I'm confiscating them."
He turns to William. "We were told he would be here. Can you
trust your man, Powell? What's his name?"

"Davies. Yes. He's paid enough for trust not to be a
problem."

He stamps from the room, shouting as he goes. "Mount up,
the bastard's not here!"

Up at Esgair Mwyn, Morris and Davies, with some workers, are
excavating a shallow pit. Several of the men are Nanteos mine
workers, the surface workings of the Powell mine visible nearby.
Morris turns to the young man who seems restless – more
interested in studying the far horizon than focussing on his
work.

"Have you got worms? You and the blasted horses can't
keep still today. Did you hear what I asked you? Go and take a
measurement of the gradient. We need to know how well it'd
drain if we dig in."

A nearby worker looks up in alarm.

"Remember, Sir – that's Powell land."

"There'll always be a way to find that statement untrue,
man. Don't think, dig!"

Suddenly a group of miners appear on the brow of the
small hill. They look to be running for their lives, shouting and
waving frantically. They are pursued by gentry militia – about
twenty-five men on horseback. Cai is in the lead, Lloyd close
behind. They drive the men towards Morris' group as riders
from the back fan out, then double back to trap them all. Soon
all Morris' men are corralled, the horses panting and whinnying
in excitement, their riders' weapons drawn. As Morris stands in
front of Davies to protect him, Lloyd smirks to see the turncoat
still trusted. Perhaps hoping to catch the Northerner off guard,

Lloyd shouts in English, "Ah! The Pig of Môn up to his old tricks, digging up our truffles, I see!"

There is laughter from some of the mounted men, but not from the miners. The few who have understood, know that Sir Herbert Lloyd can mean no good. He turns to Welsh as he harangues them.

"I see that some of you have lost your way and find yourselves on the wrong side of the mountain! You are too stupid perhaps to know which mine keeps you on its books?" He turns to Cai, "Gruffydd, do you see a face you recognise?"

"Many."

"Then there are men whose children will not eat this winter."

He turns to his henchmen, "Round them up. Take their names… if they've got cottages, evict them. If they're in the barracks, throw their possessions on a fire."

As his men move in to take hold of the miners – one in every two dismounting, the other holding both horses – a big man, roaring with fury, pushes through to Lloyd.

"Get off that beast and face me!" he challenges in Welsh.

Lloyd sneers and, wheeling his horse around, backs the animal onto the standing man. Red from the spurs stain the stallion's flanks as the haunches continue to advance, knocking the man to his knees. Lloyd's men laugh but another miner lunges for the bridle and the horse shies away in fear. Lloyd, unsteady, clutches at the front of the saddle and now it is the group of miners who are laughing. Grabbing at the girth, the man on the floor goes to pull himself up but Lloyd, incensed, lashes him across the ear and cheek with his crop. It is all the man can do to protect his eye. This is the signal both groups have been waiting for. Lloyd gives a final kick in the face to the miner, snapping his head back on his neck and, as he falls, urges his horse away to a nearby mound of old slag covered now in coarse grass. The gentry force is bigger, the miners unprepared and some fighting only with their fists. Others, hoping to take advantage of the chaos, are trying to escape from the gulley.

Powell and Trevelyan arrive on horseback with a dozen or so more men on foot. The group pitches in as Powell comes alongside Lloyd.

"Ah, the good Reverend. We have begun the fun and games already! It seems some of your men had got lost in the fog and stumbled upon the workings of Mr Morris here!"

"Arrest these men!" shouts William.

Lloyd laughs. "Why so? They will never work in Cardiganshire again."

It doesn't take long for the reinforcements to gain control and soon, two to one, Morris' miners are held trapped by the gentry forces.

"Now Morris, you will go to gaol!" Lloyd gestures to a couple of his men who grab the surveyor. He struggles. Lloyd leads the laughter. "Ah, the swine resists the butcher's boys, I see!" He manoeuvres his horse so that he can place his pistol against Morris' temple. "Maybe this will help you be philosophical about your fate?"

A fight breaks out again at the back of the group. One miner, Huw, is on the ground, a member of Lloyd's gang battering his ribs with a pickaxe handle. Cai flings himself down from his horse shouting, "Enough!"

But Lloyd's man is enjoying himself, perhaps even settling some old score. Past the stage of trying to get him off, Huw is just trying to protect himself, contorting his body in order to gain some control of the damage to his head and kidneys. Cai punches the attacker full in the face and knocks him down, getting a black eye from his nearby companion for his pains.

He is just turning to tackle him too when Powell, fist clenched around his raised crop, bellows.

"Get away, man. Who do you think you are, brawling like a Scotsman? Get some gunpowder and get this shaft filled in!"

Cai steps back, reluctantly dropping his fists. The crowd, momentarily animated, becomes sullen again. Many watch Cai as he returns to his horse; watch Powell count out £100 and give it to Lloyd; watch the latter lick his thumb to skim through the pile again.

"Easy to get two stuck together – wouldn't want to cheat you, Powell!"

William answers, without a trace of irony. "A fine job, Sir Herbert. You miss your vocation."

The party splits three ways. Lloyd, Powell and men leave with Morris, his hands tied together, someone leading his pony; Trevelyan and the biggest group drag the Powell miners away. Some are weeping. Cai and a small band of men stay to organise the sabotage of Morris' interests. As he goes to his saddlebags for the explosives, Davies sidles up to him.

"He will guess about me. I'm sure of it!"

"Move downwind of me, Davies. There's a stink coming off you."

Later, Cai sits in the kitchen, an old shirt stuffed with ice on his nose. Martha tuts to herself as she moves around at her work. "How many did you say you'd brought back with you for me to feed?" she asks.

"About twenty, I think."

"And how many of those are above stairs?"

"Three to join the family. I'll eat with the others."

"Nonsense! Mistress'll never allow that." She bangs a broiling pan onto the table by his elbow. "Who else from the house was hurt?" Cai shrugs. "Was the master injured; any of the outside servants? Well?"

"I don't know, Martha. We took them by surprise and we had horses. Lloyd's men even had guns on them. It wasn't much of a fight."

"So how is it that you were hurt, then? How is it that you're always caught in the middle? Eh?" She ruffles his hair.

Mari comes in through the hall door.

"Get this man bandaged up will you, girl. He's not fit to be seen!" She goes out to the scullery as Mari stands, eyes shining.

"A hero! They are all talking about you, Cai!"

"All talking again, Mari. You love to gossip."

"Not I. But I have got ears to hear it. They said you punched a rough miner to the ground. He had a pickaxe!"

"Not exactly. He was the one on the ground getting a beating. I stopped him losing his ribs."

Cai tips his head back and closes his eyes, melted ice soaking into his shirt. Taking a bowl, rag and some warm water from the fire, Mari stands in front of him, her legs pressing against his knees. He doesn't open his eyes. Taking the bowl and cloth in one hand she uses the other to ease up her trapped skirt a little. Although he still hasn't opened his eyes, he smiles at her boldness as he adjusts the ice. Taking care to brush her breasts against his cheek, Mari leans across him to wipe away the dried and sticky blood. For a while he lets her tend to him, the warm cloth easing the ache of the bruises.

"Why do they do it, Mari? They know they'll be found out. They'll lose everything now: families evicted –"

"Wages are better, it's said. There's even a chance for them to have a licence themselves."

But Cai is sitting up by now, Mari scrabbling to regain her balance.

"A damn lie! All it means is strangers coming in and taking their labour!"

"Not everyone likes to work for the gentry."

"And you can bet that we'll get the blame, working in Nanteos – not Sir Herbert or King George!" Martha joins in, coming back in with a brace of game as Mari pulls away from Cai. He throws the icy mess into her bowl and stands up.

"Get out of here, you two – that heat coming off you'll ruin my custards!" says Martha, smiling at last, "Mari, go and ask your mistress if it's wine sauce she wants." Mari stands, reluctant to leave. "Go on, girl! Just put that down on the side…" She leaves, the door yawning after her. Martha turns to Cai, looking him up and down with a wry smile. "Well, young man, at least somebody loves you!"

Meanwhile William is chest deep in his bath, John in attendance. There's a tap at the door and Elizabeth comes in, dismissing the servant and holding the door open for him as he leaves, his arms loaded with dirty linen.

"Elizabeth?"

She joins him in his dressing room, spreading the waiting towel over her knees as she sits on a chair.

"Well?" she says. He disappears under the water, reappears, blowing from his mouth. She hands him the towel and he presses it into his eyes. "There are rumours enough. I hear you got Morris?"

"Correct – the swine is in custody. An ugly business."

"Where've you taken him?"

"Lloyd's taking him down to Cardigan jail… and he won't get out in a hurry, I can tell you that."

"The king won't like it –"

"Old George'll have to lump it!"

He pushes up out of the bath and she hands him the towel. "What'll you do next?"

"I need to go to London. There'll be a hearing most probably. I need to be there to fight my corner, stop people bending Powis' ear. We'll try and get Jane up to keep you company."

"But I have company." He looks sharply at her as he dries himself. She continues, "I've changed my mind about a visitor. I've plenty to do with the building and the plans for the new accommodation –"

"You can forget that! Good God, the money haemorrhages out of this place! There's sweeteners to be paid now – I've started that game already, and Nanteos'll be taking the brunt of it."

"What sweeteners?"

"You don't think Lloyd and his men do it out of the goodness of their hearts, do you?"

He moves through to his room and starts to dress. She sits on the window seat. "We must at least get the new pumps into the mines, William. We'll never claw ourselves out of this if we don't go deeper."

"Good God, woman! What with? Do you know how many mortgages didn't pay up last year, and building work unpaid right back to my brother's time? Cai's filling your head with nonsense. If he wasn't such a hot-headed fool I'd take him with me and get him right out of your way!"

"He's been injured."

"His own fault. He sees a brawl and can't resist –"

"Mari says he saved one of our men from a battering."

"She'll say anything, that girl. The man was one of ours gone over to the other side; a bloody traitor. Deserved all he got!"

Elizabeth gets up and goes over to his dressing table, quietly adjusting her husband's wig where he's jammed it, all crooked, onto his head. He kisses her palm and pulls her onto his knee. For a while they sit quietly, his chin resting on her hair.

"It will be good for you to have Jane here, I believe. Another woman will settle you –" Elizabeth laughs as he continues, "And hopefully the weather will improve. Cai'll be off out. I'll keep him busy doing some surveying for our side. There must be some more good lead, or silver even, near the surface somewhere. We haven't even tried that land we bought from Pryse yet. You can busy yourself with getting the stables finished –"

"Oh, that's all right, then. Everybody safely amused and out of mischief whilst you're away."

She gets off his knee and hands him the powder for his wig.

"You know what I mean, Elizabeth. Please just look after the children... and try and make us a little more popular in the county whilst I'm away. And don't spend any money, for the Lord's sake!"

CHAPTER ELEVEN

THE HEARING, IN the Court of the Exchequer, London, is packed. Lewis Morris has brought tenants from Cardiganshire specially to testify on the Crown's behalf. Both men and women, they are of the poorest – those with something to lose knowing better than to throw in their lot with a man before being certain he's on the winning side. Many of them are wearing coats and waistcoats of the same colour, cut and cloth – as if someone has kitted them out in a job lot for the London trip. Huw is with them, standing head and shoulders above the rest, the only one to hold the gaze of both Powell and Lloyd. Morris is giving evidence. His very strong accent raises a smirk on the faces of the fine gentlemen in the chamber.

"I have a mandate! I am under instruction by Mr William Corbett, Steward of the Crown Mines. I am his deputy. These good people…" he gestures to the Welsh peasants, "These people will testify as to historical usage and precedence. Evidence has been fabricated by these greedy landlords –" his arm takes in, not only Powell and Lloyd, but many of those seated in the court. There are jeers at this, but he will not be put off. "They are trying to cheat the Crown… and the people." He repeats this in Welsh. Some of the peasants boo in response.

Lloyd turns to William. "The man's a joke!"

Morris addresses the court again, his voice loud, his stance assured. "These men are judge and jury in Cardiganshire. They rule the King's county as if it were their plantations, with the people their slaves!" He repeats this in Welsh.

This time a more vehement response from the Cardiganshire crowd follows. It is difficult to see who speaks, as almost every mouth is open in protest, but William hears clearly from the body of the crowd. "You'll pay, Powell! We'll bloody take you! Screw down the windows on your women and children at night." His face sets tight against them. Huw gets to his feet and shakes his fist in William's direction. Eventually officials succeed in quietening them.

Morris stands and makes a gesture to calm them. "These men, the MPs and JPs of the county, flout with impunity the very law they were sworn to uphold!" Again he translates. There are murmurings of unease from the English bystanders as they see the furious reaction of the Welsh crowd. Morris turns and gestures at Lloyd. "And this man clapped me in Cardiganshire gaol for six weeks. It is a lawless county they run, but the real brigands of Cardiganshire do not skulk in the hills – oh, no. They sit sipping port in the dining rooms and libraries of its fine mansions!"

This time, the reaction from the watching English crowd is so hostile that it takes him several minutes to translate successfully. When he is finally understood by the Welsh there is fresh uproar.

Lloyd sidles to his feet, holding up one, cool hand for silence. His voice is loud, but not a shout and as he speaks slowly, almost indolently, he points at Morris, though looks at the general court.

"As you have heard only too clearly for yourselves, this man is drunk with his own importance. He has run amok up there in the Wild West." He waits for the appreciative laughter to subside. "He is abusing his position as Deputy Steward, a servant of the King. Not even a native of that county himself, he is causing unrest in Cardiganshire, setting Welshman against Welshman.

I say that he should go back to that druid's island from whence he came!"

As he delivers the last sentence he adopts both Morris' northern accent and his pot-bellied stance. The English crowd erupts in laughter at Lloyd's mockery. The Welsh crowd look confused. Nobody translates for them. As Lloyd slides back into his seat William, hand on his arm, mouths to him, "Thank you, my friend."

It is raining at Nanteos, drops collecting like grease on the windows, the whole sky a pale-washed grey. Sometimes the wind casts it at the glass where it irritates like thrown gravel. The children are still upstairs and Elizabeth and Jane are finishing their breakfast from a small, informal table in the morning room.

"You'll see we keep up with fashion, Jane. No cereal pottage and ale for us. Only the best tea, coffee and rolls for our guests."

"Very impressive." They laugh.

Jane warms her hands on her chocolate bowl. "Well, how did you enjoy *Fanny Hill*, the book I leant you?"

"I almost blush to talk about it even with you!"

"Yes I know!"

"It's not what she does – that's familiar enough –"

"Oh, lucky you!"

Elizabeth laughs. "Well, I mean, it's not beyond one's imagination. It's the naming of it, somehow; seeing it written down and qualified."

"Yes, but what a sensibility – and for it to have been written by a man!"

"That is what I can hardly believe. What do men make of it?"

"I think they read it in a different way."

"Yes. With their hands down their britches!"

Jane laughs. "Men are used to reading such things."

"But surely there is no need of so much feeling in it, if titillation was the only reason for writing."

"Will you lend it to William; assuming he hasn't already read it."

"No."

Jane raises her eyebrows, questioning.

"I want to give him a surprise." They laugh. Elizabeth continues, "In all seriousness, though, I think it would feel strange, knowing he'd read it and that I had, too. I fear it would bring a sort of shame or embarrassment between us."

"I never have the feeling that there's shame between you both."

"There isn't. I just feel that reading *about* the act of love may somehow paralyse the practising of it. A stupid thing to say perhaps, but we just act –"

"Instead of feeling self-conscious, perhaps?"

Elizabeth nods. Jane goes to the Grail cabinet. "Here it is!"

"Yes."

"Do you use it?"

"I?"

Jane waits for an answer.

"Yes I would, I'm sure, but luckily there has been no need."

"May I hold it?"

"Certainly." Elizabeth unlocks the case and lifts the remains of the cup from its box. They pass it between them like a newborn baby.

"It is so delicate…"

"The Nibbling Pilgrims have done that."

"It does have a certain presence though, even so. I suppose it is just that one knows what its provenance might be." Jane sits down carefully.

"It's one's own mind that convinces, I'm sure. Yet, when I opened the parcel from William, disappointed though I was, as soon as it was in air, there was a sort of silence in the room."

Jane murmurs in agreement, her slim fingers placed lightly on the wood where it lies in her lap.

"No, that's not really it. It wasn't so much a cessation of noise as a suspension of movement… or both perhaps." She looks at the cup, takes a deep breath. "You know when you've been a long time in a bumpy carriage and you hardly notice it anymore? Then perhaps it stops to change a wheel, and you wonder up the road a way. Suddenly it's still, calm and quiet, and you realise how awful it had been before."

Jane nods gravely. "It's soothing – the weight on my legs."

"Strange, isn't it?"

"Our imagination surely: the power of the mind to persuade itself."

She hands the relic back to Elizabeth who kisses it quickly, before putting it away. Jane looks at her in surprise.

"Oh I know it's foolish! I don't know why I do it."

Elin knocks lightly, enters with a small curtsey and starts to clear away the dishes. Jane drains the last of her chocolate and puts the bowl on the tray.

"Still doing the servant's work?" Elizabeth teases.

"Cuts down on wages!"

They laugh and Elizabeth reaches for her friend's hand. "Come, you've escaped the ride I'd planned for us – I'll take you on the tour. If you're very lucky you can even see my meticulously labelled linen cupboards!"

The next day Elizabeth wakes to sunshine, pouring into her room despite the rich drapes. It is the first day since last summer that the morning light has seemed really golden. She had not bothered to have the fire lit in her room last night as she and Jane had stayed up so late. How could it be that the hours pass so quickly with a woman friend? The only reason they'd finally gone their separate ways just before two was a headache she'd given herself from talking so much. She did not bother to ring for a fire this morning either, there was really no need, and if only her undergarments weren't so tricky there would be no need to call anyone at all. She wishes she could just dress herself, like a common woman does, go down to breakfast in her own hair and move naturally amongst her household all day. This isn't London where she has to be on duty for visitors every moment of the day. It is really unnecessarily stupid to be on such ceremony!

She pulls on her robe and crosses to the window, lifting her legs onto the seat and looking out across the river to the ridge beyond. The scene still has a damp mist to it that augurs better for a fine day than a completely clear sky so early in the morning. As she watches, she sees the unmistakeable figure of Gruffydd on his mule passing the lake. He must have got up before dawn to get all the way down here so early. What could have brought him here? She jumps up and rings for Elin to dress her.

Jane is already dressed as she calls at her room. She embraces her, reminded again at the surprise of holding another woman: the corseted curves having to find a way to fit around each other, and the lovely scent. Strange too to hold someone nearly her own size – not a man, not a child. Breakfast is laid for them again in the morning room and Elizabeth dismisses Elin to serve her friend.

"A picnic today, Jane. I am determined to force colour into your sallow London cheeks!"

"But not another bone-rattling journey in a coach, I beg you."

"How feeble! But no, why bother a coach and horses. We'll have a picnic – there on the ridge, with the oak for shade. It's the most wonderful view of the house from up there. That was the first ride I went on when we took on the house. Cai took me all over the estate and right up to the mines. One of the best days of my life! You would not believe how the people live up there… there's something dark about it, almost medieval."

"They do call Cardiganshire the Wild West!"

They laugh. Elizabeth looks again to the window where she sees Cai and Gruffydd deep in discussion.

"Right," she says, unable to resist finding out what's going on. "I'll go and order a picnic. Don't rush your breakfast – I'll be back in a minute."

In the hallway she hesitates a moment, undecided whether to go outside first or go straight to the kitchens to get the picnic started. Jenkins hurries past.

"What's happening?" she asks. "Everything seems disordered today – what are we up to?"

"Ah," Jenkins falters a moment. "Mistress. Today they bring the colts in from all the Nanteos farms."

"Oh." Elizabeth looks puzzled for a moment, then she says quickly, "Yes of course; I see. Er… who is to do it, Jenkins?"

"Why, Cai, Ma'am. Cai always does it. He learned it off the horse traders at Tregaron."

"Thank you, Jenkins."

He looks relieved as he leaves. Elizabeth turns around and follows him outside into the spring sunshine. Cai and Gruffydd are just making their way to the stables and she almost has to run to catch them up. She calls out and they stop for her.

"Mr Gruffydd, are you here for the colts?" He nods his head and smiles. "So kind of you," she says.

Again he acknowledges her with a small bow of the head.

142

"He's here in case we can't stop the bleeding." Cai says, quietly.

Two men pass with a trestle table on which is an array of castration clamps and knives.

"Oh, yes; excellent, very necessary," she replies hastily.

A farm hand, leading a young working horse in each hand, passes them on his way to the paddock behind the stables.

"Right," she says. "I must leave you to get on."

Cai bows, smiles and turns away. Gruffydd stands for a moment. Elizabeth waits for him to speak but instead he just touches his hat to her and follows Cai.

Jane is standing at the window when Elizabeth returns.

"A change of plan, I think. With your permission, we'll go a little further afield after all. They're castrating." She shudders. "A horrible job!"

"Necessary, though."

"Yes, of course. I must have forgotten. I don't think it'll be the thing to be picnicking here, though."

"No, quite!"

Elizabeth rings the bell.

"I'll ask for the light chaise and a pony and drive us myself – not even you could feel sea sick then."

"What about Catherine? Should she not come with us?"

"Oh yes, I hadn't thought. I'll get Elin to ask her."

As Elizabeth is being dressed in her travelling clothes, there's a tap at her door. Catherine comes in.

"Mama? You wanted to see me?"

Elizabeth looks at her, puzzled, for a moment.

"Ah yes, my love. Jane and I are to picnic by the river – she asked if you would like to come with us. You could bring your sketchbook."

"Oh no, not today. Martha has promised to take me to gather some plants I can use to make colours."

"What plants?"

"To make dyes: herbs and things growing in the kitchen gardens and outside."

"But you've got paints; I can buy you more paints, Catherine."

"Oh, but it's not so much fun! I want to make them myself."

"I think that Cook has quite enough to do today without having to wander around the woods all morning."

"Why? She said today. She said after rain is ideal. Today is going to be a good day to start picking."

"She's got a lot of extra mouths to feed today. There are many farm hands who've brought the young horses up for… treatment."

"What treatment?"

"Well… do you know what castration is?" Elin looks up sharply. Catherine frowns a moment. Elizabeth continues. "The young colts need to be kept away from the mares. We can't have more than a few stallions on the estate; it gets impossible to separate them from each other and they can get unmanageable."

Catherine is still silent.

"Do you know the difference between a gelding and a stallion?" Light dawns on Catherine and she nods. "Well, then. Today is the day. Cook will be very busy and I don't really want you to be in the way."

"But may I just ask her, Mama?"

"I don't really want you around the stables or the paddock anyway, Catherine. Not today. It's not an attractive business."

"I won't go near, of course. But may I ask her? If she is not too busy, we could still go. I promise to keep out of the way of the poor horses."

Elizabeth is about to insist but can't bear to spoil the expression on the animated little face. It is so seldom that Catherine pushes to have her own way.

"Very well; you may ask her – but do not bully her, please."

The girl turns on her heels and disappears without a backwards glance. Elizabeth crosses to the window. Outside, a basket of provisions is already being loaded onto the trap, a sullen-looking boy holding the pony's head, his real attention obviously with the action behind the stables.

"Right," says Elizabeth. "Must be off! What will you do today, Elin?"

"There'll be plenty to do to help in the kitchens, Ma'am"

"Yes, of course. I do hope the day goes well."

She makes her way outside where Martha herself is putting a warm pie into the basket. She smiles at Elizabeth.

"Thank you, Martha. A wonderful feast! Now, Catherine has been telling me something about a hunt for plant dyes and paint materials – one would imagine that today is not the day. I'm sure you are too busy to accommodate a budding artist."

"Not at all, Mistress. In fact, it'll be a pleasure to get out on such a lovely day – and to get far away from the service yard as well. I'm not one for slaughter day or that sort of thing, despite the fact I can deal with the bodies once they're done."

"No, exactly. Yes, I quite understand…" her voice trails off as Martha bobs a curtsey and takes her leave.

Jane appears on the steps, fastening her gloves and drawing a large shawl around her.

"Oh, Jane, you won't need all that – it's a lovely spring day!"

"You never can tell how long it'll last – especially in Wales."

"Yes – too true!" They laugh and Elizabeth hands her into

the buggy and climbs up beside her. She pulls the rug over her friend's knees. "Right. We'll just tuck Grandmother in and then be off!"

Jane laughs. "What of Catherine?"

"She's decided to stay here to do something with her painting."

"Is that wise, Elizabeth?"

"Yes, yes, I've had a word with her myself."

"But who's to look after her?"

"Oh heavens – any number of people. Mari is about somewhere; Elin of course, and I've spoken to Cook personally." Jane is silent. "This isn't London, Jane!"

But Jane still doesn't answer, looking away across the river as she adjusts her shawl.

"Thank you!" Elizabeth calls to the boy, who briefly doffs his hat before running back eagerly to the stables. She wakes up the pony and they leave the house behind. Just as she's breaking into a trot to pass the paddock, Cai is seen waving her down. She stops the pony who snorts his objection, and waits. Cai joins them, holding a dejected-looking Thomas by the shoulder.

"Mistress Gardener; Mistress Powell," he removes his hat.

"What can we do for you?" Elizabeth asks, frowning automatically at Thomas.

"I wonder; could you take this young man out with you for the day?"

"May I ask why, Cai?"

"He'll be good protection for you against any highwaymen you might encounter."

Elizabeth looks at her son expecting defiance. Instead he's looking down at his boots.

"Well, most certainly," she replies, moving to the right as Thomas gets in the other side of Jane. As she gathers up the reins again, she leans over Cai and asks quietly, "What is the real reason?"

"I thought perhaps today would be an education for him, but I find he's enjoying it too much."

"Oh, I see," she nods, grimly. "Oh, I meant to ask you – how do you decide which colt to keep entire and which to cut?"

Cai looks quickly at Jane – it is an indelicate question. But Jane, having good manners, busies herself making small talk with Thomas.

"Your governess –" Cai begins.

"I didn't have one." She laughs. "My father educated me, and we had specialist tutors visit the house."

"Ah, well, you must imagine a schoolmaster then – who assesses his pupils, observes them, sets tests for them. He has watched them since they were young and is familiar with their family. Would you trust such a man to grade those pupils and to choose which one to take and develop for higher things? Which ones to let quietly slip into an unremarkable future?"

"Indeed I would."

"That then is how the gifted colt makes a stallion. Everything about him, from his eye to his gait, tells you to keep him intact." He smiles up at Elizabeth who laughs and leans towards him.

"Again you are my education, Cai Gruffydd."

"Should we not be going, Elizabeth?" Jane's tone is clipped as she cuts across. "Surely we risk being caught up in this business if we wait any longer!"

Elizabeth sits up abruptly and composes her expression. "Oh, surely you're right, Jane. Off we go, but this time with reinforcements – we are to be guarded by Thomas-the-brave!" As she gathers up the reins she rolls her eyes at Cai who turns away, smiling.

They trot down the drive, Thomas leaning past Jane and his

mother to take a last, longing look at the waiting buckets and the smouldering brazier in the paddock.

"May I drive, Mama?" he asks as they slow to go through the big gates. Only one has been opened today, the gatekeeper apologising when he sees them, still fastening his coat as he hastens to doff his cap.

"No, Thomas – not today. Jane is a very nervous passenger I'm afraid."

Though there is little talk for a while, the sunshine and heady smell of early spring soon thaw the chilly atmosphere between the two women.

They turn off the road by a stand of beech trees and make their way down a narrow lane. The pony can smell the river and picks up his legs in a smart trot. They don't cross the little bridge but pull up in a meadow where Thomas jumps down to see to the animal as the two women unload the picnic. The grass is still not very high after the hard winter, but forget-me-nots already play through it. Once unloaded, Thomas releases the horse from the traces and puts a stake in for him to graze. He goes down to collect water in the bucket that always hangs off the little trap. The two women lay the large oilskin, then the rugs, picnic cloths, cushions and blankets under the trees.

"We need a little shade. We don't want to be all brawny and hideous like Fanny Hill's Mrs Brown."

Jane starts to laugh, "Oh good grief, her horrendous wobbling thighs…"

"The 'maidenhead mines'!"

"Her 'beggar's wallet'… the 'gap… overshaded with a gggrrrizzly bush!'"

"Really, that book! What next! I think you have it by heart, Jane."

Thomas comes back and they settle themselves, their backs to the sun, the deep, slow-moving river sending up small groups of early, dancing insects.

"Look at that, Elizabeth! How lovely – like lace beneath the trees!"

"Yes – wood anemone. It's late this year."

"You know this place?"

"This is the first time this year, of course, but we have come here before, when we've stayed at Nanteos as Thomas' guests. The tenants are most kind. Once Thomas was stung by a horsefly and the wife had him in and plastered with some wonderful evil-smelling leaf pulp – he was thrilled."

Jane laughs. The air is thick with birdsong, layered by the different pitches and rhythms, every voice competing furiously for attention at this time of year.

"Mama – I'm going to paddle," Thomas announces, breaking off a fistful of cheese.

"Yes, do – but don't go out of earshot, please."

"Talking of such things, the Magdalen Charity hopes to open a home for young girls."

Elizabeth looks puzzled.

"Fanny Hill; young prostitutes. At last there is something to be done about them."

"Oh, yes of course."

"And the Lock Hospital is thriving, always full to the gunnels. If they don't change their ways, they are not welcome back. Ah, there are such reforms afoot in London, Elizabeth. It's such an exciting time!"

"I'm sure."

"We're helping raise money for the Magdalen Charity – you could subscribe."

"I'd love to."

"There are many young Welsh girls fallen into prostitution after coming to the capital. The *Cymmrodorion* are hoping to set up a school for girls from Wales."

Elizabeth hands her some lemonade.

"Now, what are you going to do about Catherine?" Jane says, suddenly.

"What do you mean?"

"She can't just meander around the house doing nothing. Will you send her to school or get a governess?"

"Well we… we had thought of one of the schools. She did go to school, as you know, when we lived in London, but it's a very different thing to think of a boarding school so very far away."

"There are none around here, one supposes?"

"No, indeed. Even Thomas would have to go as far as Hereford."

"Yes – what of Thomas? Don't you have him rather running wild here?"

Elizabeth opens her mouth ready to defend herself, but can think of nothing to say.

Jane continues, "You've been here since last September, and the children it seems have no friends of their own class and have not progressed at all in their education –"

"Jane!"

"Forgive me, but isn't this the role of a friend? How long has William been away now?"

"About five weeks. But really, Jane, we are well. Everything is well since we came to Nanteos. When William comes back we will arrange it all. Surely Thomas will go to school, and Catherine will have a governess, share some lessons with the other young girls – the Johnes', perhaps –"

"Yes, but that needs planning, Elizabeth. You do not seem

to put your energies into it. You are all about draining the mines –"

"But that's important! That's our income. Farming is nothing in comparison to the mine revenues and we are under threat! Cai –"

"Ah... Cai."

"What do you mean?"

"William does well to keep him on."

"That phrase – I hate it! Cai has a right to be at Nanteos."

"Not strictly speaking, no. William does him a kindness. Surely you can see that, Elizabeth?"

"But we need Cai... I need him; William is away such a lot." She goes quiet for a moment. "Anyway, all this talk of charitable institutions... What about behaving justly at home? It would be unchristian to turn him out and William is no hypocrite."

"Indeed not. He takes his duty most seriously – has he told you of his support for the foundling hospital yet?" Elizabeth shakes her head. "You are both so taken up with this court case and grand plans for the estate that you cannot see how unstable your household becomes."

Thomas arrives and starts digging in one of the hampers for food. Grateful for the diversion, Elizabeth jumps to her feet. "Whoa! Wait a minute, I'll help you to that – or there won't be anything left for us." She busies herself laying out the rest of the food, her face hidden from her friend by her long hair.

Jane watches her. Elizabeth has kicked off her shoes and stockings and pushed back her bonnet. She will surely turn all brown!

"A shilling for your thoughts, Jane?" Elizabeth says at last, aware of her friend's eyes on her.

"Oh!" Jane laughs. "I was just thinking how you're going to get all burnt with your bonnet off… and then I thought of our lecherous Mrs Brown again!" She shakes with laughter.

Elizabeth smiles, "I wondered what you were grinning at!"

"What?" says Thomas.

"Never you mind. What about some more mutton pie?"

The afternoon stretches ahead of them, the sun bright, but not yet really warm. Somehow, despite the late notice and the chaos of the castration party, the picnic is a feast but, though the women are content to lie back on the thick rug and doze, a couple of blankets pulled over them, Thomas is restless. Eventually they agree to go with him down river towards the mill and the river keeper's cottage.

Sparse clouds of early midges group together over the deep water and lesser celandines glow yellow against the damp, dark earth under the trees. Elizabeth has put her shoes back on but they are soon wet. Here and there large rocks protrude from the water, each streaked with droppings. Thomas points.

"What does that?"

"Ah – well spotted, Thomas. That's a dipper rock. They sit on them and hold forth marking their territory."

"And look like what?"

"Smallish but sturdy-looking. Mostly brown but with a lovely white waistcoat."

Thomas nods gravely, committing it to memory.

"Elizabeth, you really are a font of knowledge!"

"You're an expert on the street life of London Jane, and I'm the amateur naturalist."

"I'm not sure that reflects very well on me!"

"Nonsense. You're a reformer. London badly needs reformers."

Jane smiles at her. "Earlier, before we dined… I'm afraid I

spoke perhaps out of turn. I do not have living children; it is possible that I am over-anxious on behalf of yours. William is wise and a fine Christian – as are you." She adds, hastily, "I'm sure you will do what is right for your children."

Elizabeth laughs and takes her hand. They join Thomas at the bank where a small beach has formed. Beyond it the river is deep and calm, flowing slowly, the surface an unbroken sheet. The water is so clear that every individual stone can be seen.

"Why are these stones brown, Mama – and beach stones grey?"

Elizabeth opens her mouth to answer, but says instead, "Actually, Thomas, I don't know – a very good question!"

He looks away, hiding a proud smile. They pick a path across the pebbles, going downstream, the boy now and again pouncing on a colourful stone. The women find a boulder and sit, the dappled sun coming through the trees and making it just comfortably warm.

"Aren't they beautiful!" Thomas exclaims as he makes a pyramid of his finds, the deep, autumnal colours glowing as the light catches them. For a while, none of them speaks – the water and the picnic working their soporific magic.

"Do you remember us at the Vauxhall gardens?" Elizabeth's voice is low and slow.

"Ah, those supper boxes! We had a lot of fun."

"The ham – so thin you could read a newspaper through it."

"You tried once." They laugh. "I do miss you, Elizabeth."

"Oh look; the first of the year!" Elizabeth sits up suddenly and points to the tattered, dusty figure of an orange and brown butterfly.

"Look, Thomas – *pili-pala*! Oh dear, it must just have emerged from its winter sleep. It doesn't look too good!"

Thomas takes a cursory look then gets back to his collecting.

"What did you call it?" Jane asks.

"*Pili-pala*. Actually, they've got several names in Welsh: *glöyn byw*, live cinder, and *iâr fach yr haf*, little chicken of the summer".

Jane is laughing. "Oh, how delightful!"

They settle back, the soundscape of water, insects and birds, mixed with the sun's rays on their closed lids, soothing.

"How curious!" exclaims Elizabeth, sitting bolt upright again.

"What?"

"Well, I was thinking about Thomas' river pebble versus beach pebble question; another odd thing is that the smell is so different. This," she gestures to the water, "is an earthy/river smell; yet the sea is totally different."

"Oh, yes – you're right. I hadn't thought about it."

"Mama, what's that?" Thomas, his shoes and stockings off and up to his britches in the shallows, points to a still pool upstream. A spit of stones has cut off the pond from the main river. "Something strange."

"I can't see anything, Thomas. What're you pointing at?"

She holds out her hand for him to help her off her boulder and slips her shoes back on. Jane gets up and follows them under the willow tree, its trunk fissured as if claws have been dragged down it. In the still water, four small figures are floating. At first they seem to be alive – their ears pert, their paws spread out as if treading water. Even their heads are erect, some strange rigor mortis holding their spines rigid perhaps.

"Fox cubs," breathes Jane, at last. "As though you could just reach in and pluck them from the river by the ear, drop them on the bank and watch them rough and tumble."

"But they'd bite you. At least, if they weren't dead, they would," Thomas answers, his voice almost a whisper.

"Did they just fall in following their mother, or did someone drown them on purpose? What do you think, Elizabeth?"

Elizabeth watches the bodies slowly turning, bobbing in the water. To drown a fox cub – a commonplace occurrence, of course. But to leave them, displayed there! What imagination had done it?

"Let's go back," she says.

"Shall I fetch them out, Mama? I could wade in and hook them with my stick?"

But he makes no move towards the river.

"No, leave them – it might be a deliberate warning, we don't know. Anyway, it's too horrible."

They turn away, cross over the fallen willow leaves, long and grey as feathers.

"Wait a moment!" Thomas shouts. "I need to get my stones!" He runs downstream.

Jane crosses her shawl over her chest. "Even the countryside is not always sweet."

Elizabeth nods.

Thomas is trudging back dragging his stick, shoulders hunched.

"No stones?"

"No, Mama. They were all ugly and dry. They were just ordinary."

"Yes of course – I should have warned you. As soon as they dry out they're not worth having."

He turns away. They walk back upstream. Thomas points at a patch of hemlock, its tiny white flowers just emerging. "Deadly poisonous to horses."

"Yes indeed – but don't touch it with your bare hands!" she

adds hastily as the boy makes to attack the tall plant. "Let them get a scythe to it."

"Cai told me."

"It looks all innocent!" Jane exclaims

"Thomas, what were you doing that made Cai ask you to leave the castration?" Elizabeth asks suddenly.

"Nothing. Just playing about with the farm boys." He turns away upstream and shrugs off her hand. Then suddenly he explodes. "That Gruffydd – thinks he can tell everyone what to do! He hasn't even got a proper horse!" He turns his back on the river. "Anyway, I don't care about him. Cai says he'll take me to get a new pony at Tregaron. I'm going to pick one out!"

Elizabeth smiles and says quietly to Jane, "I wondered why he agreed so placidly to come with us."

"He seems very capable," says Jane, trying to make up for her earlier comments. Elizabeth is puzzled. "Cai. He seems very much in charge. How will he fare when William is back from London for good, I wonder?"

"He'll fare perfectly well, I'm sure! He'll fare just as well as he did before we ever came here. Let us talk no more of him!"

Jane looks at her in surprise, but Elizabeth has already turned away and, jamming her bonnet firmly onto her head shouts, "Back home, I think. This way we should arrive back before they panic and send out a search party for us!"

CHAPTER TWELVE

C AI AND THOMAS are dressed in their second-best clothes – Thomas even has a hat and a small cane. The streets of the little town of Tregaron are clogged with people. All classes have come to the fair. Representatives from the big houses have come to fill the gaps in their stables – seldom to sell on unwanted animals, those are dispensed with privately – but to buy at a good price from the big farmers and professional dealers. The auction rings and pens in the centre of town are for the finer horses, the riding and carriage horses. Farm and forestry animals, the heavy horses, are traded further out.

Thomas has placed himself just behind Cai's left shoulder and haunts him like a bad conscience as the man runs his hand down a leg, examines the teeth, looks into the eyes of the animals, speaking quietly to each one.

"Can I have a grey, Cai? I don't want a mare, though; I want a gelding – with plenty of spirit. Father said you should have a horse that's like you, but a wife who's different."

Cai laughs. "We're not looking at colour today – not important, unless you want to breed it, or match up carriage horses perhaps. And we're certainly in the wrong place to get you a wife!"

Thomas grins. They make a curious pair: Cai not old enough to be Thomas' father, yet too unlike the fair-headed boy to be his brother. The child seems to defer to the young man, listening to what is said, holding his stick and hat the same way, even tending to balance his weight on the left side, as his companion does. Several men stop to pass the time of day with them, their attitude to the boy depending on their own class. The farmers and grooms talk to him and tease him, the few gentlemen they meet bothering only just to acknowledge him before questioning Cai in detail about the court case in London. Everyone seems to know about it and it seems that there is not much optimism that it will go the Powell way.

Cai moves away from the ponies and to the cobs. These animals are sturdy with a steady eye. There's power in the haunches yet no lack of sense, none of the self-indulgence that would make a finer horse bolt at a hare shooting out of the bracken in front of it, or rear at a grass snake on the path.

"I want a hunter, Cai. I think I should have a hunter, now I'm at Nanteos."

This time there is no whine in the boy's voice and Cai turns to look at him.

"You will have, must have something to hunt with soon, Thomas. But for now you need a cob. I want you to ride an intelligent horse; I need help from you out on the hills – up at the mines. You need to learn the business. We need horses that are powerful and brave; that are not going to fall with us as we come down from the pass in the mist or even after dark." Thomas' eyes are shining at the vision. "When your father comes back home and this case is settled, you'll be out with the hunt and dressed up to ride out with the young ladies." Thomas pulls a face. "And you'll have to have the horse to match. But for now there's real work to do. We need a serious animal, not a leisure horse. Do you agree?" Thomas nods vigorously. "Come on then. Let's get to work."

Cai takes him into the yard of the central inn. An auction is taking place. But Cai doesn't join the crowd. Instead he moves around the back to a shadowy bar and greets a tall, thin young man with pale red hair.

"Cai!"

"Hello, Bryn. Did you see Llywelyn for me?"

Bryn nods eagerly and Cai introduces him to Thomas who makes a smart bow, removing his cap. Bryn grins and follows suit. He leads them through the alleyways at the back of the inn and down to the river meadow. There, more horses are kept in small corrals or tethered singly. They are grazing, relaxed, their summer coats mottled and shining with health.

"What are those?" Thomas points to a small circle of men. Their heads bent, they play together on their wood and gut instruments with crude, horsehair bows.

"Ah – *crwth* players, Thomas. It is an old instrument largely out of fashion now with people in the towns, but the horse traders are great musicians."

They walk towards an open tent near the river. Cai and Bryn talk fast in rough Cardiganshire Welsh, the dialect unfamiliar to the Reverend's son.

Cai looks at his friend. "Cari? Is she well?"

"She's not here. We came down from Dolgellau a couple of days ago but she stayed on. She will be here, though. Wouldn't want to miss you!"

At the tent a small, taut-muscled man with tight, dark red curls turning to grey, stands to greet them. His north Walian voice is even more difficult for Thomas to understand, though he gamely returns the man's tight handshake. Several youths lurk in the corners, but a barked order gets them up and out. The man serves them thick tea, lacing the adults' with gin.

"This must be very expensive indeed, tea being the price it is!" says Thomas. The men laugh.

"I don't pay the full price for it, lad," the man says, tapping the side of his nose. "Are you sure you won't take a splash of gin to dilute the effect a little?"

Thomas smiles at the joke but shakes his head, "No. I need to keep my wits – we have work to do to find a good animal today."

They laugh at his earnestness.

"You'll stop with us and see Cari?" says the man suddenly.

"No," Cai replies, gesturing towards Thomas.

"He's come with you on his own?"

There is a snorting from outside and the three lads appear holding young cobs. A dark bay and two chestnuts dance in front of the tent.

"Go on then, run them!" shouts the man.

The horses are put through their paces – trotted away and back up towards the party, first in tandem, then abreast, their legs moving to the same rhythm. Next, synchronised, but to no discernible command, the youths jump on their backs. Each in his turn does a perfect figure of eight before them, canters away, then gallops back up, stopping stock-still. As the horses wait their turn they circle. When the last one returns and they are standing shoulder to shoulder, Thomas breaks out into hearty applause, much to the amusement of the men.

"The dark one, Cai! Please!"

Cai smiles and examines the animals, taking each one in turn from its rider. He walks them away from the other men's hearing, calling Thomas over and quietly explaining to the boy what he's looking for.

"A kind, spirited eye." He runs his hand down the leg and lifts a hoof. "A hacking cob heeds a small hoof, must be sure-footed. And a good feathering on the leg for the water to run down and away from the foot."

"If you look at a horse and like it today, you'll look at it and like it tomorrow," the man shouts over.

Thomas chuckles.

"Llywelyn's not making a joke, Thomas. He means that you pick a horse with a kind of instinct; it's a feeling of rightness between one animal and another that makes you pick out your horse from any number of suitable beasts." He turns to the trader, "They're all sound, of course."

Llywelyn nods haughtily, "You'll find no mealy-muzzled nag here."

Thomas has a chance to watch their paces as Cai leads them. Then he rides each in turn, taking them down to the river, up the far side of the meadow and back at a slow canter.

"Any, Thomas," he says, dismounting at last. "Though the mare with the white blaze may need protecting from the sun."

Thomas is quivering with excitement as he looks from one to the other.

"Get the tack," says Llywelyn to the boy holding the bay cob.

"No need," Cai speaks up. "He can sit without."

Taking Thomas' hat and cane from him, he flicks the boy up onto the horse's back and Thomas takes off over the field. The pace is too quick at first, the boy's lightness spooking the animal, but Thomas manages to stay on, gripping the mane with one hand but succeeding in sitting deep and back, and the horse soon settles. There's a wobble at the corner as they turn to come back, but both horse and rider soon recover and Thomas slows sedately before the tent.

The man laughs. "I've never seen the gentry ride bareback. You must have some gipsy blood, youngster!"

Thomas opens his mouth, indignant, but then decides to laugh along with the others. As he gets to the ground, he holds the bridle, the horse nudging him between the shoulder blades. He looks eagerly at Cai, who nods in confirmation.

"A sale, Sir, I believe. How much do we owe?" asks the boy.

Cai tosses him a bag of coins and he goes to count it, being reluctant to let go of the bay gelding. Giving up, he hands the reins to one of the young men and steps forwards into the tent. The man holds out his palm, and when it is finished, shakes Thomas' hand. Thomas bows deep, as if he was asking for a lady to partner him at a ball. Again there's laughter, but Thomas, though he knows he's the cause, doesn't care.

"Can I ride him back, Cai? Can we go now? We'll need tack and I –"

Cai holds up his hand.

"We need some refreshment first, at least I do. Mr Llywelyn will find the leather goods for us and deliver the horse to the livery stables."

"What time?" Llywelyn asks.

"Whenever's convenient. Give us a little time in the tavern."

"If Cari comes, I'll tell her where you are – though I doubt you'll be in a position to see much of her!" he gestures with his head to the boy.

Before they leave, Cai puts three more coins onto the table. "For your daughter. Please tell her… I'm sorry."

Llywelyn nods. "Gruffydd?"

"He's well," says Cai as they turn to leave.

They push through the crowds, whinnying from the horses in the auction ring loud and shrill with panic at being in a confined place with so many people and their noise.

Bryn shouts into his ear, "I'll go on and get a table in the upper room, shall I?" Cai nods and gives him some coins. Bryn disappears almost immediately. As Cai pushes through the crowd he realises that Thomas is no longer behind him. He stops abruptly, feeling people butt up against him. There is no possibility of seeing the boy through the crush and no calling him either. Cai starts to push the people aside. Taller than most, he can see over the heads to where the crowd has thinned by the stables. There, a woman is bent over, stuffing the straw back into her shoe, and when she straightens up he thinks he sees Thomas, head in his hands, sitting on the mounting block. He crosses the flow of people, handing them off. As he breaks free he shouts out. Thomas looks up and the clutch of people around him backs away.

Kneeling in front of him, Cai takes Thomas' chin in his hands, moving his head slowly one way, then the other. "Who did this?" he asks, quietly. Thomas shakes his head and looks down. For a moment Cai is still. Then he stands, looking intently from one to another. "Who did this to him?"

No one answers. He takes a clean handkerchief from his pocket to replace the dirty rag staunching the blood over Thomas' eyebrow. Without speaking or looking up, an elderly man moves forwards and takes the cloth off him, tucking it in his belt. Cai addresses him directly. "Who hurt him?" The man presses his lips together and shakes his head. "No. Someone will pay!" He pulls Thomas to his feet.

"He's gentry," says the woman, her voice almost inaudible, face impassive as she looks pointedly away, as if to disown her speech.

Cai frowns at her, then bends to pinch the two sides of Thomas' wound together. Lifting the boy's hand he puts it on the cut. "Hold it firmly like this. We'll go and wash it." He takes the boy by the arm, gets him slowly to his feet and leads him to the tavern.

The serving man knows him and ushers them straight upstairs. "Get clean water and rags, please," Cai throws over his shoulder. He sits Thomas down as Bryn comes up the stairs with jugs of ale.

"There're all asking about the Morris case down there…"

He stops and peers at Thomas. "What's gone on here? Has he fallen? Have you fallen, lad?"

"Knocked down, more like," Cai answers, his voice grim. The water and cloths arrive and Cai takes the boy's pinching fingers from the wound. "Doing well, Thomas."

Thomas smiles shyly and holds tightly to the wooden arms of his chair as Cai tidies up the wound.

Bryn bends down in front of his chair. "Did you see them 'as did this?"

Thomas bites his lip and goes to shake his head, wincing instead at the pain. Food and more drink is being brought up the stairs. Bryn straightens up and looks to Cai, who shakes his head. Bryn gets the message and sits down again without speaking.

"There, Thomas – you'll live!" Cai throws the cloths, only slightly tainted, into the bowl and takes his place at the table. "Don't move from my side again. You understand?" The boy nods. "Right, food. Eat, young man."

With his mouth full Thomas asks, "Did Mr Llywelyn know about us – the Powells, Cai? I didn't hear him ask about London. Mind you, I'm not sure I always understood him."

"Mr Llywelyn doesn't care for gossip, he has his own ways of finding out what goes on. Nor does he have to care what the gentry do. Now eat, please – there has been plenty enough talking for one day."

After drinking some ale and eating more than it would seem possible for so slight a boy to eat, Thomas is soon asleep, his head resting on the wing of his chair. The men settle back, Bryn lighting a pipe.

"My sister asks after you."

"How is Gwenllian?"

"Well – as beautiful as ever – but lonely."

Cai laughs.

Bryn reaches into his pocket. "We came down from Shrewsbury Saturday. I got this."

He passes a small, poorly-bound book to Cai who studies it, holding it to the window to see better, turning it to look at it from different angles.

Bryn leans forwards in his chair, his hands clutching the arms, "All shapes and sizes, Cai, dark ones too – a world of women! I'll sell it you, if you like."

"Indeed! But not a nipple amongst them!"

Bryn snatches back the book and quickly flicks through it.

"You're right man!"

Cai takes the book back and studies it, turning it a right angles and bending over it. He starts to laugh.

"Which one?" smiles Bryn, eagerly. "Which one're you looking at?"

"The wheelbarrow!" Cai is really laughing now. He gives the book back and drains his beer.

Reluctantly, Bryn puts the book back in his coat pocket. "I hear there's a new wench come to Nanteos with the family?"

Cai nods.

"Very pretty. Brunette. She doesn't have a suitor?"

"Not that I know of. You interested?"

"Me?" Bryn snorts and rolls his eyes. "And I could flap my arms and fly to Ireland! But you could –"

Cai shakes his head and stands to go, but Bryn puts his hand on his arm. "Why do you stay on?"

"Stay?"

"At Nanteos. You won't get anything. Even if something was to happen to this one," he gestures to the still sleeping Thomas, "there's another one."

"I'm not there to get anything."

"Why then?"

He shrugs.

"No. Tell me why, Cai."

Cai sits down again and leans forward. "Look, it's just beginning, Bryn. The mortar's not even dry between the bricks. I can help develop the estate, get the new machines into the mines. We can get some life back into the people up there; some pride into them."

"We? You and your partner William?" Bryn mocks.

"No – he doesn't see it. Elizabeth Powell's the one with vision."

Bryn smirks, "And she's a looker, so they say!"

Cai looks sharply at him but the other man has his face buried in his tankard. He scrapes back his chair and gently shakes Thomas' shoulder. The groggy boy smiles and pushes back the curtains of fringe from his sweaty forehead. Cai bends to examine the cut. "Good – won't leave much of a scar – except to the pride of course."

"You won't tell Father?" Cai doesn't reply. Thomas looks quickly at Bryn. "Please don't tell my father. It was an accident, to be sure."

"I will not tell him." Bryn turns to Cai. "They'll be ready. You should go straight back."

"Are we going now, Cai? Are we going to get the horses?"

Cai nods and helps him on with his jacket. As the boy looks out of the window, eager to be gone, Cai takes Bryn aside. "Put him between us. Don't let him out of your sight, particularly if there's any fighting, human or animal." Bryn nods.

The three of them leave, pushing through the crowd gathered for the cock fight. Thomas looks longingly at the cockpit but runs to keep up with his mentor, nudged in the back by Bryn. They pass another tavern on their way to the livery stables. The drinkers are overflowing onto the street, rough sawn planks balanced on barrels to make an extra bar. As they pass, a stone hits Cai between the shoulder blades. He wheels around. There in the road is Huw, his face blotchy.

"Cai, you bastard!"

"Hey, shut it, you!" Bryn shouts back.

There's some catcalling and mocking laughter from the men at the bar.

"You bloody bastard!" shouts Huw again. He seems close to crying. "Lost me my job. I'm nothing but digging for peat now and we're turned out of the cottage."

The crowd seems to focus. As they move nearer, a tense quiet descends on the scene. Thomas looks up at Cai. The man's face is expressionless. He stands still, though his feet have moved apart and his breathing has deepened.

Huw staggers nearer, ripping off his shirt. "My wife," he chokes, continues, "She's picking sheep's wool with the tinker women and the children are on the hills like monkeys in all weathers looking for lichen!"

"Go home, man – you've had too many!" Bryn shouts, his voice drowned out by jeers from the crowd.

By now Huw is near enough for them to see his sore eyes. He is at least a head taller than Cai, his face, neck and arms burned brown and covered in coarse orange hair. The contrast with his torso is shocking. It is so pale it seems grey, a long scar running from below the shoulder to just above the belly button. Cai pushes Thomas away from him and begins to remove his own clothes.

"Don't be stupid!" Bryn's voice is full of panic. "Walk away from him. He's a drunk, he's nothing!"

"Get the boy out of here," are Cai's only words.

Taking his friend's coat, waistcoat and shirt with him, Bryn drags Thomas by the arm, but only as far as the edge of the crowd. With a roar, Huw lunges forward and smacks Cai across the side of the face with his forearm. He staggers, his hands breaking his fall. Huw grabs him and whirls him around, flinging him into the crowd who toss him back. Cai, head down, uses this momentum to slam into Huw's abdomen. The big man grunts in pain and staggers backwards, but is kept on his feet by his supporters. By now a big crowd has gathered. Many don't know either man, but one is threadbare, the other seemingly a gentleman, so the favourite is obvious.

Huw straightens and grabs for him again, but Cai dodges and smacks him hard on the temple with his fist. The crowd's gasp shows their allegiance. Huw tries to claw at Cai as the ring around the two men gets smaller. But Cai knows that his only hope is to avoid the much bigger man getting hold of him. Again he jabs at Huw's face and springs back. There's a groan of anger from the onlookers as the big man's face opens and he bleeds about the eyes. The two stand, heavy breathing for a moment, legs planted square, heads down, like two bullocks in a pen. Then Huw roars and comes at him again, but Cai dodges it. The space between them is getting smaller as the crowd close in, others on the periphery trying to see better, closing the circle. Soon Huw will be able to grab Cai by just stretching out and the younger, lighter man's better agility will no longer save him.

"You brought it on yourself!" Cai shouts over the noise of the crowd. "Go somewhere else. Go to Dylife or somewhere they don't know you. No one'll employ you around here now, not after you worked for Morris!"

"They won't have me at Dylife – your lot'll see to it!"

"We'll do no such thing – I won't be telling anyone up there."

"Ah, shut up and hit him, Huw!" comes a voice from the crowd.

Huw lunges forwards but Cai trips him and he sprawls to the floor.

"Grab the bastard!" A shout rings out from the crowd and several men grab Cai by the arms. One has his forearm around Cai's neck.

"Get up and punch 'im, Huw!" More voices join in as the crowd's excitement grows. Huw, helped to his feet, is rolling up his sleeves, the fight becoming pure theatre. Suddenly there's a woman's screamed commands and a scuffle of alarm as people push in desperation to move away from something. The crowd melts back in revulsion as a tall redhead appears, struggling to control a stinking bucket of lye.

"Here you – have a bit of this to sober you up!"

She swings the half-empty bucket behind her and the crowd scatters, calling in panic as the foul mixture splashes out at Huw. Though part-blinded with blood as well as drunk, he manages to stagger out of the way, some catching his boot. Cai, his captors having fled, laughs as she flings the bucket away from her.

"*Ych a fi!*" she howls with laughter.

They move away from the noxious pool.

"Saved by the piss bucket!"

"Who says you don't need a woman?" She reaches up and kisses him, her soiled hands held behind her. "My father said you were after leaving without seeing me," she says, stepping back and looking at him.

"I'm not alone. I've got the Powell boy."

"He can put up at an inn, can't he? We'll send someone to the house to tell them where you are."

"Not this time, Cari."

She looks past his shoulder to where Bryn and the blotchy-faced Thomas are standing. The boy's voice is still unsteady from sobbing.

"I thought he was going to kill you – he's a giant!" He points to the figure of Huw, one hand holding his face, being led back into the tavern.

"Poor sod was drunk. I'm all right. Thanks to a woman and a bucket of lye."

They laugh.

"Not just any woman," says Bryn, looking at Cari in admiration.

She winks at him. "I need the water pump, I fear. Are you sure you'll not stay with us this time?"

"No – not this time." He takes her around the waist as she holds her arms safely away from her body, and kisses her deep.

Thomas is hypnotised.

"What I didn't like was the crowd against you, Cai. That's dangerous," she says quietly.

"They always hate the gentry," he shrugs.

"Better make sure those snakes are on your side then."

As she leaves, she looks over her shoulder and mouths, "Goodbye."

"You're a fool, Cai!" says Bryn as soon as she's out of sight.

"No. I just know my own mind," he says, reaching for his clothes.

CHAPTER THIRTEEN

In THE NURSERY, Catherine is looking out of the window, watching the huge trees beyond the lake dip and bow, their branches shaken like a besom broom. Wind screams through the gap in the corner of the window frame and rumbles deep in the chimney. She experiments: first as normal; then she tries the same scene with her hands over her ears. Without sound effects the storm has a comic quality – loses its bite. "Interesting," she says to herself. Thomas is busy slamming marbles against the wall. Curiously, it is not so much how hard one pitches them, more something to do with the angle at which they hit the wall that makes them occasionally ricochet right across the room and hit the fireplace. Mari doesn't take much notice, bobbing Little William up and down on her knee and looking listlessly into the fire.

In the small study Elizabeth and Cai sit close, drafting plans for the improvements. Their heads bend over the same map. Both the same shade of darkest brown, Cai's hair is curly, Elizabeth's sleek as a mermaid's. Cai is superimposing the plan for the water-powered drainage system across the paper; Elizabeth marking possibilities for improved workers' housing.

"Jane has written again." Cai grunts in reply. "She warns that our case is not terribly well-received in London. We are viewed as provincial idiots."

He looks up sharply. "She used that term?"

She nods. "I think that Jane and I did not part entirely easy with one another." She sighs. "I told her of the attack on Thomas at Tregaron – she was horrified." Cai sits upright and looks at her. "She could not believe that we were not doing more to arrange for them to go away to school; that we were allowing them, as she puts it, to 'run amok' on the estate, with little regard for where the line between above and below stairs lies…" Her voice falters.

"No regard of the barrier between above and below stairs…" He pauses. "I didn't know that things had been so difficult between you. Perhaps you should take it in hand."

"But William is never here and there is so much to do. Besides, we are all so happy."

"Perhaps it was not only the children she was referring to, Elizabeth." Cai bends again to his work, his shoulder masking his face from her gaze.

She waits for him to explain himself but he does not. Looking pointedly down again at her task she says, "And William writes that Morris brought eighty of them to London to stand as witnesses, country people, never having been further than Aberystwyth! He really is an extraordinarily able man."

"It'll cost us."

At that she straightens up and looks at him. "So there won't be much money to do this."

"We can't afford not to do it. For years I tried to persuade… Thomas to invest. Since you've come I feel that anything's possible, I –"

"I can't believe the time I used to waste in London! There's so much to do here, so many possibilities!"

Neither sees Mari watching them from the hallway. She holds Little William by the hand. Suddenly he calls out, "Mama". Elizabeth hears him and laughs, holding her arms wide to him.

"Come on then, Little Man. Come and see the grand plans!"

He rushes in and, in doing so, pulls on the overhanging tablecloth. Red ink spills, splashing across the papers, oozing through the material. For a moment they freeze, then chaos ensues: William bursting into tears, Cai and Elizabeth trying to save the documents, Mari the handsome carpet. Red spreads through Elizabeth's pale dress. She stands, arms held away from her body, laughing. Mari sees the red seeping through her stomacher and into the skirt. "Oh no! Mistress!"

"Don't fret. I didn't like it anyway." She tries gingerly peeling it down from the shoulder. "Mari, help me please. I can't walk through the house dripping red! Go and fetch an old sheet or something for me to stand on."

She turns her back to Cai. "Would you mind undoing me, kind Sir?" She gives a little bow. He smiles and begins the arduous job of unfastening her, easing open the laces with his fingers. "You are surprisingly adept at this, Cai!" She raises her arms for him as he teases the bodice up her body and over her head. As he brushes her sides and under her arms she starts to laugh, William picks up on the mood and chuckles.

"You are ticklish, Elizabeth!" Cai smiles.

She nods and bites her lip. Behind her he bends to breathe in her scent as the tight garments are opened. As Mari hesitates, turning back from the doorway in surprise at the laughter, Elizabeth looks up sharply.

"Hurry please. I'm starting to drip!"

"Wouldn't it be better if you came upstairs to change properly, Mistress?" she says, boldly, but Elizabeth's waved hand dismisses her.

The girl leaves. The thick stomacher has protected the finer linen beneath it but the ink has soaked right through the layers of thin skirts. Cai works to untie them, and she wriggles free, letting each drop onto the carpet. Soon Elizabeth stands in her stained petticoat and shift, Cai in front of her. She smiles up at him. "You would make an excellent ladies' maid, Cai – except you are perhaps rather too handsome." Realising what she's said, she bends over and reaches across the table to check the documents, hiding her face behind her hair. "Thank goodness these seem to have escaped!"

Cai can't suppress a grin at the sight of her in her underwear, cap dislodged, hair dishevelled, peering hungrily at the plans.

"Right, where were we?" she says.

Thomas dodges around Mari as she comes in through the door with clean clothes for Elizabeth.

"There you are, Cai! Can we go riding? Can we go and find the badger set, Sir Herbert –"

Cai turns from his task to look outside. "Well, there seems to be a bit of blue sky at last – we should take advantage of it. You can come with me to the weir if you like. The nets have been torn again."

"That bloody beast!"

Mari, laying rough linen on the carpet to try and take up some of the stain, turns on him, "Thomas! Apologise at once!"

"Sorry, Mama. Are we going to kill him? Shall we take the dogs? Can I…?"

As Mari, her lips pursed in disapproval, takes over with Elizabeth's dress, Cai moves the remaining papers onto the mantelpiece.

"Slow down, slow down! We're only going to move the site of the nets –"

"But Cai, why don't we catch him and stick him. Father would be so pleased with us. I could stick him in the head and –"

"Enough! We don't have time for that and it's begun to rain again already. The estate doesn't run itself."

"But Sir Herbert –"

Elizabeth intercedes. "That's enough, Thomas. Sir Herbert

is a man of leisure. He has the time and most certainly the inclination to spend days searching the countryside for something, anything to kill. You will make your choice: go properly with Cai and learn something useful, or stay with us here. I could indeed do with some help embroidering the seats for the music room like I promised Jane. These papers can wait until tomorrow."

He pulls a face and they laugh.

It is raining heavily up at the Powell mine. Women and children are sorting the washed ore, their heads bent against the downpour, their clothes as drab and grey as the sky. Other women empty a truck of raw galena out from the level entrance as a party of men struggles, trying to get the damp gunpowder to ignite to start a fresh shaft further down. The surface windlasses are not coping: sometimes two to each lever, the men's feet are slipping, their raw hands losing their grip and one in five turns folds back on itself, their efforts lost. A horse-gin squeaks and shrieks as it lifts a laden kibble from the vertical shaft.

Trevelyan's figure stands out from the rest. Though he isn't afraid of heavy work, his clothes still retain some of their colour. His hat is pulled down low and his riding boots and thick gloves protect him. For a while he hovers at the deep shaft entrance, taking care to move out of the way of the blinkered horse who trudges, as if in a trance, in tight circles. Having assured himself that the metal containers are still getting filled, he moves to the hole from which the men and women emerge, baskets of rock on their backs.

He helps steady a young woman as she clambers out. "What's it like down there? Are the pumps still coping?"

She looks at him blankly.

He turns instead to the man behind her, speaking as slowly and clearly as he can. "Is the mine filling up with water? Are the lower levels still safe?"

The man shrugs, slipping on the final rungs of the wooden ladder at the surface. But whether it is a shrug to say, "I don't understand your Welsh, Cornishman", or "I neither know nor care about your blasted mine", is impossible to tell.

Underground, work is continuing. Each level has its own hand-driven windlass for circulating air – a popular job, but usually only given to those too infirm to dig or carry rock, so that even these crude machines don't operate at their full capacity. At the lode face there is no sign of trouble, the men fire-setting to break up a new seam. They talk easily to each other, recognising each speaker largely by his voice, the meagre light only illuminating a shape if the man stands within a foot of the candle stump.

"They say more ore's found hard by Bwlch Gwyn. Morris had ordered an open rake on it. Powell wasn't pleased."

"I thought the boss'd lost that battle already. There're *lluestai* on that land. It's common for sure. The Powells've been trying to pretend it's theirs since my father's time."

"They say Morris'll pay better wages – especially to locals. He'd rather local men." The speaker stands against the wall, letting the cold water soak through his shirt to bring some relief from the heat and sweat.

"You thinking of it, Tal?" Tal replies with a laugh, lost in the dark. But his friend is unconvinced. "And what if Morris doesn't find ore, or he loses in court? What if he never comes back?"

Another man joins in. "If you get caught you'll lose your job here. You'll lose your cottage. They'll hunt you down, Tal, like they did the others."

"It's only the bastard who'll recognise me under all the filth!"

They laugh. The fire set, they take a break before lighting it up.

"What's his game? Why's he still here?"

"Days gone by, a *plentyn siawns* could inherit."

"Not now. This is English law. But that Cai knows a lot. He could get a lease like Morris if he started working for the Crown."

"Who are you, talking like a lawyer!" Tal pulls his bulk upright and, lighting up, walks towards the face. "We're not paid enough to mind others' business for them! Let's get this rock down."

Cai and Thomas are saddling up ready to check the nets. Thomas can tack up himself now and talks quietly to his horse as he fits the bit and places the saddle.

Cai looks at him in approval. "We'll take that new cob out tomorrow, Thomas." He scans the sky beyond the ridge. "There's some weather coming in by the looks of it. Better get a move on."

The boy smiles and bends to pick out a hoof.

Suddenly the dogs start barking their frantic warning and the horses prick up their ears and shift nervously. Thomas' pony snatches his foot away.

"Hey!" shouts the boy. "Give it here!"

But Cai holds his hand up for quiet. The barking is frenzied now and they have to hold the horses steady as a rider can be seen by the lake. The man has no hat and is already shouting, although it's impossible to hear any words at this distance. Cai calls over a couple of boys to take the horses and sets off down the drive, Thomas running to keep up.

The man's horse is sweated up dangerously, its eyes wild,

froth covering its flank. The man too is desperate, hardly able to speak. As he yelps out his story, Cai holds the animal's head.

Then, "Go and ring the bell, Thomas. Run," he says.

Thomas streaks away shouting and soon the alarm bell fills the air.

"Good man," Cai says as he turns towards the house. "Get off that horse and give it in to the stables. Tell them what's happened then go in and have something to drink."

"But I can't – I must go back up!" He gathers up his reins again.

"Don't be an idiot, man! You can't ride that animal back up again – you'll kill it. I'll tell someone to get up to the mine and say we're on our way. Rest up for God's sake, you're no use to us like this!"

The man does as he's told. Already people are swarming over the service yard. Several of the more senior men rush to meet Cai as he pounds up the drive, shouting orders. "There's been an accident at Bwlch Gwyn. Hafod level's flooded and there's a shift down there. Get the wagons hitched up with supplies. You," he points with his crop at a slim, alert youth, "get out to Gogerddan and tell them we need help. We'll need as many hands as we can get," he says, almost to himself.

The big stable doors are flung open and anyone who can ride is getting saddled up. Every spade, shovel and pick axe in sight is collected and dumped on the first wagon. Three or four of the younger men jump aboard as it moves away.

Elizabeth runs from the house. Cai meets her, both his hands holding her arms tight as he looks at her.

"Send anyone who's left to the other big houses for help. We need everything they've got. Get them to meet us at the Bryn Glas adit, we'll try and lower the level and drain it off down the hillside."

"Will you bring the injured here?"

"No – too far. Get any medical help up to Hafod, we'll bring anyone who's hurt there."

"Food, Cai?"

"Send up whatever we've got to Hafod and get the other houses to send food." He glances at Mari, Elin and the other women who are running with bundles of linen and blankets and dumping them in the second wagon. "Yes – get blankets from them too if you can."

Elizabeth nods and, as light as a whisper, kisses his face, then turns on her heels.

For a moment, Cai stands unmoving, looking in shock at Elizabeth's slim back as she rushes back to the house. He's distracted by Thomas who's standing with his hands on his hips, shouting in Jenkins' face.

"But I'm a big boy. I'm Thomas of Nanteos. I will come!"

There is no time for this and he'll have no opportunity to take care of the boy up at the mine. Vaguely conscious that, in one sentence, he will be undoing weeks of work with his young charge, Cai shouts, "Get inside, young man. There will be sights to see not fit for young eyes."

Brought up short by his tone, the nearby activity stops and all eyes turn to Thomas. Tears of frustration and embarrassment brim up, but the boy viciously brushes them away with his fist. His face tight, legs stiff, he walks away towards the front entrance of the house. With regret written across his face, Cai turns and calls for his horse.

Later, the rain reaches the mansion. Elizabeth and Mari watch the river from the music room windows. It has scorned its banks and slumps across the field, creeping towards the low earth platform they'd built to protect the house. They stare as a heifer passes, upside down in the water, her mouth open and her legs rigid – stiff and straight as table legs. Her bloated body turns and waltzes slowly in the flood.

"Martha says it's coming up through the cellars already."

Elizabeth grunts in reply.

"I can't understand why the river's so high. It's only just started raining really heavily, and anyway, it's April – it shouldn't be that bad!"

"It's how much rain they've had in the mountains that counts, Mari. Jenkins said a flash flood's come down from Pumlumon."

The two are quiet for a while.

"Will they bring any injured here, Mistress?"

"I hope not. That journey would surely kill an injured man. Cai has the sense to get them treated on site and kept nearby if at all possible. I've sent for Dr Edwards to go straight to the mine. Oh I wish William was here!"

"Have you let him know?"

"I will have to. We'll have to see about food for the children. Can you see Cook, Mari?"

The girl nods and leaves. For a moment Elizabeth is alone. It is growing dark and the candles are reflected in the glass of the Grail cabinet. She opens it and picks up the fragile cup, presses it to her cheek and prays for the miners. The rain and the murmured prayers work to comfort her.

She is disturbed by Mari re-entering the room. "It's Thomas, Ma'am. I can't find him."

"What do you mean? I mean, where have you looked? He must be here!"

"I've called all over the house. Catherine says she hasn't seen him for hours."

"Why didn't she tell us? Silly girl!"

"She didn't know he was missing. They're often apart. She thought he'd gone out with the rescue party to the mine."

"Oh, Lord help us, perhaps he has indeed! Have you questioned the servants?" Elizabeth throws the Grail down on the sofa and makes for the door.

"None has seen him. I'll ask if the few still here know anything about him going with the men."

"Who is left for me to send after the rescue party if he is not to be found?"

"All that can ride have gone."

"Then I must go myself… no, wait, I must ask if anyone has seen him. Please go and stay with Catherine and William."

She rushes down the stairs and into the servants' wing. Only Martha and Annie are left, cooking in a frenzy of steam.

To Elizabeth's frantic questioning, both women shake their heads, though Martha adds, "He won't have gone far, Ma'am; he's not taken food."

Jenkins comes in as she's going out, his hair dishevelled, he has no cap to remove in respect.

"His pony! Is his pony still here?" Elizabeth crics. "No, wait, I'll go and look myself…"

She runs out to the stables in the rain. The huge doors are banging in the wind. The other women have followed her out, bringing lanterns. Elin carries an old coat which she boldly tries to put across her mistress' shoulders.

"No!" she shouts, shoving the girl away. "Saddle up my mare!"

"Mistress, you can't go out in this! … And all the horses are gone, Ma'am!"

By now Jenkins has joined them and stands between Elin and Elizabeth, gesturing for the girl to take the coat and move away. "We don't know which way he's gone, Ma'am. If he's with the men he'll be safe and sound, but he might have gone another way." Elizabeth darts behind him and, grabbing the coat off Elin, struggles to put it on. "Madam, please!" Jenkins puts a hand out as if to stop her, then thinks better of it.

She spins around and addresses them all at once. "Go to the village and find me a horse. Anything!"

Martha steps forward, speaking firmly but not shouting. "There won't be a horse for miles around. The call's gone out of the accident. Everyone 'as can will be there. He'll have gone to follow the action, God's truth. By the time we've gone up there to find him he'll be on his way back."

For a moment Elizabeth casts her eyes from one to the other, her mouth open, as if to issue another order, or perhaps a scream. Then she seems to subside, the fingers that had been frantically working to close the top buttons, dropping down by her side.

"Help me batten down these doors!" Jenkins says. Gently they push past her and secure the stable and barn.

She stands in the big coat, her dark hair loose and plastered to her face, the fine silk slippers wet as paper. Martha steps forward and places her hand on Elizabeth's arm.

"Won't you come inside, Mistress?"

All night the rain comes down. Elizabeth is put in the nursery with Catherine and William but every time they lead her to Mari's bed and lift her legs in, she slides out again. Martha has given her the Grail to hold and she sits on the floor by the fire. Though there is no sound, her lips move in prayer. Mari wakes several times in the night to see her mistress hunched there but she doesn't want to wake William, whose bed she shares, or Catherine, who's cried herself into a fitful sleep. What could she do for her anyway?

As dawn collects itself, grey and weak at the window,

Elizabeth gets to her feet and goes quietly downstairs. She takes up her vigil at the parlour window where she can see far down the drive and to the lake. The fire is cold in the grate and she wraps part of a curtain around herself, the Grail inert in her lap. After a while the dogs begin to bark and she thinks she sees figures pass the far side of the lake.

She runs outside, bare feet bruised by the gravel. Yes, the dogs' barking is desperate now and a large party of men straggles home from the mine. She keeps on running across the stones as Jenkins, alerted by the din, apprehends her.

"Mistress Powell! Please, Ma'am, stop!"

He can do nothing but grab her and hold fast as he shouts for help across the yard.

His wife, Sarah, is first to the scene, helping him restrain Elizabeth, who struggles and frets in Jenkins' bear hug. Next are Martha and Annie – the girl open-mouthed with horror to see Elizabeth so wild. Martha takes charge and grabs Elizabeth firmly by one arm, Sarah has the other.

"No, please; I must speak with them. I must know! Where is my boy?"

"Mistress, stop it! Jenkins will go to them." Martha gestures urgently for him to leave. The first men are rapidly approaching and it would not do for them to see her in this state. "Get inside, Annie, and warm some wine." She sees Elin, hanging back by the kitchen door. "And you, girl, fetch your mistress some warm clothes and some proper shoes, for pity's sake!"

The two older women march Elizabeth inside the house. Martha keeps talking quietly to Elizabeth as she sits her down and makes her drink the strong liquid, now and again throwing a brusque command over her shoulder. She has put Sarah to stand behind the chair, the big woman on the alert, just in case

Elizabeth tries to run out. As Martha talks, Elizabeth nods, though her eyes never leave the door. Annie has been posted just outside to divert the exhausted men away from the kitchen and out to the service quarters above the stables. Elin works to dress her mistress, taking her feet from the bowl of warm water and drying them. When she is finally properly dressed, she goes to brush her hair, but this is the final straw and Elizabeth can't tolerate it.

"Enough," she says, pushing Elin away. Then, looking at last at Martha, "Thank you," she mouthes.

She gets to her feet and Sarah hovers in alarm until told to stand down by a quick gesture from Martha. The cook gets slowly to her feet and steps back a few paces.

"Thank you, dear friends," says Elizabeth.

For a moment she hesitates, looking from one to the other. Annie's face appears around the side of the door but she has the sense to keep quiet.

Elizabeth turns to Elin. "I need to see Jenkins, Roberts and any of the senior men who have come back. Please send them in to the study immediately." Then to Martha she says, "Please make the men as comfortable as you can; they will have to go out again."

Nobody moves as she sweeps from the room.

Once inside the study she closes the door. For a moment she just stands. At last she has men and horses, though both are exhausted. There must be no more carelessness. Decisions she makes now might be all that is left between Thomas alive and… not found in time. She scrapes her hair tidy with her fingers and pushes the thick, loose bunch down the back of her dress out of the way. A knock and Elin puts her face around the door.

"The men, Ma'am," she says.

"Thank you, Elin. Please arrange for a fire, warm drink and some sustenance."

"In here, Ma'am?" The girl is shocked.

"Yes. Now, please. Send them in."

Elin's face disappears and Jenkins is the first of three men into the room. Elizabeth gestures for them to sit, but none will.

"Please, gentlemen; you have been up all night on Nanteos' behalf. Please do sit and be comfortable." They hesitate. "There's no time for ceremony. I want you warm and comfortable as I talk to you." Jenkins sits and the others follow. She remains standing. "Firstly, I must thank you." Roberts goes to protest, but she holds up her hand to stop him. "The men down the mine – how are they? Do we have casualties?"

"No, Ma'am," says Roberts. "By some miracle, no one was killed or even badly hurt but two levels are horribly flooded. The mine is set back months."

Elizabeth nods. "I am assuming that there has been no sign of my son up at the mine or I would have been told."

The men shake their heads but do not look at her. Elin and Martha come in with hot food and drink and Annie crouches to lay a fire. She waits for them to finish before continuing.

"Thank you," she says as the women leave.

She gestures for the men to take food, but they cannot bring themselves to do it. Impatient, she goes to serve them but Jenkins rises in alarm and snatches the flask of drink from the table just in time. She smiles slightly and concedes. As they drink and eat – awkwardly, delicately trying to balance their platters on their knees, she speaks. Her voice is calm and steady but fast. Now and again she breaks off to look at them or to wait for an answer to her questions.

"Thomas left within an hour of your departure for the mine." Jenkins winces slightly at her failure to use 'Master' in front of the men, but tries to hide his discomfort. "If he had come after you, someone would have seen him, and I understand," she looks at Jenkins who nods, "that he knew the way to the mine having been there several times with Cai. Therefore, I'm ruling out him following you."

Roberts grunts his assent.

"Where therefore might he have gone?"

"Does he have friends, Mistress Powell?" Roberts asks.

"No – but good thinking. His greatest confidant is Sir Herbert Lloyd." A quick look passes between the men. "But Lloyd is still in London with my husband and Martha says he took no food with him. That leaves me baffled." There is no response from them. She continues, "The first thing I want done is for Cai to be informed of Thomas' disappearance. He knows him as well as anybody." Jenkins raises a hand to offer and she nods gratefully. "You three then, please split up and organise a search party."

"We'll take the dogs and horns. The young master could never resist that, even if he is holed-up sulking somewhere!"

Elizabeth smiles weakly. "Good idea, Roberts. Will the men be able to make it out again, do you think?"

"There'll be no shortage of volunteers, don't you worry, Ma'am. The horses may be a problem, though."

"We'll take the Gogerddan horses. They were just spares and were led most of the way," says the coachman, daring to speak at last.

"I'm sure Pryse won't mind," she says. "Have you any other ideas? Anything I've missed?"

They look at each other.

"Or is there anything you need from me? Anything I might have missed?"

None of the men speaks.

"In that case, please let us get to work. Jenkins, you must take anything you need."

He nods and gets to his feet.

"Thank you," she says simply as they bow their heads and make to leave.

As Roberts reaches the door he turns back. "Thomas is a strong boy and not without sense. He'll come back to you, Mistress."

She nods and bites her lip as he closes the door. In the hallway the three men pause for a moment.

"It takes a good master to ask for advice from a servant," the gamekeeper says quietly.

Jenkins nods. Roberts continues, "The boy loves to hunt; I'll take a party to the badger woods."

"I'll go down to town," says the coachman. "Has he taken a gun, Jenkins?"

"That's an idea. I'll check. If so, I'll get down to the rookery – but my first job's to send for Cai."

"He'll know," the other two say together.

"Get what you need from the stores." Jenkins throws Roberts the keys and the three men part.

As the door closes behind the men, Elizabeth drops into a chair. Head in hands, she shudders. Trying to pull herself together she reaches for a drink but her arm is shaking so much she cannot raise the cup to her lips.

"He's a strong boy – he'll come back to me," she mouths.

Cold to the bone she wraps her arms around herself and rings the bell but she is standing still, warming herself by the fire when Elin arrives.

"Please bring my things, Elin," she says calmly. "I need you to do my hair."

When all is at last quiet again outside, Elizabeth, Grail by her side, settles herself in front of the parlour window for the long vigil. Mari comes in with William and Elizabeth takes him on her knee, repeatedly, absent-mindedly kissing the top of his head, though her eyes never stray from the drive. As the afternoon stretches on, he falls asleep on her lap, his head resting on her arm like a puppy's.

She is the first to see the solitary figure passing the lake. As she jumps to her feet the child's head bangs against the side of the table. He howls, and she thrusts him at Mari as she runs out onto the drive. Others from the house quietly appear behind her.

The one lad leads Thomas' pony. Though wet, the tack is undamaged. Elizabeth walks to meet him.

"Where? Where was he?" she asks.

"We didn't see him, Ma'am. But we found this with the pony." He holds up the otter spear.

Elizabeth's hands fly to her face.

"Where?"

"Down by the river. Down by the weir."

Elizabeth groans. "Dredge the river," she says and turns away.

"Pardon me, but we can't Ma'am – it's too high. Men have gone downstream. Cai Gruffydd is there now."

Elizabeth drags herself back to the house.

In the parlour she sits, the Grail in her lap, rubbing it against her thigh through her dress. She faces the window. Upstairs Catherine is also keeping vigil, her shame and guilt driving her loneliness. She is the first to see the men out beyond the lake. She careers down the stairs and into the parlour. As she pauses at the doorway about to speak, she is silenced by the expression on her mother's face as, still seated, she looks at her. Slowly Elizabeth turns back to the window and Catherine, holding her hand, crouches down beside her. The party draws up to the house. Though there is noise from the dogs, the people are silent. Elizabeth does not turn around. Finally there is a knock at the parlour door and Jenkins enters.

"Ma'am, I beg your pardon, Cai is here, they've –"

Still facing away, Elizabeth puts up her hand to silence him. Then, dropping Catherine's hand, she gets to her feet.

Cai is standing alone with the drowned boy in his arms. He cradles the head to his chest and it is impossible to see the child's face. Elizabeth walks like a somnambulist down the main steps and towards them as Catherine hangs back, tears running down her face. It has stopped raining and a blackbird is staking his territory from a yew tree by the house, the notes rich and sweet. Without fuss, the men have taken the dogs away behind the house, the horses to the stable. Those workers who are left stand, their hats in their hands, eyes lowered, paying the proper respect. As Elizabeth is almost there she stumbles, lunging over to one side. She utters a single cry. Cai shifts the body and grips her arm, raising her up. She reaches out for the body of her son, cleaving to it, trying to pull it into her. Cai tries to help her, lowering the torso into her outstretched arms, gathering the legs and supporting the lolling head. But the boy is too heavy and she staggers, her legs crumpling under her. As she goes down, Cai drops to his knees, holding the body for her as she kisses his face, his hair. She moans: a low, urgent litany that makes many of the onlookers shift with discomfort.

Jenkins gestures for the remaining men to leave and to Mari to take Catherine indoors. Finally only he, Sarah and Martha remain. By now Elizabeth is limp and quiet, her head resting on Cai's chest as he supports her around the waist, her dead son sprawled across her lap.

CHAPTER FOURTEEN

CAI SITS IN the study, still churning from the letter he'd written William in London, sending it by special courier. His head is thick with grief. He'd known somehow, with a sick jolt under the ribs, that the boy was lost, even as the messenger had panted out Elizabeth's desperate summons to him. His journey down from the mine had not been filled with urgency, but dread. He had been grim and hard, knowing the boy was dead. No one had asked him how he knew to go to the weir – he had not even questioned it himself. Finding Thomas' horse was the first sickening slip down that shaft of pain, each stage horribly inevitable. He had known what Elizabeth would understand on seeing the youth return with the animal, with no one there to hold her through that first wounding, but he had to go on, had to stay, to finish it at the river.

He groans – tormented by all the snatched pictures from those last hours and sometimes whole sequences played back for seconds at a time. And the feel of them, the terrible cold of the dead boy; and his mother – clutching at him, scrabbling to hold him, clawing at his body. His clothes are still damp from them.

"Elizabeth!" he cries through clenched teeth, his arms clamped across his chest, pressing down on the ache where she'd been.

The door clicks open and it is Mari's blotchy face that answers his groans. But Cai's eyes don't see her. His arms ache where he supported Elizabeth as her body realised that her son was dead, his collarbone still remembering the weight of her forehead as she slumped against him.

"Cai?" Mari's voice is tentative.

He shakes his head, and as she leaves, she begins to cry afresh.

It takes William five days to get back from London and it is Cai, his face closed, his movements restrained, who has to manage the first business of death. It is the women's job to lay out the body of the little boy and Sarah and Martha are joined by a woman from the town who specialises in such things. The house is muted, the staff appearing, efficient and quiet to do their work, then dissolving away. Words of condolence arrive, even from families who have not been directly informed, but each messenger is greeted at the door and sent on his way.

When William finally returns, he goes over the arrangements in obsessive detail. When the burial ceremony is at last secure in his mind, he turns to the drowning itself. Everyone is to be interviewed, there is no one who does not have to give an account of themselves. No one without guilt. Cai is first to be summoned to the study.

It feels unfamiliar. William is in his usual chair but does not look up from the fire as Cai knocks, waits, then enters. He stands for a moment, but the older man makes no move; says nothing. William's hair is thinning and Cai sees his scalp. It has a yellow tinge. Impatient to get the inevitable ugliness over with, Cai finds a seat. "May I help you with any arrangements that are to be made?" he says at last.

William doesn't acknowledge the comment. This is the first time the two have been completely alone in weeks. As Cai looks at William in profile he is shocked to see how gaunt he looks; how his cheeks are sunken, his jowls loose.

"William –"

"No!" William's hand gropes for the Bible at his side. Cai

tenses, makes to rise, but it is not as a weapon that the book is to be used. At last William looks in his face. "This, this," he shakes it, holding it upside down, the covers in each hand. Loose papers, covered in writing, fall to the floor. "This is… empty!" It is a howl of despair, horrifying from a man so disciplined. Cai bends to the floor, trying to recover the papers as William kicks at them.

"There is no drowned son!" He shakes the Bible so violently that the text starts to tear away from the binding. "I told you!"

Cai goes cold with dread. Has William heard of the threat to Thomas at Tregaron? He and Elizabeth had decided not to tell him until he had returned from the trial in London – but maybe he had received word some other way? Cai gets to his feet. The terrible shadow of that possibility – that Thomas did not slip, that his death was not an accident, has hung over him, unvoiced, since the boy's drowning. The accusations, the recriminations, he has been expecting them. He will not tell the ravaged father that he doesn't need his reprimands, that he has drilled each one into his own skin so deep they will never leave him. He stands, determined to let William vent his grief against him.

"I said to you, 'Look after the mines whilst I'm gone, Cai.' I said you were in charge. But I said nothing about Thomas. Mammon drove me!"

"But, you –"

"Revenge! It was court cases and ore, but Thomas was dead." The Bible slips from his fingers and lands, broken-backed. William's knees give way and he slumps in his chair, forehead buried in his hands.

After a few minutes, Cai bends to retrieve the book, closing it, uselessly pressing the pieces of the ruined spine back together. He gathers the papers into a pile beside it. For a moment he waits, helpless, realising that the sorrow he himself feels is a poor relation of this in front on him. As William sobs, dry and bitter, he realises he can never tell him of his fear.

Cai takes the opportunity to leave the house for a while. It is a relief to be away from the place with its strange noises and ravaged faces. He takes his horse up to the offering cave, careful not to let her drink from the river, poisoned with lead. With the ghost of Elizabeth tiptoeing towards the entrance, her shocked face turning questioningly back at him, he sits with his head in his hands. The evil water sounds innocent enough as it runs over the flat rocks, skids around the boulders. Only the absence of birds, with no flies or larvae to feed on, would warn the unknowing not to drink. Why had he not taken Thomas to the mine with him, kept him close? The question swings like a pickaxe at his mind. He had been so self-important, so wrapped up in his duties, relishing the responsibility with William away, that he had not taken proper care of the boy.

The wind shifts the carved sticks and bones suspended from the trees and bushes overhanging the cave. Some knock together, the hollow sticks even more resonant than the bones. These tokens had protected a shift full of miners from the flooding of a whole level. Why then had they let a young boy die? The mare whinnies a warning; perhaps some of the miners are coming to tend the offering cave? He goes to her. The grass around where he's tethered her is beaten flat. She is restless, twisting from side to side and pulling on her halter. Maybe she can smell the poison in the water? Perhaps the skulls and feathers in the cave still retain something of death in them. There is no tinge of green in the light foam around her mouth that would tell him she feels relaxed enough to graze.

"All right, Lady, not long now."

Briefly he lays the flat of his hand along her flank. She is starting to sweat up, though it is a cold sweat. Then he hears it too as the wind blows stronger – metal clinking on metal, coming from near the cave.

As he draws close to the entrance, it is clear that there has been recent activity at the site. The moss has been cleared away leaving the bare rock at the cave-mouth looking sore, with black crumbled soil remaining lodged in the ledges and fissures. The empty eyes of the goat's skull give nothing away. But now the sound seems to be coming from above the cave. He scrambles up the twelve foot of wall to the cliff overhang. It feels good to struggle for a hand hold – to haul himself up and feel the muscles between his chest and arms take the strain. He takes care to move away from the drop behind him before straightening up. He sees now that the dead metal clack, the ring, the chime, is coming from a series of large poles, sunk into the ground, from which hang used animal traps. Hare, weasel, a small badger, a polecat; each occupant is shrunken and desiccated, suspended in their iron cages. In some the bones show through, others are better preserved, twisted faces recording their last agony. All the eyes are missing – gone to crows or flies no doubt, but strangely no one has come to take the valuable pelts or tails as trophies. He fights himself, forcing his feet forward. The strange 'wind organ' is right in front of him, the skulls of the creatures about head height. He counts seventeen, the metal teeth trapping mainly their limbs. They swing and bob against each other, weirdly animated by the wind. He shudders – they have been displayed here, left until their bodies rotted away, like Sion-y-Gof in his macabre headdress, displayed at the crossroads to ward off evil.

A wave of despair wells up in him. The flood at the mine killed no one, but it had lured him away from Nanteos. Some malicious spirit had sucked him in, tricked him up to the mine and kept him busy there; pandered to his vanity while, down on the mud flats below, it had drowned her son. With a roar he kicks out at the nearest pole, hammering at it with his boot until it comes down. He cuts off the rope attaching the obscene ornament and uses the first pole as battering ram to strike down the others. It is hard work, effort having gone into erecting the sculpture, the posts being sunk perhaps a foot into the peat. Once on the ground, the totems are quiet. He throws down the weapon and crouches on his haunches to get his breath. How long had they been here? Had they been here all along, even when he was here with Elizabeth, some change of the wind direction preventing them from hearing the obscene music. "Elizabeth!" he cries out as he sees her face, trusting him, looking intently at him, the last time he saw her before she lost her son, the time she kissed him, like a moth's wing in the night. There is no one to hear.

Elizabeth is not judged fit to attend the funeral at Llanbadarn. When it is done William cannot be still. Even when not dealing with the urgent business of the Morris case, he moves from chair to chair, room to room as if his spirit would somehow find his son, reach through into some other dimension and arrest the small body before it lost its footing to the swollen river. Sometimes he sits for hours by his wife's side, his words useless against the grief's granite. She will not crack from her waking coma and now many in the household, having waited so long, half hope that she will not return, so great is their dread of seeing her pain. For days she would not eat, would not even sit up. When they carried her to a chair it was as if her spine had melted and could not hold her. When the master is at home, he or Martha feed her thin soup or milk, the only thing she'll open her mouth wide enough for.

But Cai will not let her starve herself to death. When William is out he takes her in his arms, tucking her under his coat, rocking her gently as he feeds her, taking food himself from the same spoon. Though her eyes remain fixed and blank, she opens her mouth properly and swallows. At first the women are outraged to see their mistress, so vulnerable, in the young man's arms; but how could they let her die, and who would dare to tell her husband or the doctor about him? She is losing so much weight that her skin has a blueish, translucent tinge, like the enamel tip of a front tooth.

"She will need the antimonial cup – to convulse her stomach and shock it into wanting her food," the doctor says on his ninth visit in as many days. William has had to go to Peterwell and Cai is up at the mine from which no ore has come since the flood. Elin looks at him in horror.

"Come on, girl, take this and fill it with acid white wine and leave it overnight, then make sure you get it into her. Do it at midday and I'll come back here to monitor the results."

"But, Sir – she's so weak! What if the retching pains kill her!"

"Will you argue with a physician? Get on with it – do as you're told."

And the next day Elizabeth takes the warmed wine as the doctor is sighted riding up the drive. Her retching is terrible to see. So weak is her body that she can only whimper at each convulsion. She can't manage to hold herself over the large bowl so Martha and Sarah hold her up by the arms, with Elin, kneeling on the bed, holding back her hair as the spasms bring a thin liquid into her mouth which dribbles from her lips. After she is quiet, the doctor takes her pulse and frowns.

"She must be bled."

"Not again, for pity's sake!" Martha exclaims.

But it is the only thing he has left to try. It takes seven stabs to find and keep the vein in her arm running. When Catherine and William are brought in that night to kiss their mother, she seems calm. The staring tension of the last weeks has lifted and, though the breath is shallow, her expression is relaxed behind her closed eyes. Catherine, herself a guilty little skeleton, sleeps that night, for the first time since her brother's death, on a dry pillow.

Cai returns from the mine for breakfast, having left as the first light of dawn began to catch the winding gear. It had been a terrible struggle, but at last the drowned levels are clear again and work can resume. As Martha prepares an enormous tray for him, he goes to check on Elizabeth. There is an unpleasant smell in the room, as if some small creature had died and is rotting unseen behind the wainscot. At first it seems that she is not there in the bed, but Elin is deeply asleep on her couch and, as he draws nearer he can see that she is there, her hair trapped in a plait so that it does not even frame her face against the pillow. Both skin and linen are the same colour. He shouts out as he crouches by her bed and Elin struggles awake, crying in panic.

"What's the matter? What's wrong – oh, is she dead?"

"Get Martha – get…" he looks up, his face tight with shock.

He pulls back the bedclothes and drags Elizabeth up into his arms. Her body has a brittle quality and the breath, just discernible, smells foul. He rushes to the door with her and shouts for hot water.

The whole house is churning with panic. The call has reached the outside staff and he can hear men running in the yard.

"Martha, thank God." He has wrapped Elizabeth in layers from her bed and is rubbing her all over through the covers. She stirs slightly and opens her eyes.

"Warm milk and brandy," says the cook as she rushes out.

Elin appears, Sarah at her heels.

"Warm water. Get warm water – now!" The women do as he says.

Jenkins arrives. "The doctor, I'll send for him now."

"What's been done to her whilst I was away?" Cai barks.

"I – I'm not sure."

Sarah is back and Cai gestures for her to fill the sick-room bath. Jenkins turns on her.

"What did you say the doctor did to her?"

"Vomiting," she looks fearfully at Cai. "He used the vomit cup."

"Damn him!" Cai starts to unwrap Elizabeth, tearing open her nightdress but the shock on Jenkins' face stops him. For a moment he holds her to him, his torso bent over her, crouched, defensive as a buzzard on the ground. Mari and Catherine are in the doorway, the young girl's face grey with shock. He looks up from face to face then, suddenly, straightens up. "Get her in warm water as soon as you can." Wrapping the covers back tightly around her, he puts her gently down on the bed and leaves the room, passing Martha on the stairs. "Make her drink it, Martha – make her. Then put her in the bath. Let me know how she does."

She nods and hurries past him into the room.

Every vessel Cai can find in the kitchen he sets to work, heating water to bring her back. Mari comes in for more warmed milk.

"Is she drinking?"

She gulps and nods.

He is still for a moment. Then, "Take William in to her," he says, suddenly.

"Little William?"

"Yes – maybe he will stir her. There're stories of animals

nearly dead who've rallied after their young are brought to them."

"Nearly dead!"

"Go, Mari, quick – please try."

The girl takes the toddler into the stifling room. As Sarah and Elin help support Elizabeth, Martha alternately sponges her body and spoons the warm liquid into her mouth.

"What's that little mite doing in here?" she snaps.

Mari hesitates to come forward in the light of the woman's anger but she notices Elizabeth's eyes on the child.

"Cai said," she replies, simply.

She comes nearer with the little boy who stretches out his arms to his mother. Mari is uncertain for only a moment before exclaiming.

"Right, William, in for your bath!"

Quickly she strips his clothes off and lowers him in, his feet on his mother's thin legs. He giggles at the strangeness of it all and Martha splashes him. Soon he is chuckling loudly, and surely hurting his mother as he bounces up and down on her thighs, Mari's hands supporting him under his armpits. Then, wobbling, he lunges forwards, his fat arms around her neck and she reaches out for him, wrapping her own arms around his chubby chest she nuzzles his hair. Martha acts quickly to stop him slipping and the three women watch, hardly daring to breathe, as Elizabeth kisses her son. But his tenderness cannot last and he is easily bored, pushing out of her weak embrace, intent on grabbing the sponge. As Mari scoops him out there is an urgent knock at the door.

"Tell Cai she'll be all right," Martha calls as Mari, the naked, dripping William clinging to her bodice, opens the door.

CHAPTER FIFTEEN

IN LLANBADARN CHURCH the congregation wait for the parson to begin the Sunday morning service. The unforgiving light of early June is filtered by the stained glass and blesses Elizabeth's face as it falls. Her skin, white and unmarked, is perfect for mourning and this is the first time she's been seen in public since Thomas' death. The people are quieter than they would normally be, given that an unwed mother is doing penance in front of the altar. The girl stands in her white sheet, a white wand in her hand, open-faced with the paper of accusation pinned to her breast. But even she is of little interest compared to the gentry woman, a mother, gone insane with the loss of her son. Elizabeth sits like alabaster and her form has a magnetic pull for every woman there: oh, the tragedy; oh, to be so beautiful; oh, the fineness of the tuille and lace! Most of all it is the sight of her surrounded by her family: the vigorous husband; the charming daughter; the chubby toddler with his fluffy hair, that impresses. Elizabeth is beloved and privileged. Even the retainers, sitting either end of the family pew like bookends, are superior. That young north Walian girl is a beauty and the bailiff, though nobody would really trust him because of his breeding, is as handsome and proud as any naval officer.

The service begins and the white-shrouded woman melts away. Although the preacher is viciously denouncing the Methodist Revivalists, his face red and flecks of spume at his lips' corners, not a flicker passes across Elizabeth's face. When it is time to sing, to read, to pray, Catherine finds the place for her mother and puts the book into her hand, even closing her fingers around it. Only at the end of the service does she stand and, with William guiding her by the elbow, walks down the aisle with all the grace and poise of a new bride. As the family leave, a sigh seems to pass just before them, running through the congregation. No one, not even one of the other gentry families, has made a move, and they are soon outside in the sunshine.

The penitent woman is there again, her painted sign ragged in the light.

Catherine frowns and whispers, "Mari; what is for-ni-cation and bastard-bearing?"

Mari presses her finger to her lips.

"What lovely writing she has!" says the child, turning to Cai.

"Not her own, but some clergyman's surely," replies Cai, grimly.

He moves to stand next to Elizabeth who sways slightly from the hips, though her feet remain stoic. First the vicar, then the better-dressed members of the congregation, give their condolences again to William and Catherine, acknowledge the toddler in Mari's embrace. Although they look in Elizabeth's direction, not one goes near her.

As the vicar shakes his hand, William exclaims, "God deliver us from the Ranters. They should be whipped from the county, or better still, stoned like that devil in Hay-on-Wye!"

The clergyman nods his assent but moves quickly away, embarrassed by such a display outside the proper arena of the pulpit. An old woman presses a bunch of flowers into Catherine's hand.

"We are praying for your brother," she whispers.

As William prepares to usher his family down the path, one of the Nanteos grooms rushes through the churchyard and thrusts a letter at him.

"Urgent, Reverend Powell, Sir. Sir Herbert's man said I had to find you and give it to you, just in case you were out to dinner in the town and not coming back straight."

William's face darkens, his features pulling tight as he reads it.

"They've found against us!" he cries. People are turning to look at him but he cannot stop himself. "We are stripped of our offices and they find in favour of Morris. They are sending a militia to Cardiganshire to guard the mines against us!"

"I'll get everyone into the coach and home." Cai is already moving towards the gate.

"No. I need to think. I must get to Peterwell, Lloyd'll know what to do. Take them somewhere... oh, go and look at the ships, or something, Cai. Think of something. I'll write to Jane, try and get her to come to Elizabeth."

As she stands on the path, a ragged woman appears from behind a gravestone and presses something into Elizabeth's gloved hand, closing her fingers tightly around it. It is arranged like a small posy of flowers but made of black feathers. In the middle is a large magpie's feather. The lot is tied at the base with black ribbon secured to an upturned crow's claw.

"Lose it in water," the woman whispers, bending forwards to breathe the words into Elizabeth's ear. She disappears as William strides up the path, taking his wife firmly by the shoulders and kissing her passive face.

"Elizabeth?" he calls, softly, but she just stares through him.

He leaves, taking only John with him. Mari, having given Little William to Catherine, tries to take the bundle from Elizabeth and put it out of sight. It is attracting the attention of the passing congregation, people looking at it out of the corner of their eyes, their bodies bending away from it, like horses shying from a dead hare. But, though her face still betrays no emotion, her fingers have found a way into the bundle and she will not part with it. Mari is afraid of causing a scene and it is only when Cai comes, putting her free hand through his arm and supporting her round the waist, that Elizabeth is prepared to move through the crowd towards the coach. Cai makes their excuses as they pass and the carriage drives away towards Aberystwyth.

Inside, Mari is doing her best to entertain the two children. By now William is used to his mother's state and takes very little notice of her. Catherine though keeps glancing at her, a quick, sideways glance that has become almost a tic in the young girl. Cai rides beside them. Elizabeth has let the window down though it is chilly. Now and again she lifts the feather posy to her face as if to smell it.

They reach the mouth of the river as it flows fast into the harbour and Elizabeth bangs on the roof to make the coach stop.

Before anyone has a chance to restrain her, she leaps out and down the bank, her feet sinking deep into the shale. As she moves forward, the small stones slide and roll. Her feet and legs are sodden as she throws the bundle in as far as she can, a great howl of effort escaping from her chest. Mari and Catherine try to follow but Cai shouts at them to get back. He has followed her into the water and stands downstream, ready to catch her if the current tries to take her. The driver has jumped down and is fighting his way through the loose stones, stumbling with every step. As he reaches them he stands, awkward and embarrassed for a moment, not knowing whether to lay hands on the woman. Cai gestures angrily for him to stay away.

The bundle is taken by the current and starts to sink, but then snags between a rock and the far shore. Elizabeth cries out and tries to get it, wading out fast into the deep water, her arms outstretched, her eyes fixed straight ahead. The current is strong here and she is knocked off her feet almost immediately. Cloak, dress and petticoats drag her down, and she seems to make no effort to resist, keeping her eyes fixed on the strange bundle as she keels over and begins to move downstream. Now both Cai and the coachman are in the water trying to get to her. Catherine is screaming and a small crowd has gathered. Suddenly the totem breaks free. It turns pirouette after pirouette in the water and is carried away.

Only then does Elizabeth move her legs and help as the two men, up to their chests in water, drag her from the estuary. Cai pushes the coachman away and lifts her in his arms, stumbling up the shingle and sinking to his knees as he claws the hair away from her mouth and eyes. Some of the women and Mari try to detach them but he will not let her go. As Mari watches in horror, he kisses Elizabeth's wet face. As she turns away, the servant girl is sobbing bitterly. Several people come forward to offer their cloaks but he will have none of it. He heaves Elizabeth to her feet and scoops her up once more, boots sinking in the shale as he staggers towards the road.

"Get us to the Gogerddan Arms for God's sake!" he shouts at the driver as they bundle her inside. Catherine, calm now, holds her mother's hand. Cai holds Elizabeth to his chest, his riding coat spread across them both. Mari cannot bear to look.

At the tavern, Cai leaves them for a moment, giving orders to the publican and his servants. Then he turns to the coachman. "Take them back to Nanteos. Hurry – the master was preparing to go to Peterwell. Then take the chaise and bring Mari back here."

"Will do, Sir."

"Take them home, Mari, then come back as quick as you can. Bring everything you need."

He brushes Mari's miserable face with his hand, then struggles to get Elizabeth out of the coach.

"She'll be well, Catherine, don't worry," he says as the young girl, unwilling to leave her mother, starts to sob.

In a darkened bedroom at the tavern, two maids are undressing Elizabeth and trying to make her comfortable. She makes no effort to resist them. She seems calm, her eyes focused on the near distance, as if remembering something.

Cai stands on the landing outside her door. His shoulders are slumped, fists clenched, his forehead pressed against the cool of the window pane. One of the maids appears at his side.

"She asks for you, Sir."

They leave as he enters, whispering together as they close the door. Elizabeth is sitting on the edge of the bed dressed in a thin, borrowed shift. Her hair is down across her back and still damp. Cai tries his best not to look at the contours of her body.

"Thank you," she says, simply. He looks at her, his face confused. "For my life today. For finding my son." He feels a barb turn in his chest. She continues, "It was my fault. I never saw him go."

"No, Elizabeth! The accident... William wasn't there. You had to organise everything, you –"

"I never missed him. I never thought about him. I never saw him go."

"I should have taken him with me. I should have found him!"

"You did," she says quietly.

She beckons for him to come and sit beside her on the bed. She takes his hand, drawing her bare legs up underneath her. For a while they sit, each chest clenched against the onslaught of guilt, the re-playing of the endless, hopeless images of grief.

206

Elizabeth starts to squirm restlessly. "Jane told me it would come to no good. She said we should send him to school, or to one of my cousins – but William was always away and there was no time to make decisions." She starts twisting her fingers hard in her hair, pulling at the scalp. He tries to release them, but this seems to make her worse. "And we seemed so happy – I was so happy, Cai!"

She looks at him.

"I know," he says.

She sinks towards him, her tears soaking into his shirt, still tacky from the salt water. For the second time that day he holds her, and it is as if his arms have been shaped for her, as if his torso and chest will never stop remembering where they felt her weight rest against them. He hears her quiet sigh and the sobbing subsides as she curls onto his lap. Her hair still smells of the estuary and is sticky to the touch as he gathers it away from her body, tries to stop the water seeping down her back. They are together for a long time. A knock at the door, a maid's voice asking about refreshment.

"Leave it outside," he orders.

At the noise she raises her head and half opens her eyes, but he kisses them closed again, holding her even tighter.

After a while she stirs luxuriously and begins to rub her cheek against his nipple through the cloth. "You're so warm," she murmurs.

He suppresses a groan as her hands find his belly, resting one on top of the other as if swearing on a Bible. There is a blindness about her movements – like a cub pushing, driving for milk. Her eyes are still closed, the lashes so dark and glossy, as though dipped in wax. She finds his mouth, pushing, burrowing into him, as if she wants to climb inside. The discomfort is unbearable and he gently shifts her off his groin, rolls her onto the bed. She lies still a moment as he looks down at her.

"Elizabeth, you… I… You are not yourself."

She shakes her head then rolls onto her side, pulling up her legs as if in pain and sobbing again. "Oh Thomas, my boy, my son."

He tries to comfort her, dragging her up again, back onto his lap, where he used to feed her in those terrible early days of Thomas' death; pulling her towards him, squeezing the pain from her. She tears at her clothes as if they're suffocating her, calling on Thomas again and again. Cai feels tears behind his own eyes. Her calling is like a curse. But slowly her body uncurls, the tension seeping away and he dozes for a while with her in his arms.

He is woken by her face, moving down on his belly, nuzzling him. He groans with pleasure.

"Beautiful, beautiful boy; my beautiful boy," she murmurs as she climbs astride him, tightening her legs against his thighs.

He finds her mouth again and it tastes like nothing in his life before.

"I love you," he breathes into her.

"Please, Cai, please…"

CHAPTER SIXTEEN

A S THE SHORT afternoon gives way to dusk the October bonfires begin. From her room, Elizabeth watches the thin line of people with blazing torches walking along the ridge and on to the hills beyond. The animals have been settled early tonight in preparation for All Souls' Eve and only a skeleton crew are left at the house. Elizabeth rings the bell and it is Mari who attends her.

"What is tonight?"

"Beg your pardon, Mistress?"

"Tonight. Where do the people go?"

"Oh," Mari hesitates a moment. "*Noson Calan Gaeaf.* They go to the bonfires, or the churchyard perhaps."

"There are spirits abroad?" Mari nods. "You do not go?"

"No, Ma'am. I'm staying with William. Anyway, I don't want to see the *Hwch Ddu!*"

"I'm sure there is none," Elizabeth says quietly. "What else comes to these parts? Different places have different spirits."

"Oh there are many! The *Ladi Wen*, I would not wish to meet her – and the *gwrachod* come out tonight and are very powerful!"

Elizabeth looks intently at her. "You believe this?"

"Well," again the girl hesitates. "I would not like to anger them or even to see them, if indeed they did exist."

Elizabeth's laugh is hollow in her throat. "The spirits are enough." She looks at her hands and the spectre of Thomas, wet and flopping, his drowned head lolling from his neck as he lay in Cai's arms, comes into the room between them.

"There are spirits of the dead on every stile and in particular at the crossroads, Mistress. Tonight they have permission to come back."

Elizabeth reaches out for her and the two women sit for a while, watching quietly as the main procession passes from sight.

Eventually Mari gets to her feet, releasing Elizabeth's hand and gently folding it back onto her lap. "I must go to Cook. There is some business that she wants me to attend to." She looks at Elizabeth. "You are well tonight, I think, Mistress." She waits for an answer but none is offered. "Will I get Elin to sit with you?"

Elizabeth shakes her head, manages a small smile, though her eyes slide again to the window.

"I'll leave you for a while then; let you rest a little?"

Elizabeth nods her assent and Mari pads softly from the room.

Elizabeth moves quietly, putting out the candles until only the fire is left. As the room darkens, the sky grows clear. She sits back down on the window seat and watches as the dark lumps become defined, become leafless thickets; as boulders emerge, densely black against the pale grey near the top of the ridge. There is not much traffic now on the hill and the stars are gathering. There is no black sow, only the night animals shifting, wary through the dark, and what would the witches want with a grieving woman like herself? There is nothing to fear from the night. Yet, perhaps on this one evening, the first All Souls' Eve since his death, Thomas will be allowed back. She lets her mind move amongst the images of her son, inhabiting again all the places where her eyes had seen him. Sometimes he's laughing, sometimes turning sharply as if he could see her, as though she had disturbed him.

After a while she rises stiffly and finds her way to the stables, taking with her the heavy lantern from the porch. It is chill and she's forgotten her cloak, but a feverish excitement drives her on. As she opens the heavy doors, some memory of that other desperate night haunts her. There is not much wind and the horses, though surprised to see her, are calm. Damp from the straw seeps through her thin slippers and she is momentarily irritated by her lack of preparation, but Lady's low whinny brings her back to her purpose. She moves quickly about the stall, fitting the tack, preparing to ride.

The door bangs suddenly and Jenkins shouts in alarm, "Mistress – what are you doing?"

She cringes from the voice, concentrating on the stiff leather of the girth that seems to resist her cold fingers.

"Mistress!" Jenkins is at the stall door but still she ignores him and he disappears.

Soon the mare is ready and she leads her out, knowing this time that she is not dressed properly, but also realising that to delay would mean to be stopped. Like a thief she takes the horse to the shadows and tries to mount up, but she is weak from months of little food and no exercise. She makes another attempt to mount, struggling to heave herself into the saddle. A strange, strangled sound escapes from her mouth as two figures lunge forward out of the dark. One grabs the bridle.

"Elizabeth, where are you going? Elizabeth?" She ignores them, carries on her struggle to mount up. "Elizabeth!" Cai holds her shoulders tightly and looks directly at her. "Tell me what you would do."

"Thomas will be looking for me tonight. I must go to him."

She turns back to her task. Cai hesitates for a moment then grabs her flailing leg and pushes her up onto the horse's back.

Immediately she feels the saddle under her she settles herself, shoulders hunched, head bowed and is quiet.

"What are you doing?" Jenkins grabs at Cai's arm. "You shouldn't be helping her!"

"Go and tell Mari to fetch warm things for her. Then saddle a horse for me."

"This is madness! Wait 'til the master hears of it!"

"Do as I say, man!"

Jenkins turns away towards the house. Elizabeth's furious energy of earlier seems to have seeped away and she sways slightly. Cai props the torch in its holder and fits his arm around her, though still holding firmly onto the mare's mouth. She slumps against him, resting her head against his shoulders.

He talks quietly to calm both the woman and the horse: about the long, waxy grass of spring; the way the butterfly clouds rise and fret as someone walks through the hay meadows in high summer; the intoxicating scent of the new hay in the warm barn as the white light turns to the yellow sun of autumn, coming in through the open doors. When Mari arrives, Elizabeth seems to be asleep, though she shivers sometimes underneath his coat.

"Get shoes for her too, please, Mari," he murmurs. "I'm glad Catherine isn't here to see her like this."

Like a young child she is dressed by them. Finally, the grumbling Jenkins having delivered his horse, Cai gathers up the reins and puts them in her hands. She wakes like a princess from a spell, and sits high in the saddle.

"Wait 'til the master hears of this – and the mistress with child!" Jenkins says, again.

Cai rounds on him. "And what of it! She hasn't sought to go out in nigh on six months – would you stop her now?"

"There are spirits abroad!"

"You're a Dissenter! Have shame, man. She'll not rest easy tonight, thinking of the boy roaming abroad. We'll ride as long as she has strength and then maybe she can be quieter in her mind. Now go and fix a lead rein to that mare – she mustn't take fright."

"How can she not take fright tonight!"

Cai looks past him to Mari. "Make sure you're there when she gets back. Have food, spirits and a warm bath."

Mari nods. They ride away into the dark, lanterns bobbing from the saddlebags.

"That horse could stumble and toss her; she could see something should never be seen. That baby will be deformed by this," he mutters, but the girl has already disappeared.

Later the house is quiet as Martha had predicted, All Hallows' Eve having pulled everyone away. Only Jenkins has stayed, reading his Bible in his quarters above the stable as a shield against the dark old ways.

"I'll see to the Mistress when she comes back, but the Maid's Trick should really be done after the household has retired to bed, you know."

"Yes," answers Mari, "You said."

"You must accept it as it is. Have you the spring water?"

"Yes. I put it behind the door so no one would take it."

"Fetch it."

Martha begins to lay the long table, putting out food.

Mari returns with the full pail, putting it in front of the flames to warm. "But what if some of the others come back before midnight and eat of it? I won't see him."

"He's the only one likely to come back before midnight – he and the Mistress, that is. The others won't be back 'til light, until every spirit is chased away by drink and mischief."

Mari nods, gravely.

Martha goes to the range to prepare the toasted cheese as Mari takes off her clothes. She stands in her thin shift.

"You look like a spectre yourself!" Martha laughs as she brings the meat plate, loaded with food. "There, you must place it."

Mari puts it in the centre of the table, fussing, moving it a hair's breadth one way, a sliver the other.

"No need to fuss, girl! Just put it there – he'll find it. Now take that thing off and wash it full in the special water." She turns away to make up the fire.

Mari hesitates for a moment, glancing towards the door but there is no sound, and the dogs would have alerted her if anyone was abroad. She slips the material off her shoulder, but makes no move as it pools around her bare ankles. Martha turns around.

"Come on, girl. What are you afraid of?"

Mari shakes her head.

"Mari?"

The young woman is hiding her face. The candle flames, disturbed by the hungry draw from the banked-up fire, lunge to the side, making darker all her pits and hollows. Martha looks her up and down.

"You've not been eating enough. You must get yourself downstairs and eat with us more."

"I usually eat with the children."

"Well, you're missing out somewhere – that's the problem with a nursery maid, you don't fit in anywhere."

Mari shivers, bringing her hands across the concave sweep of her belly.

"Yes – I believe it now," Martha says quietly. "You *are* a maid."

Mari's eyes are wide with the boldness of it, but she doesn't dare complain.

"Right, I'll leave you now. You remember what you have to do?"

The girl nods.

Martha makes to go then turns and retraces her steps. Mari still hasn't moved but her head is lowered again, strands of hair hiding her face. Gently Martha moves the wet hair aside and tucks it behind her ears. Brushing her lips lightly against the girl's tear-stained cheek, she says softly, "Even if he does love somebody else, you may still turn him." Then she leaves, closing the kitchen door softly behind her.

A log spits and Mari snaps out of her stupor, stepping away from her clothes, gathering up the white material and taking it to the bucket. She crouches on her haunches as she rinses it again and again, mouthing the special rhyme. For the first time that evening, a smile lifts her mouth as she gathers her loose hair back to stop it dragging in the water. She squeezes out the material and lays it on the back of the chair he most uses, unable to drag her eyes from her own body as she moves about the dimly-lit room. It is not often that she sees herself naked but hopefully, soon another will see her too.

She is reluctant to leave the room, all set for his return. She scans the table once more, committing it to memory so she may see it again as she lies in bed, waiting for his spectre to come to her.

Elizabeth sits at her washstand. Her shift is pulled down around her waist and she holds first one, then the other breast in the sponge and squeezes. The soapy water dribbles into her clothes. The mound of her pregnancy sits on her knee, taut and mottled and sometimes her finger strays to fiddle with the button that now stands proud of the belly. She is quietly humming. The Grail is on her bed in the mahogany and glass case, resting on its cushion. She abandons the sponge to soak into the varnished wood of the washing table and climbs onto the bed, lifting the Grail and propping herself up with pillows. She puts the cup over the left breast, rubbing the wood against herself. Her eyes are closed and she is praying.

There is a quiet knocking at the door and Mari comes in. She calls out, but is ignored. She fetches Elizabeth's shawl and wraps it around her, gently unfastening her fingers from around the cup and replacing it on its cushion. She tries to encourage Elizabeth to get under the covers, lifting each arm in turn as she tries to hitch the nightgown back up. Eventually she has succeeded in easing the blankets over her mistress' legs, taking over the prayers or the hymns as they rise, in isolated phrases or in snatches of tune, on Elizabeth's lips. Climbing into bed next to her, she strokes her hair for a while. It grows dark in the room and, as Elizabeth sinks into sleep, she eases herself from under the covers, takes the case with the Grail in it and slips out. She meets Cai on the stairs.

"We must help her!" her whisper is a hiss of fear.

"What are you doing with that?"

"She… she was misusing the cup."

Cai looks full at her.

"I think she was trying to do a spell or praying. She was rubbing it on her body… I cannot tell you!"

Cai snatches the Grail casket from her and, glancing once at Elizabeth's closed door, turns to go downstairs. "We should lock it away," he flings over his shoulder at her.

Mari follows him, grabbing onto his arm in the hallway. "What are we going to do, Cai? She needs help. The clergy are not enough! She cannot get comfort from their God's will."

"She doesn't believe enough."

"The master's getting impatient, the children don't understand, they're grieving too. I'm grieving yet I have to comfort them. They need their mother."

"I'll speak to him!" He shrugs off her hand and moves away. "Maybe he will know of another doctor, in London perhaps. Maybe she will see Jane's husband."

In the drawing room, he puts the casket on a small table as he searches in his pocket for the key.

"Cai?" Again she puts her hand on his arm, tries to turn him around. "Why don't you look at me?"

At last he does so.

She takes a deep breath. "People say…"

"Again! What do these people say, Mari?"

"That you, and Elizabeth…" Her voice falters and she looks down, bites her lip.

He watches as tears gather in her eyes. She makes no effort to check them, perhaps she hopes he will not notice. Suddenly he has her in his arms and he is kissing the warm, salty skin of her face – silencing her. As she releases her breath in a sigh, her body relaxes against his, seeming to cling around him, enclosing him. There is the sound of shouting and barking dogs and Cai pulls away. Mari reaches up and snatches another kiss as he turns to leave.

In the hallway William is raging, shouting for servants to take his boots, bring food and dry clothes. He sees Cai. "Blocked from my own mine! And Ranters everywhere – seducing people. They're worse than conjurors. Where is my wife?" A servant is struggling to remove his boots. He kicks him away. "God alive, must I do everything myself? No wonder my brother had an apoplexy and died on the street in London! Everyone wanting a piece; all the wolves snapping at the door." He notices Mari hovering in the doorway. "Where is your mistress?"

"Not well, Sir."

"What ails her?" He stops wrestling with his boots and looks up. "I said, what ails her?"

Mari looks quickly at Cai who turns away. "A broken heart," she says flatly.

For a moment William is silent, then, still wearing the filthy boots, he moves away. "She is not alone," he says grimly. Looking back over his shoulder, he barks, "You two, come into my study."

William sits himself down and gestures for them to do the same. Elin brings food and drink for him.

"Shall I bring something more, Sir," she asks timidly, looking towards Cai and Mari.

Cai holds up his hands to decline the offer.

"That will be all, Elin." William takes a gulp of wine. "Well?"

Cai turns to Mari. "Tell him."

"She grows bad, Sir. She can hardly rise at all now and we have to force her to eat. When she does come down she sits for hours at a time at the window looking down the drive or worse, Sir..." she falters. "She cannot leave the cup alone."

"What do you mean?" he snaps.

"She... worries at it, bothers it. She takes it to her bed, Sir."

William turns to Cai. "Have that window bricked up." He drinks deep from the glass and relaxes back in his chair. "The Reverend Forbes – he has been to see her? Offered the sacrament?"

Cai shakes his head. "No good."

"What about that doctor?"

"She refuses to have him near her after last time. I wondered, Sir, maybe Gruffydd –"

"That old charlatan! Pardon me, Cai," he adds, then continues more calmly. "He's good enough for horses perhaps, but a gentlewoman?"

"He can treat anyone," Cai says, quietly.

William pours himself another large measure and takes a draught. The silence is awkward, Mari shifting uncomfortably in her seat, unused to being asked to sit in this room.

Suddenly William brings his fist down on the arm of the leather chair. "I won't have witchcraft in my house! Spells, superstition! Let Elizabeth have her prayers! Instead of your rabbits' feet and crows' beaks, let her hold the cup: sleep with it if she wants to." He looks hard at Cai. "What harm can it do?"

Mari half rises to her feet. "But she doesn't nibble at it like a Christian pilgrim, Sir, she…"

Cai silences her with a dark look.

William looks from one to the other. "Thank you. You can go now, Mari. Go and look after your mistress, or the children." Reluctantly she leaves. "See to it, then, Cai," he says as the door closes behind her. "Do it so the gossips won't know. Take my wife to Gruffydd, if you think he can help her." Cai doesn't answer. "You won't do it?"

"Of course I will!"

"Then what's the matter with you?" William leans forwards, looks closely at him, then, smirking, gestures with his head at the closed door. "Ah, Mari is it? You do not need my permission to take her for yourself. You could do worse than a nurse maid." He pauses and bites into a fowl's leg. "Why so silent? Perhaps you are holding out for something better? A little heiress, perhaps, who doesn't care, as long as her bastard is handsome and has good manners?"

Cai rises to his feet, his face contorted with anger. "It is only the fact that I know you're in grief and not yourself that stops me from breaking your head against that desk! How dare you! How can you presume to know me!"

William looks at him and it is a mixture of surprise and a new respect. He puts the leg down and wipes his mouth. He's about to speak when the door opens and Catherine enters. She looks unkempt and tired.

"What's the matter with you, then?" her father asks.

"You were shouting, Papa."

"It wasn't me, my love. Cai was shouting."

Alarmed, she looks at Cai. "I'm sorry, Catherine," he says.

She comes to lean against her father's chair. "Mama won't answer her door. Mari won't let me in to see her."

"Come, let's go and see her together." William gets to his feet, pushing the tray away. He takes his daughter's hand. Before leaving the room he looks back, returns to the middle of the room and stands, looking down at his boots.

"My apologies for earlier, Cai. It seems that nothing goes right for us since we came here. As though there were some sort of curse on us." He utters a bitter laugh and looks up at the younger man, extending his right hand.

Cai holds his gaze for a moment, then shakes the hand. Quietly he replies, "I'll see to the window. I'll take her to my grandfather."

It is enough for them both and William, putting his arm around his daughter's shoulders, leads her from the room. As they mount the stairs she remembers her mother's bedtime litany and stops in front of the animal trophies.

"Goodnight, my darlings. Don't think of the hounds. Dream of the lush grass and rabbits. Oh, and fish!"

"There will soon be another head to keep that one company, God willing."

"What do you mean, Papa?"

"I mean that great dog otter that Thom…" he clears his throat, "that your brother was after."

"I wish he could be left to swim in peace. If I see his face on the wall I will always think of Thomas drowned!"

"That is why he must be taken, Catherine. Somehow I must find the time, before someone else finishes him."

They have arrived at Elizabeth's door on the landing. William knocks firmly. Mari opens it. She shakes her head and squeezes Catherine's hand as the girl begins to cry.

"Take her up to bed." William's voice is stark.

"Don't worry, Catherine. Mummy will soon be well," Mari murmurs to her as she leads her away.

Elizabeth is sitting on her bed, her hair and clothes are loose. She seems calm as she looks out of the window at the dark sky, except that her fingers rake again and again through the items in her jewellery box. William snatches it roughly from her.

"These!" he says, bitterly. "Do not get so fond of these trinkets, Elizabeth. This case is crippling us!"

He picks up the necklaces, one at a time. With each string of gems, he names one of the Nanteos farms. "Pendre… Hafod y Gau Uchaf… Brynmawr… Ysgubordau… Banc y Llan." Elizabeth shrugs. "Do not scoff, Elizabeth! There is more than one thousand pounds spent defending this case already!" Her fingers pick again through the jewels. "We are all grieving, Elizabeth." He snatches the box, snaps it shut and returns it to the hidden compartment in the panelling behind the bed. Elizabeth starts to knead at her breasts. "Good God! What are you doing? You are like a wild woman!"

"They're heavy. Hold me, William, they ache so!"

He begins to weep as she holds him hard against her, forcing his hands on her breasts. Her skin smells of musk and rose water as he kisses her, finding the hollow at the base of her throat that is always so warm and soft. She slides down the bed and rolls onto her side, holding his hands hard on her breasts. She moves her bottom against him, small sounds escaping from her lips, like a baby suckling. He shifts away from her a moment to deal with his clothes and to pull the covers around them but as she loses his warmth she moans, lurches up, disorientated, her hand clawing at the air.

"Here, my love. I'm here!" He moves quickly to reassure her, taking them both underneath the blankets and pressing his body hard against her, wrapping her in his arms, his cheek pressed against the side of her head. He feels her relax and she draws her hands up to her chest, one nestled in the palm of the other, as he makes love to her. She closes her eyes and smiles a little, it is a kind of prayer between them, a kind of healing. There is a quiet knock on the door which goes unheard.

Cai turns away from Elizabeth's door and stands for a moment. There is the distant sound of Catherine crying in the nursery above. Taking the stairs two at a time he finds himself out of the house and in the comfort of the dark. Though cold, the night is still as he makes his way to the stables. Small bodies shuffle away into the shadows as he walks with a lantern towards Lady's stall. She whinnies at his approach, though he has nothing for her. Moonlight shines through the bars as he stands, his cheek against the mare's neck, watching the faint light of Elizabeth's window. He remembers her body, her scent, not just with his mind's eye, but in his skin. He groans, burying his face in the animal's hide, feeling her muscles work as she chews the fodder.

He hears a voice calling his name – Mari. He doesn't answer her but, rubbing his face quickly with the back of his hand, stands up straight. Releasing the horse's stable rug and letting it fall, he starts to brush her flank. She stamps in alarm at the girl's approach.

"I knew you'd be here," she says. "Didn't you hear me calling?"

He shrugs. She watches him.

"Cai? The night of Little Thomas –"

"Hush, Mari."

She stands hesitant at the doorway, her weight poised on one foot, her small hand gripping the wood as she lowers her lantern to the floor. "No I won't. It's not only you that feels it. That night, I was not thinking of the children. All day they'd been arguing and you and Elizabeth shut up together, your voices so alive, talking over one another. I couldn't bear it, and then when you saw me watching –"

At last he turns to look at her. "Stop. You do no good!"

But she is determined to continue, "And then her dress covered in red like blood and I thought, 'Yes! I wish you'd die. Die and go from here!' I wished her all the ill in the world, and I kept thinking it, and then suddenly Thomas was gone." She breaks down. "I made it happen!"

Her body crumples and she comes to rest in the hay, her face hidden in her hands.

Cai keeps brushing for a while, but the horse is restless with the stranger and there is no comfort in it for either of them. Mari continues her loud sobbing. He goes to her and, crouching down, pushes back her hair. The young face is shining with tears where the lamp light catches it. Though there is no colour to her eyes or lips, they too gleam as she looks up at him, putting out her arms. He kneels and holds her tight to his chest as her breathing calms. She is warm and heavy and fits to him as he turns and lies back, still holding her, her face nuzzling into the hollow between his shoulder and chest. Slowly, rhythmically, their bodies begin to move together and the mare takes herself away into the darkness at the far corner of the stall. She doesn't touch her hay net but shifts restlessly from foot to foot.

Afterwards, Cai reaches for the horse rug and pulls it over them – a gesture almost automatic, as a dog scrapes with its back legs to make a covering of leaves. He lies in the deep hay, Mari's head rising and falling with his breath but his eyes are fixed again on Elizabeth's window as her candle is extinguished.

CHAPTER SEVENTEEN

INSIDE GRUFFYDD'S COTTAGE a good fire of wood burns under the wicker hood, throwing shadows on the walls, even though it is not yet dark outside. The room is small but dry, thick flags cover the floor, and there is glass in the tiny windows. A wooden partition divides the space in two, with a rough ladder leading up to a raised platform where he sleeps. Cai and Elizabeth sit on the settle, steam from the drinks he has given them making their faces shine. From the little room behind the partition comes a regular, murmured incantation. In rhythm and power the sound is like a Latin mass, yet the words are Welsh. Elizabeth, sitting broken and silent, shivers, though Cai has her pulled close to him.

After a while, Gruffydd comes in from the back with a stranger. The man has tangled hair and seems afraid, holding out his arm, as if he would disown it. On the top of the hand is a large lump under the skin. Gruffydd puts him to sit down at the far side of the hearth and bends over the lump. The man looks away, his eyes wild in the flames' light. The conjuror rubs at the growth with a leaf until it becomes green with slime, then gives the man a drink from a small pot near the fire. Slowly the man seems to relax, lying back in his chair: the lump catches the light off the flames. Gruffydd straightens and looks at them.

"Come, Elizabeth," he says, putting out his hand.

He draws her through the door in the partition wall. But before she will stand and go with him, she reaches out to Cai and the three go together into the back room underneath the sleeping platform. It is small and has no fire. A tallow lamp smokes. Gruffydd gestures for Cai to sit but he and Elizabeth stand. From somewhere he takes a red cord, gives the end to Elizabeth to hold between them and begins to make the spell. Moving to the full length of the cord, back and forth, doubling it, tripling it to get nearer to Elizabeth, then back again. All the time he is chanting quietly and calmly, his steps moving exactly with the words. It is as though the woman is hypnotised. Half-closed, her eyes seem to slide back in her head and she sways slightly, forwards and back, as the man moves towards her or away. Cai is very still, but there is a terrible tension in him and his eyes never leave her face.

When the ritual is over, Gruffydd presses down on Elizabeth's shoulders and she sinks into a chair. He crouches down holding both her hands and looks deep into her eyes. "*Yr edyn wlân*. This must be tied to your leg until the grief and melancholy releases you. When you are ready, you will break it. No one must break it for you."

She nods once as he puts the cord in her fingers. There it hangs loose.

"It must be tied to the leg, Elizabeth," he says, gently.

It remains limp. Without looking at him she hands the cord to Cai.

Cai looks at the older man.

"You tie it, then," Gruffydd says.

Slowly Cai lifts her skirts. She is wearing tight wool stockings and he is at a loss where to put it. Gruffydd smiles. Elizabeth rolls her skirts higher. As is the custom, she wears no underwear. Her birthmark is revealed just above the stocking, perfectly round, as if someone had drawn around a coin and shaded it in. Gruffydd leans forwards, looking intently at the mark.

"Where did you say she was from?"

"Rhiw Saeson."

"And what family?"

"The Owens."

Gruffydd is still for a moment.

"What does it mean?" Cai asks quietly. Gruffydd shakes his head.

"No – you know. Tell me; I need to protect her."

Again Gruffydd shakes his head. "She will be known."

"What do you mean by that?"

"She will be remembered... that is all I have to say." Suddenly he snaps at Cai who is still fumbling to tie the cord around her leg. "On skin, boy. Come, I know what's been done between you."

Cai looks sharply at him, but Gruffydd's face is impassive, his pale eyes fixed on Elizabeth. She shifts again and lifts herself slightly to allow him to tie the woollen cord around her thigh but makes no move to pull her skirts back down. Cai does this for her too.

Gruffydd turns away. "Come and warm yourselves a little before you leave," he says.

The man with tangled hair is still there slumped deep in a chair. The two sit as before, though Elizabeth is no longer shivering. Gruffydd sits on a low stool and, taking a blunt knife, pokes the growth on the man's hand. The man is watching this time, but doesn't flinch. Gruffydd takes a sharper knife and, slowly burrowing into the lump from the side, peels back the lid of it. Watery blood exits, but there is something else there under the surface, black – and moving. The man watches, now shuddering with horror, as Gruffydd digs around then under it, disturbing a writhing mass.

Suddenly, the knotted tangle rears up, pauses for a moment, a black silhouette against the flames' light. Then it drops and, rolling across the floor, seems to gather itself. Like several large spiders tied together it scuttles away towards the gap under the door. The man makes a strangled shriek as Gruffydd deftly picks it up and tosses it into the fire where it sizzles, shrivels and disappears.

"What in God's name was that?"

Gruffydd laughs, the sound that of a much younger man. "I told you, Cai. Once you've finished sticking your fingers in the gentry's pie, you should come and find out."

With wooden tongs he takes some large leaves that have been soaking in a pot on the fire, applies them to the wound and then bandages it up with clean rags. Again he makes the man drink from the small basin by the fire. Finally he puts a cushion under his head, a blanket over him and turns away. He comes to sit on a stick-backed chair by Cai.

Suddenly Elizabeth is on her feet and moving towards the entrance. She walks as though in a trance, stopping, disorientated, when she reaches the closed door. In a moment Cai is at her side.

"Are you ready to leave, Elizabeth?"

She does not answer him but walks forwards a few steps before faltering again. He reaches past her to open the door and she stands on the threshold, her eyes closed, her face offered up flat to catch the weak sun's rays. Gruffydd appears at her side and draws her arm through his. She leans on him calmly as Cai readies the horses. When all is done he fits a heavy cloak across her shoulders, fastens it, then lifts her onto her horse. She makes no move to take the reins.

"A beautiful woman," Gruffydd says, shaking his head. "She will be well again, but it is never the same woman after the death of a child."

Again Cai urges her to take the reins but has to give up, mounting up behind her and leading his own horse with one hand, the other reaching around her waist for the reins. As they pass out of sight Cai looks back, once. Gruffydd has both hands raised high above his head as he watches them go, his palms open, white and stretched towards them.

The sun is growing low in the sky as they pass through the gates onto the drive. The gatekeeper's wife bobs a curtsey as they move past, but Elizabeth doesn't seem to see her. The woman stares until they are out of sight. They meet a group of workers on the drive returning from the woods with festive greenery. Roberts is anxious to clear the road for them to pass, but Cai stops him and their animals fall into line behind the heavy horse who bends to his chains, pulling the great tree trunk that will be the Yule log for another year.

Later Elizabeth sits in the parlour facing the blocked-up window, her back to the door, the Grail discarded on the floor. William comes in with a tray, puts it down and closes the door. She doesn't move.

"Will you eat, Elizabeth? Feed our child?"

His words by now a mere formality, he sits in front of her and feeds her, his mouth opening involuntarily as he spoons in the rich, milk and mace pudding. Since her pregnancy she has been prepared to eat, but only when someone has come to feed her. Though she has not gained weight all over her body as some women do, her face is a little fuller and has lost the absolute pallor it had in the first weeks after Thomas' death. William talks constantly as he lifts the food and carries it to her mouth, the dipping in, wiping, offering and emptying of the spoon, fitting the rhythm of his murmured words.

"Feed the child, made by us in our time of grief, perhaps with the spirit of little Thomas in it. Feed our child…"

Christmas passes and Elizabeth, heavy now with the child, has to exaggerate every movement to shift her cumbersome shape and weight. Carefully she stretches up, takes the box of jewels from the secret cupboard in the headboard behind her bed and turns the key on it. Ripping at a pillowcase from her bed, she wraps it around the box then uses the curtain cord, binding it around and around the bundle. A noise from outside sends her to the window. Unseen, she looks out, absent-mindedly playing with the cord above her stocking as she watches Cai washing himself at the pump, the wet, dark hairs on his chest and belly lying flat and sleek as a pelt. She sees as Mari sneaks up from behind him, an empty feed sack in her arms. As he bends to put on his shirt she jumps up and flings it over his head. He wrestles it off and she hurtles away squealing as he follows her, laughing. She ducks and runs into the hay barn.

Now the yard is empty, yet the significance of what she's seen between them remains like a spectre to Elizabeth. Suddenly, the cord snaps in her hand and she stifles a cry of surprise. A sad smile plays across her face as she gathers up the threadbare wool, kisses it and puts it deep inside her bodice. For a moment she looks at the hurriedly wrapped box on her bed, unable to remember what she had been doing with it.

In the barn, Cai freezes and pulls away from Mari. His hand silences her. He is listening intently and soon she too hears faintly the sound of the harpsichord. He takes the main stairs two at a time, then hesitates outside the music room door. Elizabeth doesn't look up as he enters. He stands and listens for a while. Though she plays much slower than before, her fingers have remembered the fugue, the bass line urgent and repeated, her right hand celebrating in a cascade of arpeggios.

Only her slight shifting on the stool so that her face is deliberately hidden by her hair, suggests she knows he's there. He crosses to the instrument and stands behind her, watching her hands. Bare of any ornament and pinched by the cold of the fireless January room, they seem to have a will of their own. At last they falter. He crouches on his haunches, covers her hands in his and holds them.

"How?" he says, breathing his words into her back.

Slowly she turns to face him, pulls the cord from her bodice and gives it to him. Her voice is shaky, unused to speech.

"Tell William…"

Unable to stop himself, Cai puts his arms around her middle, lays his head on the mound of her pregnancy. She kisses his head, her fingers tight in his hair.

He looks up at her. "The child… this child?" His hands are spread wide across her skirt. Elizabeth slides his hands far down and under her belly, presses them hard up against her so they hold the weight of the baby. She gives a deep sigh, closing her eyes and tilting her head back. "Mari says that William lies with you." She nods slightly. "The child…"

But others have heard her playing too, and there are sounds of people on the stairs. She loosens his hands and turns away, begins again at the Bach. He gets to his feet but cannot bring himself to leave her. "Elizabeth?" But she will not turn again for him. He goes, passing Catherine on his way out, the girl's face open with joy.

Finding Elizabeth improving, William accepts an invitation to a gathering at Gogerddan. It is hard to let go of the Old New Year and, all through the county, rich and poor alike are using it as an excuse to prolong the festivities. The morning, though chill, is clear and, after hastily ordering that Elizabeth receive a final check by the doctor, William can find no excuse for them to stay at home. Since the return of her wits the doctor recommends she go out for short periods, pleased though bemused that she is suddenly eating for herself and reputedly starting to manage her household again.

"She may easily revert to her former state, however, when any strain is put upon her – and we must be especially vigilant around the birth," he warns as he bleeds her for what he hopes will be the last time.

William nods gravely, but, as Martha turns away, she rolls her eyes and spits at Elin under her breath. "How much is he paid to tell us what we know too well ourselves!"

Gogerddan mansion, three times the size of Nanteos, is not a lovely house. It is too wide, the patterns of windows elongated, repeated too many times for the eye to sigh with pleasure. Whereas Nanteos would have been an excellent model for any discerning child's dolls' house, Gogerddan is a working building – more administrative than decorative. They had been there before when William's brother had been in charge at Nanteos but then they had been the poor relations, not the Pryse's near social equals. Although others in the county were to stay for a dinner party that night, it was thought enough for Elizabeth just to attend for tea, and they had invited the Powells on their own.

As Elizabeth, William and Catherine arrive they are honoured by the Pryses coming right to the door to greet them, a tide of small dogs washing around the women's huge skirts.

"Look, I told you Mama – we need miniature dogs!" whispers Catherine fiercely to her mother as she sees the toy pack. Elizabeth smiles faintly.

Even though it's only afternoon, the men do not join the

women for this gathering – instead William joins Sir Pryse in the library where business is surely on the menu again.

Lady Pryse holds court in the saloon. Inside the house is much more pleasing, the plaster work new and fresh – painted in cream and pastel blue. Elizabeth stops to admire a long case clock to the left of the door. Lady Pryse glows with pleasure.

"Oh you are discerning, my dear – an eight-day clock with a lacquered case, just up from London!"

"I'm glad I haven't lost my taste," she smiles, wanly.

"Come, please, we must have you sitting down in comfort," she fusses, arranging the cushions herself as Elizabeth comes to rest by the fire.

Once the business of settling everyone is completed, an awkwardness descends on the room. Catherine, having made the compulsory fuss over the dogs, sits on the edge of her chair, her face set and tight, almost scowling at the Pryse daughter, home from her travels with relatives. The girl is tall for her age and has big feet. Lady Pryse rescues the situation.

"I've arranged for an artist to attend us from Shrewsbury – I thought young Catherine would enjoy it; I know how much she cares for drawing (she smiles in Catherine's direction, the young girl's eyes are shining with pleasure). He's most expert at rendering portraiture from card – it's all the rage, a type of cameo technique..." she tails off. Elizabeth is no longer looking at her; instead her gaze is focused somewhere beyond the window. "Well, let's have our tea and then invite him to join us later."

"Is drawing of silhouettes what you mean, Lady Pryse?" asks Catherine.

"Yes indeed. You know the technique?"

"No, but I have seen it in a catalogue – I would dearly love to try!"

"Excellent!" Lady Pryse beams. "Sophia isn't much interested in drawing, but is developing into a fine horsewoman –"

"Do you ride?" Sophia's voice is abrupt.

"Not really," replies Catherine. "Only when I have to!"

"Oh, shame indeed." Sophia bends to scratch one of the dogs on his tummy. "I would have liked to show you the stables," she adds.

"I do like horses, though," says Catherine quickly. "And I love to draw them. Would you take me anyway?"

Sophia nods and grins. Again the conversation is becalmed.

"I thought of asking him to return later in the spring to stay for a while and give more lessons. I want the girls ready for when the new governess comes. Will Catherine have a governess, or will you find a school for her?" Lady Pryce looks directly at Elizabeth. "Mistress Powell?"

Elizabeth turns to her daughter. "Catherine, have you made your decision?"

"Yes, Mama; I've decided. To school I'll go!"

Lady Pryse raises her eyebrows. "Surely it is not the child's choice to make!"

Catherine looks at her a moment, then continues. "It is too lonely and glum at home and, now, well, now there's only me to need a drawing master and any other tutors (William being so young), I would be better off at school with others of my own age."

"Well, I think you're very clear about what you want, young lady, and I wish your Mama and Papa luck in finding you a place in a fine institution." No one answers her. "And now I'm going to ring for tea!" she says, hastily.

After the lavish refreshments, the girls are dispatched to 'survey the stables and their inmates'. Elizabeth, hoping to relieve the pain in her back a little, stands to admire the landscape set into the mantelpiece.

"Very much a work in yellow and green," she says.

"Yes – it's a likeness of the estate, of course."

"It's so beautiful here…"

Lady Pryse waits for her to say more, but nothing else is forthcoming.

"I wonder…" she says. Elizabeth sits down again. "We have had such trouble finding a music tutor for the girls – you haven't yet met my eldest, I don't believe, since you took Nanteos – I wondered, in fact we both wondered, my husband and I, if you would condescend to take them under your wing for a couple of months. You are such a wonderful musician."

"I am not qualified –"

"Oh, but you are by your enthusiasm and performance alone! And it would be a fine thing to have the girls mix more regularly, I believe."

Elizabeth smiles softly and nods.

"You will do it?"

"I will indeed."

"And Catherine will be brought here to enjoy the services of the drawing master, until she is sent to school?" The older woman smiles, the olive branch almost visible, suspended in the space between them.

Elizabeth nods. "Thank you," she says. William would be delighted with her – the Gogerddan trip everything he had hoped it to be. She wishes the same good fortune for him in the library.

Suddenly Lady Pryse leans forwards. "The King's Drops, perhaps? What was it finally healed you?"

The words shimmer like heat haze in the cold room. Elizabeth looks down at her hands.

"Or perhaps the regular ministrations of the Grail cup…" her words trail away. A log shifts, spits and settles. "I'm sorry." Lady Pryse is flustered. "I didn't mean to be indiscreet, I –"

"I'm not healed." Elizabeth's voice is suddenly loud. She falters and swallows.

"No, no of course, one never forgets I'm sure or –"

"I am not healed," she says again. "I simply remembered that I have other children."

Back in the coach, heated flasks in place and the furs pulled up over them, William is animated. "All is not lost, Elizabeth; we will pool our resources and plan a combined and improved sorting mill halfway between the two mines. Our shipping burdens too we must share, for the better. Just a little initial investment, and we will soon reap the rewards. I hope we will never see the likes of yesteryear again, my love!" Elizabeth doesn't answer. "How did your wooing go?"

"She needed no wooing, William. Lady Pryse was contrite and I believe only too eager to bend over backwards to be friends with us. It is a marvel what the loss of a child will do to soften unpleasant neighbours."

He looks at her sharply, but she does not seem distressed. Instead, eyes down, she is loosening the ribbons of her bonnet.

"I liked Sophia," interrupts Catherine. "She is not as stupid as she looks."

William laughs, turning again to his wife. "Well, Elizabeth – do elaborate."

She gives up on the ribbons, her arms dropping heavy on her knee. "We are to be bosom friends with the Pryses, as I understand it. The Pryse girls come to Nanteos for their musical instruction; Catherine to attend on an artist at Gogerddan."

William hugs her tight, relief flooding his face. "I am reformed, as you see," she says, putting her head back against the seat and letting her eyelids close.

CHAPTER EIGHTEEN

THE SECOND OF February – Candlemas. The day had been a short one, the mist not rising from the river until well past nine and hovering just under the ridge all day. William had gone to petition Lord Powis who was visiting Cardigan. The whole house, holding its breath as he banged about preparing to leave, sighed with relief to see his back, straight and stiff, disappearing at a canter down the drive. Though he was taking the coach to use later, he always liked to start a long journey on horseback.

"Riding helps me calm myself, Elizabeth," he had said. "And anyway, it's quieter and smoother – a man can think away from the rattle of that damned contraption. I just hope the bridge's holding or it'll be a wasted journey!"

This evening Martha had produced dinner early and Elin had encouraged Elizabeth to dine alone in her room in front of the fire. There was no need to keep a constant vigil over her now; maybe the late stages of pregnancy released some calming vapours, or maybe the soul of this new child was winning its battle with the shade of the dead boy for the mother's heart? Whatever the reason, Elizabeth could once more be expected to choose her own clothes and plan a menu though, God be praised, she no longer rode out to the hills or bent herself over extravagant plans in the study.

Downstairs, candles blaze in every window. The days are at last growing longer and it will soon be possible to feed the animals in daylight so, as tradition dictates, the dairy maid can give back her candle to her mistress. In the kitchen and scullery, there is candlelight in every pane and the wassail bowl, empty since New Year, is scoured and dressed ready. Small candles, ready to be lit at a moment's notice, have been fastened around the rim and it is Catherine's job to check that, from now on, water is kept hot to warm it.

"First we do our divination!" says Martha, in her element with a kitchen full of expectant faces.

Annie claps her hands with glee. "Who first?"

"Age or rank?" asks Mari.

"The spirits pay no heed to rank! Age. That is myself and…" She looks about her.

"Jenkins won't come, Martha, Ma'am," Annie replies. "He's muttering to himself over a prayer book in his rooms."

"I should have known it. He bans his wife too I expect – peevish man!" Martha stabs an escaping curl back under her cap. "Well, who's next, then?"

Elin points at Mari, who grimaces with excitement. "What do I do?"

"Sit here between these two big candles." Martha slams the pewter candlesticks down on the table top. "I sit on this chair next to you. Close your eyes, drink deep and toss the goblet back over your shoulder and onto the floor."

"What happens then?"

"Get some gin in here, will you, Elin?" Martha interrupts her, holding up two wooden cups. "And pop some warm water in with this one – a third water in one, half for the other. That'll be yours," she says to Mari. "Right then, where were we…?"

"What happens when you've thrown the cup?"

"Well, if it lands upright, you'll live to a ripe old age. But if bottom up, you'll die young."

Mari shudders.

"Shawl?" asks Martha.

"No, just excited!" the girl replies.

Elin puts the two goblets on the table and Martha takes a swig. She smacks her lips. "Right, down the mine!" she gulps hers down in one and throws the cup – it hits the wall and lands on its side, rolling under the table.

Everyone laughs, William giggling and throwing his arms about.

"Can't count that," says Martha in disgust, holding out her hand. "Fill up another, girl, and I'll try again." Noticing Mari wincing as she sips the liquid, she slaps her on the arm. "Get it down you!"

Mari swigs deep with screwed up eyes and then throws the goblet behind her, coughing and spluttering. It rolls against the wall and stops on its side.

"Oh no, I'll have to do another one!"

"Never mind, don't bother," says Martha. "Next! Who's next?"

Annie and Elin look at one another, but before one has to step forward, the door opens and Sarah Jenkins slides in, closing it softly behind her.

"They're on their way! Roberts' boy says he's seen their lanterns pass by on the top road."

"Come in, for goodness sake. You're ancient; you can go next. Come and sit down and tell your fortune." Martha gestures for a refill, calling out to Elin, "And don't water mine as much this time!"

"Oh, I can't! Edward –" says Sarah, shocked.

"Nonsense. Sit down woman, he'll never know." Martha grabs her arm. Elin returns, reluctantly putting down two more goblets. Martha drains the cup and throws it again. This time it hits the wall so hard the wood cracks. "Blethering thing!" she shouts. "Go on then, Sarah!"

Sarah, her eyes tight shut, downs the alcohol and throws her cup. It bounces once and lands on its base.

"You lucky harlot!" Martha shouts.

Everyone claps and William, so proud now of his talking shouts, "Throw it, throw it, Martha Cook!"

Elizabeth, having worked her way through nearly everything on her tray, opens the curtains to look out. Dimly she sees lighted torches shining through the mist. Suddenly, the old panic sinks its claws into her belly; the spirit night! But it can't be. That was before she was recovered. She pulls her wrap around her. No one has come for the tray; not even Mari has come with William to say goodnight.

She goes downstairs seeking company, hears hilarity from the kitchen. She knows now she's not welcome – had always known, really, except that now, at last, she will admit it to herself. The main front door stands slightly ajar, cold air sidling through the gap, but instead of simply closing it as she knows she should, she feels instead the old mischievousness creeping up. She smiles, glad to greet a familiar friend. But she is not so rash that she will risk her child to a February fog and goes as quickly and quietly as she can back upstairs to her room to reinforce herself.

Armed with Annie's stout boots that she hid in her travelling chest those months ago, and a heavy felt cloak, she goes back outside. Something other than mist is in the air – faint, inexplicable sounds and a smell of burning pitch. Keeping to the flags set up against the walls of the house, she can avoid the betrayal of the crunching gravel. She sees the lighted candles blinking in the windows, seeming only to emphasise the darkness outside. She looks in through the library window. The fire blazes uselessly in the empty room. Looking up to the nursery window on the second floor she sees it is dark. Where are her children? The grinding panic grips her again and she thinks she will have to go inside to use the commode but she can hear laughter coming from the servants' wing, light spilling from the open door and candles dancing in their windows too. Keeping close to the wall, she walks right around the back of the house.

She can see into the kitchen from here and, going up to the window, looks through the rows of lighted candles into the room. Everyone is busy and she sees her daughter warming her hands on a big wassail pot taking pride of place at the table. Her little boy is sitting on the chair beside his sister, swinging his legs and no doubt being kept out of harm's way by a huge biscuit that looks as hard to chew as ship's rations. She smiles.

Martha is tending a big pot suspended over the fire and takes liberal comfort from a goblet by her side, surely being topped up from the open bottle of gin next to it. Elizabeth suppresses a laugh.

Suddenly the door to the men's quarters opens. She hears shouting and laughing and is suddenly made aware of her ridiculous position – sneaking around in the cold, spying in at her own windows. Such behaviour will look to them all like the actions of a mad woman again! She acts quickly, crossing the yard on tiptoes, avoiding the shaft of light bleeding from the kitchen. She presses herself into the shadows of the hollow where the water pump is against the wall of the stables. For a moment she thinks that all is lost as she sees a couple of terriers with them – surely they will betray her? But the animals are too excited to find her out and focus instead on the party of eight or so men who take off down the drive singing.

As soon as their noise has passed, she comes away from the wall. The baby is churning and sometimes, when she's sitting quietly and wearing only her shift or her nightdress, it's possible to feel the lump of a foot running underneath the surface of her skin. Though her feet are cold, the little brazier that is the child is keeping the rest of her warm. But she hasn't had to stand for so long in ages and she feels the weight of her pregnancy pushing down on her – a heavy, swollen sensation between her legs and an ache in her calves. She retraces her steps back around the house – she must get back in her room quickly, before she's discovered, before anyone starts panicking about her. But just as she has almost reached the front of the house, she hears and then sees another party of men singing, laughing and carrying torches, coming up the drive this time. She can't try and bolt for the front entrance – it's heavily lit with lanterns and she'll definitely be seen. She scuttles then, as fast as she can, her hand rammed up under her belly supporting the bulk of her pregnancy, back to the hollow behind the water pump. What the devil would William say to her now? She smiles to herself as she pushes her back up against the wall for support.

The party of men come straight around the back and the door is flung open by Elin, who grins from ear to ear. They start singing for admission and one by one the women appear in the doorway. Martha takes up her place at the front of the house contingent. It is amazing that no one can see her, Elizabeth, skulking in the shadows, but the flame of the torches must be dazzling their eyes, stopping them seeing into the darkness across the yard.

The women make their answer. Led by Martha and Sarah who know all the words, they sing the familiar duel. Only Catherine is unable to join in. As they finish, Martha bites her thumb at them then flings wide the door and ushers everyone inside. Leaving their torches propped against the outside wall, the six men go into the kitchen, the door left open behind them.

From inside she can hear more singing, different this time, and laughing. Suddenly there's a woman's shriek.

Elizabeth comes out of her hiding place and hurries to the window. Inside she sees her daughter, draped in blue material, with William on her knee. The men and women are parading around her chair singing a new song together. On the table the wassail bowl steams, its candles blazing. She sees one of the men grab at Annie's bottom as they circle the chair and the girl squeals and giggles, holding up the procession as she leans on the table, beside herself with laughing. Martha turns around and prods her and they do two more turns around the chair. Then a man in a large hat holds up his hands and shouts, "Halt!"

The noise subsides and he and a bearded man carefully lift the bowl off the table. A couple of the candles lurch ominously and they quickly put it back down. Martha clicks into action, melting up some more wax and repositioning some of the less stable tapers. As she does this Annie happens to look towards the window and lets out a scream. They turn around as one, drawn to the direction of the girl's trembling, pointed finger. One of the men bounds to the door and it is too late for Elizabeth to hide herself. She sees his face, all confusion, then Martha's behind him. She peers past him.

"Mistress Powell, what on earth do you do out here alone in the cold? Come in at once!"

In a moment, the woman has come out and, grabbing her by the arm, propels her inside. The light and the warmth take her breath away. Catherine's face is a picture of horror as she struggles to her feet, the cloth slipping down. William is hastily set on his feet.

"Please, don't let me disturb you," Elizabeth says, gesturing expansively to the room in general. The men have moved away from the table and stand quietly warming themselves by the fire, watching what will happen next. "Sit down again please, Catherine," she says firmly and turns to Martha. "As I understand, this is Candlemas?" The older woman nods. "Though it's an old-fashioned practice, I don't see any harm in it. What do you do exactly?"

"The Candlemas rhymes, Mistress – the entry carol, the carol of the chair…"

The lead man, his hat now respectfully removed, takes over the explanation. "And the carol of the wassail bowl – from which we drink together. The ritual is interrupted. Our Mary," he gestures at Catherine, hiding her face behind the blue caul, "has not even drunk yet." He shakes his head in disgust.

"Well… it is similar to the practices north of the Dyfi where I grew up. I see no harm in it. It is not as if we practise divination here." Elin and Sarah exchange a look of panic, unseen by Elizabeth, who continues. "Please carry on with your celebrations."

Grateful, the man bows to her and, rather self-consciously, they take their place again around Catherine's chair.

Suddenly warm, Elizabeth's body starts to shake uncontrollably and, anxious to deflect attention away from herself, she sinks into a chair. Elin takes off her boots, Elizabeth almost laughing out loud as she sees the shock on Annie's face when they are placed by the fire and the girl recognises them as her own. She is brought a warm bottle to rest her feet on. Martha loosens her cape and puts a goblet of warm milk in her hands. As she bends to do so she plants a kiss on her mistress' forehead. Catherine, anxiously watching her mother, gasps in shock, but Elizabeth doesn't mind. So much has passed between the two women during the time of her illness that such closeness, especially after gin, seems entirely natural.

"We will repeat the chair carol, then," says the man. "Then we will drink from the bowl."

More than a little subdued this time, they repeat the carol. Elizabeth hides a smile as she watches Annie, tucking in her bottom and holding her hands behind her, determinedly putting space between herself and her would-be tormentor in the circle. They stop and the man holds up his arms again.

"Call for the man of the house to offer the bowl!"

The women look at one another. "There is none," says Martha.

"What about Jenkins?" Elin asks.

Sarah shakes her head vigorously.

"Will I do?" asks Elizabeth.

They look at her and she shrugs her shoulders and smiles.

"The lady of the house will be the best of alternatives!" shouts the man at last, breaking the ice.

Again, the two pick up the heavy wassail bowl but this time the candles are stable. With bent knees they walk on eggshells to Elizabeth's big chair near the fire.

"What must I do?" she says.

"Give your blessing and proffer the bowl, if you please – no need to stand," he says hastily as she struggles to her feet.

She clears her throat. "As the lady of the house, I hereby proffer to you, the wassailers, the wassail cup on this Candlemas Eve!" She bows her head and there's a round of applause.

"The carol of the bowl!" the man calls as they break into yet more song.

The men mince back with the bowl and, taking a ladle from her belt, Martha offers Catherine a drink. Catherine sips carefully, her face grave.

"Give some now to the Christ child," says the man, gently.

She gives William a sip. He screws up his face in disgust, then asks for more. Everyone laughs.

Soon they have all drunk from the bowl and, as the level goes down, the men lift it to drink straight from it, risking singed whiskers as they blow out the candles and causing great hilarity as they slop the concoction down their fronts. Catherine, released from her role as the Virgin, comes to sit on the rag rug at her mother's feet.

"Will you play with my hair, Mama?"

With William on her knee, cuddled around her pregnant belly, Elizabeth reaches down and sleepily curls her daughter's hair through her fingers.

Mari comes over to her. The girl has been silent since her mistress came in, avoiding her gaze and now stands uncertain before her. "Shall I take the children, Ma'am?" she says at last.

Elizabeth nods and Mari reaches down to pick William up. He's heavy now, and it takes both the women to get him safely into Mari's arms. He cries a little as he's disturbed but is soon a dead weight again against the girl's body.

"Come on, Catherine, you too," Mari whispers, sticking out her hand from under William's bottom. Catherine stretches up and uses Mari's hand to get to her feet. She kisses her mother on the head and then kisses the bump. Elizabeth smiles.

"Off to bed, now, my darlings. I will come soon."

"Thank you, Mistress," Mari says quietly, as she turns to go.

Martha, the other three women and the wassailing men seem to have forgotten she's still there and are seated around the table, finishing off the last of the pot with long spoons, digging into the delicious mess of cake and fruit at the bottom. Leaning on the chair arms, Elizabeth pushes up and gets onto her feet. A couple of the men who are facing her, make to get up in respect and Martha turns around, leaning back in her chair.

"Mistress – wait. Elin, help your mistress up to bed!" Elizabeth waves her hand in rejection of the offer. "Get up, you lazy girl –"

"No, no – I insist!" The tone of Elizabeth's voice is a clear pulling of rank and Elin drops gratefully back into her chair. Elizabeth leaves quickly before she causes any more disturbance.

One stair at a time, she makes her way towards her bedroom, stopping on the small landing part-way up. As she looks at the familiar dead faces, tears, welling up from the water table of grief which is only ever just below the surface, run down the side of her nose. She stands for a while looking into the otter's glassy eyes.

"You will have to be moved, dear friend," she whispers. "I cannot bear to look at you any more." Turning away she wipes her face and enters her room.

Without help she is stuck in her clothes and, the fire having burned down low, she lies on her bed, wrapping the coverlet around her.

Dimly, as she dozes, she registers men coming back, probably William as it is the front door that slams shut, and then the hallway is full of voices. As she drifts away again she hears angry shouting coming from the back of the house this time. But William is away, surely they weren't expecting him back for days? Suddenly, with this thought, she is properly awake, propping herself up on her elbow. Definitely William's voice and coming from the service wing. She eases herself around and off the bed, shivering as she casts off the covering. As she makes her way downstairs William is still shouting and now she can hear a woman crying. As fast as she dares, she reaches the bottom of the stairs and makes her way through to the kitchen.

John is standing outside the door and shakes his head vigorously at her. She ignores him and goes in. The last of the wassailers is making a hasty exit. As he leaves, William picks up the man's hat and spins it at him. It hits him between the shoulder blades and skids across the floor. The man picks it up and disappears.

"Get that thing out of here!" He pokes the pot with his stick and a sobbing Annie swoops it up and out to the scullery. "Antique practices! And what on God's earth is this?" He lifts the blue material onto his cane. "Well?"

As he looks at her, Martha bobs a curtsey, but doesn't answer. He looks at Elin – she looks down. "A good job the bridge was down. Can I not leave my property without some foul play being done?" He turns to Annie. "You, girl – what was done here?"

Through her sobs, in a voice full of gulps and hiccups, she tells him. No doubt aided by the gin, she warms to her story and it becomes a garbled tale of vice and superstition. William, his face white, is very quiet.

Then he turns to Martha. "Popery! Get out of my house."

As he turns to leave, he suddenly registers Elizabeth, standing quietly by the door. "Come upstairs out of the way – you should be in your bed!" He turns to Elin. "You, slovenly girl, get your mistress undressed and into bed or you'll be out too!"

He kicks one of the wooden goblets, still on its side on the floor, as he slams out. Martha says nothing, but starts to clear away. Elizabeth feels desperate to speak, but can think of nothing to say. She bends down awkwardly and retrieves the goblet from the floor.

"Where might this go, if you please?" she says to Annie who, still hiccupping, is trying to clear up as Elin hovers nervously by her elbow.

"Oh Mistress Powell, please give it to me!" she exclaims, mortified, holding out her hand to take the dirty vessel.

Elizabeth goes to pass it to her but slips on a wet patch on the flags and, as she pitches backwards the goblet flies out of her hand, hitting the table hard behind her and spinning across the floor. Elin lunges forwards and steadies her in time to stop her falling.

"No harm done," Elizabeth says, briskly, yet she is shaken up and sits down quickly on the chair put behind her legs. The room has gone quiet and, as she looks up, she sees the face of every woman looking past her, deathly silent, down towards the floor. She turns around quickly, "What's the matter? What are you looking at?" No one will meet her eye.

But Martha snatches up the goblet and the other with it and takes them to the scullery. Elizabeth sits, trying to calm her breathing for the baby's sake. It takes a while for Martha to return. When she does, she is without her apron or her proper cap. "Goodnight, Mistress," she says quietly and takes Elizabeth's hand.

"Don't worry, Martha. I am mistress here. The house servants are my domain. Nothing will happen to you."

Elizabeth squeezes the cook's hand once then puts it firmly down. As she gets slowly to her feet she says, "Go to your quarters now and stay out of his way for a few days." She turns to Annie. "Make sure Cook doesn't waste her time packing. She'll have a lot of work on tomorrow, preparing the master's favourite veal and ham pie to win back his heart!"

CHAPTER NINETEEN

S O SLOWLY, ELIZABETH creeps down the stairs and opens the door to the study. The stain on the carpet is still there, though more brown than red now, and she forces herself to register, wearily, that she must have it removed. Cai, his back to her, bends over the table. In his hands is a scale model of a water-powered winding machine. She watches him, unseen, smiling at his intent interest in the little contraption. Though she hasn't moved at all, some instinct must convey her presence to him, as he turns around.

"Elizabeth! You've come down!"

She smiles at the obvious statement, shrugging her shoulders slightly. He is already on his feet, pulls out a chair for her and closes the door behind her. As he bends to build up the fire she finds her eyes travel up his legs, linger on his haunches – she smiles to herself to feel the familiar sensations returning, and she with child too!

He comes to sit opposite her, a grin the width of his face. It is all she can do not to reach out and put her palm flat against his cheek to feel his relief. She smiles back at him.

"What is this you play with?" she teases, picking up the contraption.

"Ah – it came today. This is what we shall have working for us by the summer!" He picks up the model and, like a youth, demonstrates every possible pulley and lever of the machine.

"Oh! Um. Very good. Good heavens," she nods, pretending awe at the projected improvements in efficiency, the multiple functions of the thing. Eventually he runs out of steam. Her eyes are sparkling. At first he thinks, with a jolt of pleasure, that she's holding back laughter at his enthusiasm, but then he sees the tears seep from her, without a sob or a groan, as effortless to her now as breathing.

"Oh, Elizabeth!" He longs to hold her, but there is no excuse, now that she has recovered enough to feed herself and the baby.

"You were as silly as Thomas demonstrating his catapults or his homespun bird traps, that's all. No matter." She gathers herself, managing a weak smile. "I would like to go out." He waits. "Will you take me?"

"Of course." Cai is aware of his heart banging in his chest. "Where?"

"I think… I think to the ridge. Yes, I would like to see Nanteos from afar."

"When?"

"Now." Her lovely smile is back.

He gets to his feet. "You then – warm clothes, especially boots, and something very soft and comfortable to sit on. I'll get us the trap."

He puts out his hand and they shake on it.

"Right, my marching orders – better get moving!" she stands, carefully.

Neither Elin nor Martha is at all happy at the plan. In fact, the front steps are crammed with long-faced figures as they prepare to leave.

"We're only going up there, Catherine," Elizabeth points to the oak on the ridge. "You'll be able to see me most of the time. Why don't you take your sketchbook to the front window in the music room and do a landscape for Papa when he comes home?"

The girl, always quick to be brave, nods, but Elizabeth notices how tightly she holds onto Mari's hand. Elin, Mari and even Jenkins have offered to come with them, but Elizabeth, uncompromising as ever, has made her wishes clear. As Cai urges the pony on, each is uncomfortably conscious of the eyes on their backs. Elizabeth, turning briefly to wave at her daughter, catches a tight-lipped frown on Jenkins' face.

But as soon as they pass the bend in the drive, the suffocating tentacles of worry drop away. Elizabeth sits up straighter in her seat, pushes her fur hood back a little. Cai glances at her and laughs.

"I can hardly see you behind all those clothes!"

She has been almost mummified by the attentions of the women, only the features right in the middle of her face visible. He can see her smiling even so, her eyes closed as she feels the slight breeze on her face.

Luckily the gates are still open after the delivery this morning, and they don't have to see or explain their movements to anyone else. Though every corner of the estate is some sort of signpost reminding her of Thomas, for once she is able to recognise each as it hurts her like a squeezed bruise, wince, then push it away.

They pass no one else as they take the road up to the hills, and Elizabeth presses herself up against Cai under the furs. He leans against her and there is no embarrassment between them as the pony trots through the chilly morning. Cai takes her hand and soon she boldly pushes off both their gloves and wraps his one free hand in hers.

He takes it back to manoeuvre the trap as they reach the oak. For a while they sit there, overlooking the valley, Nanteos below them. Though no one can be seen, it is hard not to imagine the prying eyes.

"I want to get down," she says, pushing her hat back off her head.

He goes round and helps her. He can't take hold of her around her waist because of the baby, so he puts his hands under her armpits instead. As her feet touch the ground he kisses her hair. She does not move away from him but lets her forehead come to rest against his shoulder.

He makes a nest for them on the ground underneath the leafless tree. The earth is surprisingly dry and hard amongst the roots. Martha has made them pack a small hamper though it is hardly two hours since her breakfast. Elizabeth puts her back to rest against the tree's trunk and reaches out for him. He comes to sit near her, holding her hand.

"Do you remember –?"

He nods. The pony nibbles at the yellow, washed-out grass.

"Thank you for finding the money, Elizabeth." She looks at him quizzically. "For the pumps," he adds.

"Oh – there was really no use for such fancy outhouses, and I don't need diamonds to make me sparkle!"

He looks at her in delight – the first joke! But her cheeks cannot stay smiling for long. She shifts, her back uncomfortable against the bark, the baby's weight grinding down on the base of her spine.

"Come, Elizabeth…" He moves to sit up against the tree, his legs bent in front of him and gently places her to lean back on his chest, her body supported by his. Now she is warm and sheltered in his arms, but he can no longer see her face.

"I regret nothing," she says suddenly. "Only Thomas." She feels his body tense around her, but he doesn't speak. "And I know you're leaving." She sits upright and moves away from him. "William told me."

For a while neither moves nor speaks. Then he reaches out, easing her towards him, gently angling her legs to lie across his thighs and off the cold earth. "I can't stay. Can't keep looking at you with William; can't keep holding Mari, wishing it was you." Elizabeth nods, but the tears are back. "She knows it too. We'll both go away. We could go anywhere – new mines in Nottinghamshire, best of all, they need engineers abroad."

"I could not bear to think of you separated from me by water!" she cries.

"Don't, Elizabeth, it's hard enough!"

He holds her close, still sideways on so they can fit against one another without the baby in the way. She squeezes his arm tight where it rests on her leg, lifting his hand and kissing his warm palm. Her body, made both vulnerable yet voluptuous by her pregnancy, is heavy and he moves her further onto his lap. She rests on him, sinking deeper as she begins to relax, and he remembers the tavern, his body jolting alive with arousal at the memory of her. Every breath is full of her scent, his arm supporting her under the heavy breasts. He groans and shifts under her.

She stirs slightly. "Please stay until the child comes."

He freezes. Taking a deep breath, he asks her at last. "Is it ours, Elizabeth? Did we make it that day you came back from drowning?"

But she only shrugs slightly, closing her eyes as she presses against him, her hands folded together and calm on her lap, like two birds asleep, and it is his turn to weep. This may be the last time he holds her in his arms. She sighs as she dozes, warm against his chest, her hair tickling his nose with the rise and fall of her breath and he knows that he too could never bear to be an ocean away from her.

"I love you; I have always loved you," he murmurs, his lips against her hair.

"I know it," she says sleepily, burrowing deeper under his coat.

But sound carries far across the shallow valley, with little breeze and no leaves on the trees and, though he is sitting too low to see the ground floor of the mansion, he's aware of activity there. He shifts Elizabeth into the crook of his arm, slides her legs off his and lowers her gently off his lap. His limbs are stiff and cold as he stands up – he must get them both home.

The noise is unmistakable now, definitely coming from Nanteos, and when he hears someone beating a copper pan, he knows their time is at an end. Standing at the edge of the ridge he waves his arms high above his head to ease their worry back at the house; stop someone coming out to find them. Elizabeth stirs and sits up, her face wet where tears have come again as she slept.

"They are calling us back, Elizabeth."

She nods and he helps her to her feet, picking up some of the rugs to take to the trap. There, nestling sheltered between the roots of the great tree is a pale, brave cluster of primrose flowers. "Oh Cai, look. The very first of the year!" she calls as she bends towards them.

He kneels down and, with his knife, eases the tiny bunch out by the root. Carefully he wraps the spider of roots and soil in a handkerchief and folds her hand around it. She bends her face to the petals. "Oh, no smell. I thought there would be a little scent."

Holding her hand he leans down to smell the flowers and smiles. "You can put it in water with a little sugar and it'll come alive in the warmth of your bedroom. I'll see to the trap."

Whilst he tightens up the harness and loads the trap his gaze returns to Elizabeth waiting by the tree, looking out at her home. Even now at nearly nine months pregnant, it is impossible from behind to see that she is with child. She stands straight and still, cradling the posy in her hands. He leads her to the vehicle and, taking her in his arms, lowers her gently onto the seat. They make a half-hearted attempt to wrap her back up, as though they could somehow hide improper feelings inside layers of clothes. Trussed like a ham again, she looks ruefully out from under her hat. He laughs and she joins in and soon they're howling with mirth, a sound that changes to sobs for her as he turns the pony ready to leave. She looks back for a final view of her home, blowing a silent kiss.

"You did it that day in Aberystwyth, to the ships – do you remember?"

She nods, "I remember everything."

Leaning on one another for the journey back they are silent. Only once does Cai have to speak to the pony, comforting him as he rears in the traces, frightened by a brown hare. The wild creature, suddenly finding itself in the open on the road, a trap bearing down on it, dances with fear – darting ahead of them, zigzagging in panic, its eyes bulging in its head. There is nothing Cai can do but halt the pony until the animal has turned the bend and disappeared from sight. He looks quickly at her face but, to his relief, she betrays nothing of the fear that a local woman in her condition would feel to see a hare cross her path. Too soon they reach the gates, the lodge keeper hurrying out to touch his hat to them.

"Mistress Powell, so glad to see you abroad. God be with you!"

She nods and tries to smile, but can think of nothing to say to him. Cai walks the pony slowly for the last half-mile – it will end soon enough, this bubble of quiet, sacred privacy, and as they round the bend by the lake, figures push forwards to meet them. She squeezes his hand tightly, fitting her fingers between his, as he pulls up in front of the house. Cai, after helping Elizabeth down, can stand it no more, sickened by the prospect of composing his face for so many. As he walks the pony back to the stables, William, coming from the building work at the back of the house, apprehends him.

"What do you think you're doing?" His breath forms angry smoke in the cold air.

Cai stops, looks straight ahead.

"I'm talking to you." He waits. No answer comes; Cai does not even acknowledge him. "Your irresponsible, faithless behaviour… careless of both my wife and our child. I sheltered you as a Christian but – enough. Look at me when I'm talking to you! I've tolerated you too long!"

Still Cai does not react, though the pony is impatient for its feed and nudges at his shoulder with its nose.

"Your leaving cannot come too soon! What have you to say, man?"

Finally Cai speaks. "She wished it," he says, simply, and looks down. The words hang in the air between them. Then he looks full at William, the two men the same height, though Cai is broader. "The model for the pump has come. I'll let them know we'll take it this afternoon."

"Oh." Disarmed, William hesitates for a moment – Cai is waiting to be dismissed. "Right, good, yes. That'll be all, Cai," he says.

Meanwhile Elin ushers Elizabeth inside. "The master is home, Mistress. He asked for you and… well he was much displeased to hear you had gone out." She eyes the posy, but says nothing.

Her women have become bold during her illness – unavoidable surely, but something she will have to reverse, firmly and gradually, after the baby comes.

"Thank you, Elin," is all she says now, as she stands in the inner hall for the girl to unwrap her. "Have food brought up to my room, please."

The girl curtseys. The onlookers disperse, reassured that she has returned unharmed but robbed of a scene between Cai and Mari or Elizabeth and William. She goes to her bedroom alone.

Her breath comes with difficulty after climbing the stairs – the trip has been more taxing than she realised. As she enters her room she looks at the Grail in its casket. She is tempted to get it out and hold it to her but, although she's been allowed to have it back with her at last, she is loath to seek comfort from it when people can see. It frightened them. She turns her back on it and, brushing them lightly with her lips, puts the wilting flowers in the glass by her bed. She struggles into her house robe, desperate to be out of the layers and layers of clothes, but trapped inside them until someone comes to help.

She brings a chair to the window and looks out across the valley to the oak. Clouds are forming now behind its proud skeleton but she hardly notices the tears seeping from her eyes. There is a light tap and William comes in. She turns and manages a weak smile.

"What do you do, Elizabeth?" he brings another chair to sit beside her and takes her hand. "It is hardly March and you ride out, nearly full with child!"

"I didn't ride. I went in the trap."

He smiles, exasperated by her stubbornness, but pleased to hear the old wit and wilfulness resurfacing. Her hands are cold and he rubs them. Clasping them both he leans forwards. "You will agree to releasing more of the jewels, Elizabeth?"

"Of course."

He brings her hands to his lips, kissing each in turn. "And those stables can wait. I've given the foreman the new, trimmed-down designs – they'll be finished by the end of April, so he says." Her gaze strays back to the tree. "Thank you, my darling." He lets her hands go and watches her for a few minutes but she makes no more acknowledgement of his presence.

Elin taps at the door and enters with a tray of food. "Shall I stay and help you eat? You must make sure that you take enough food. Shall I aid you?" he asks her, relieved perhaps to have some other function here. She shakes her head.

"I'll eat, William, don't worry." Finally she looks properly into her husband's face. Through the mist of her misery she notices with shock the changes wrought there in less than a year. He is suddenly middle-aged – his skin thick and dull; his lips colourless and the once fine, fair hair now thin, gone to the colour of ash. "But thank you, William," she squeezes his hand. "We have neither of us come to harm." Her eyes take in the unborn child.

"May I sit with you while you eat?"

She nods.

"May I bring you some refreshment too, Sir?" Elin asks.

"No – but thank you."

The girl leaves. Despite her hunger Elizabeth is too tired to manage much, though just to please her husband she forces herself to finish the potted venison.

"I need to sleep now," she says then.

He helps her undress, kissing her neck and shoulders as they appear from the layers. He gets in beside her to warm the chill sheets, propping himself up on the bolster and tucking her under his arm. She sleeps on her side, the bump of the child resting comfortingly on his hip. He too dozes, waking briefly as Elin comes to fetch the tray, but it is a long time since he has been so at peace.

CHAPTER TWENTY

THE MEN ARE gathered in the stable yard ready for the hunt, about eight of them and the pack of otter hounds. They carry special spears and nets but there is none of the usual jollity. As they wait there is no flagon in sight – not even a hip flask makes its way from man to man, and the fog seems to shroud the endeavour.

"Where is he? I cannot wait any longer!" Even William is on foot this time, the better to pick up any signs on the ground.

"Cannot say, Sir." Jenkins looks down at his boots.

"You know, Cai, Sir: never around when you need him!" John turns away to hide a smile of triumph.

William rounds on him, the broken capillaries in his cheeks livid in the raw air. "Minding the business here while I'm gone is your job. In fact you can get yourself inside – see to your mistress; useless blaggard."

John, chastened, goes quickly inside. William looks about him again. "Do any of you know where he is?" William's crop flicks again and again against his boots.

"No, Sir – cannot say…" Roberts replies.

"Will not say, more like! He's up at the mine again playing with that engine – that new toy, is he not? Has he forgotten Thomas so easily? God damn him!"

The men fall silent and even the dogs shrink away from him – their legs bent and heads low.

"Sir…" Roberts hesitates but then comes forwards, the lead dog at his heels being careful to put his master in the way of the whip. "Would it be better to leave it today?" Seeing the reaction on William's face he adds hastily. "The fog will surely lift by tomorrow or later in the week and, as I understand it, Sir, you are not due back in London for many days."

With a roar, William turns and brings his crop down on the side of the water trough. "Christ help me! Can not one of you understand? I cannot rest until I find that devil, that most unnatural of creatures – half-fish! He haunts me! Did you hear me? Thomas' spirit cannot be at rest whilst he lives!" The men are all standing in an arc, tense and dismayed at this display. The dogs have slunk away behind them. "We will wait for him no more – let him go to Hell!"

He gestures for Roberts to call up the hounds and the party leaves, disappearing into the mist before they even reach the bend in the drive.

Elizabeth watches them go from the long window in the first-floor corridor, leaning against the sill for support.

"No longer like a moonstone – more of an agate. Cloudy like an agate stone," she murmurs to herself. Elin appears at her side. "The sky; just like an agate stone."

"Beg your pardon, Mistress?"

"Like an island." She sighs. "The mist makes this place an island. You feel you are all alone. In London it is dangerous – people die in it. It chokes you or you are run down by the terrible traffic on the street."

"Indeed, Ma'am. I'm sure London is a terrible dangerous place. Won't you come and sit a while? May I find some refreshment for you?"

Elizabeth shakes her head. "Will they find him, do you think?"

"Find who, Ma'am?"

"Thomas' otter. Will they kill him and mount his sad head on the wall?"

Elin grimaces. "I'm sure I cannot tell. I hardly know whether to hope it or no!"

Elizabeth's knuckles are white with the effort of supporting herself. Alarmed, Elin takes her arm. "Please, Mistress; won't you sit a while? Why not rest a little on the bed?" Elizabeth shakes her head. "Or perhaps play a little – play one of your lovely tunes on the keyboard?"

Elizabeth smiles slightly into the girl's earnest face. Humouring her, she nods and makes her way to the music room where she lowers herself onto the piano stool. She gestures for Elin to leave. Slowly she plays a Bach pavane but her hands hover over the keys from time to time as she winces in discomfort. Catherine enters and comes to sit by her mother, perching on the edge of the stool. Elizabeth stops playing to stroke her daughter's hair but it is clearly an effort. At last, putting her arm around the girl she kisses her head and says quietly, "Go and fetch Martha, Catherine. I'm… not well."

As Elizabeth, leaning on Elin's arm, creeps into the bedroom, the copper pans are hurriedly lifted out from under the quilt, the servants standing back for her to pass before exiting with their loads. Even though it is only late morning, the fog makes the house very dark.

"The fog in London; sometimes it lasts so long and it is a thick thing that you can smell. It leaves a residue…" She is still talking, though to no one in particular.

Elin undresses her, taking her time, waiting for each of the pains to subside before moving her. Martha builds up the fire.

"It is like a bog of the air: bog – fog!" Elizabeth laughs. "Tregaron Bog. Borth Bog. In London we have to travel by chair sometimes; too dangerous for the carriage, and people walking are dead, often dead."

"Indeed, Ma'am." Martha helps lower her onto the bed and lifts her legs, then turning to Elin, hisses. "Close those curtains, will you – keep that blasted fog out!"

At last she is safely tucked in, the sheets up to her chin. The room continues busy for a while, the women making ready with the water, cloths, crib and even the ingredients of the womb poultice. Elizabeth's legs see-saw under the bedclothes, she is only just managing her discomfort, but still she speaks, her words coming fast, so intent is she on telling her story.

"We are late. Ah, always late and William is beating his riding crop against the top of his boots like a silly boy; or striking the flint again and again without purpose in the way that makes me seethe and I have to wear the jewels. All the time something different! Have to remember who has seen it, where each piece has been. 'For they think us yeomen, Elizabeth. They think you rub unscented lanolin into your skin!' I laughed at that but it was no good, it didn't cheer him at all. 'Nanteos! That is who we are. I can speak the English as good as they and soon silver and lead will do the talking for me!'" Her voice falters and she grimaces, twisting and kneading the sheet in her fist.

Elin looks at Martha's face for reassurance, but there is none. She whispers to the older woman. "It's early, isn't it? Isn't the baby coming too early?"

"What do I know – you're her personal maid." Martha yanks on the bell.

Elizabeth resumes her monologue, half-turning to Martha, though not really seeing her. "No, the pains are not as the times before. Each one is a pinching pain, a grinding thing that makes you see stars; a bang-on-the-elbow pain. I am used to the rolling waves of pain that change to massive breakers. The sea at Aberystwyth – all brown, all grey. Why do the poets say it's blue?"

Annie comes in and Martha turns on her. "Have you done as I asked? The Reverend? The doctor?" Annie nods. "Where is that Mari?"

Annie shakes her head, dumb. With a swipe of the hand Martha dismisses her and sets about bathing Elizabeth's hands and face, but she has clearly been touching herself under the covers and her right hand is covered in blood. Horrified, Martha takes some of the shredded sheets and they tie her arms to the bed. She moans, corkscrewing her body from side to side as they fasten her down.

Martha leans over her. "We need to clean you, Mistress, for the doctor coming. It's for your own good!"

Elin yanks the drapes aside and looks out. A groom is clearing horse manure from the drive but there is no sign of anybody useful.

"Maybe we should send for Myfanwy?" she says. "I know the master said, but..."

"If she comes anywhere near the birthing chamber we're out of a job – you know that," Martha snaps. "Annie, get a fresh nightshirt for your mistress – and tell someone outside that we need a clean oilcloth up here."

They bathe her, the fresh red blood staining the water pink. Elizabeth's body, stretched out like someone on a rack, flexes and tenses as the pain squeezes her, her cries turning to whimpers as each subsides.

Mari sidles in, her face hidden by her hair, and crouches by the pillows. Elizabeth whispers at her, groping for her. Annie comes in with a clean nightdress and Martha bends to untie Elizabeth's hands. Together they sit her up and pull the soiled gown over her head, easing the new one down, lifting her hips and settling it underneath her. Mari looks in horror at the deep, fresh stain. She turns to Elin, "Is she meant to bleed this way?" Elin shakes her head quickly and moves away.

Elizabeth stretches out her hand again and Mari sits down by Elizabeth's pillows, bending her head to catch the fast-whispered story. Although Elizabeth's speech is urgent, her face earnest with the need to communicate, her voice is now barely audible and she repeats the same words in nearly the same order, her nails digging into Mari's palm as she talks of the fog. Then, "Please, I need to relieve myself!"

Together the women lift her onto the pot, Mari holding up her shift, Martha holding it in place. When she's finished, Martha wipes her, putting the cloth over the bowl and thrusting it at Elin. "Take that downstairs and put it in the scullery – the doctor might want to see it." Elin's face twists in disgust. "Do what I say... Now!"

Elizabeth, her hands free again, seems more peaceful. She looks straight at Mari as she tells a different story. "My cousins, they brought an otter pup to the house once, when we were young. An evil-smelling thing it was, but endearing. Fluid as mercury, it was more snake than dog, with whiskers that quivered and shimmered. It tormented the servants, drove the dogs wild, could climb and jump like a cat but had more a sense of humour. They made a collar for it and took it on a lead but it was more weasel than dog – had no shoulders for a collar to grip. Then it disappeared... I forget. For a while the boys would not hunt lest they hunt it down, but we all forget."

As she speaks, Martha lifts up the covers and slips her hand under Elizabeth's bottom. When she pulls it out it is covered with blood.

"And where is he, this great man, this doctor!?" She turns to Elin in despair.

But Elizabeth, seeming oblivious, her pains only a memory, is talking again, her face flushed. "Then you came to me with two boxes. 'Jewels!' you said, and the healing cup. I opened both in turn but must confess, liked the gems best! When I opened the treasure chest there was a loud sound as of trumpets or the clash of cymbals. I liked the bright sound, the colours. When I opened the second I heard nothing. Inside was a broken bowl made of wood but mended in metal. The whole room seemed to go quiet but the goblet did not speak. I closed it up again. Later, when I used to open it, I noticed the silence like a wind suddenly dying down about the house. Made of olive wood from the true cross it can heal; but that's a secret…"

Having gathered other landowners and their men on the way, the otter hunt is about twenty strong by the time they reach the salt marshes. The men have fanned out and the dogs move constantly between them. They keep up a continuous calling because of the fog – even the experienced hounds finding it hard to smell, hear and see in these conditions. Roberts is at William's side.

"I would say we should go back, Sir. Leave it for another day."

"Again!" William stops and looks hard at him. "I wouldn't have put you down as so feeble. You do what you like, man – but that animal dies today. Or I die in the taking of him!" He stumbles on, his boots slipping on the treacherous ground but his body held stiff.

One hound hurls itself into a ditch from which a startled heron rises. The bitch manages to jump for its legs and drags the bird to the ground where it breaks its wing, though still snaps with a fearsome beak. But others of the pack have joined the fight and soon the wild creature is dead. Roberts whips the dogs away before they can tear it to pieces and spoil it.

"An excellent bitch that, Duchess! You'll sell her to me, Powell?" Johnes has joined them for the sport. William only smiles grimly.

The gamekeeper holds up the heron. Its head lolls from the broken neck and the long legs dangle. Like a poorly-handled puppet it jerks and bobs as he speaks. "They are edible by all accounts, Sir, although I've never tasted the meat myself. Hardly seems worth dragging the blasted thing back to Nanteos!"

For a moment William looks at the bird, seeming about to speak, then does not. His eyes are fixed on the beak, broken and hanging open at an unnatural angle.

"Sir?" Roberts is uncomfortable and at last holds the body still.

"Yes," William replies at last. "Give it to the marsh bailiff. Blow that horn will you, Roberts. We must move on."

The doctor sweeps into Elizabeth's bedroom followed by Annie who struggles with the oilskin. He turns to Martha. "Who's in charge?" She nods. "Good God, woman – it's far too hot in here! And get those drapes open, it's like a cave!"

He flings down a large bag and pulls out a baize cloth, setting out some forceps, a small saw, scissors, rolled cat gut and a large needle. He thrusts a bottle of unlabelled red wine at Elin. "Get this heated up, will you." She stands dumb. "To sterilise the instruments! We're not in the Middle Ages now." Elizabeth seems to be dozing, not even registering the man's presence. "Right, an examination's in order, I think." He turns away, rubbing his hands.

Mari and Martha move Elizabeth onto her back, bending her legs at the knees and hitching up her nightdress. The skin of her belly has a bruised look, dark purple stretch marks having been clawed from her navel right to her pubic bone. As the man turns his face back towards them, they put a sheet over her. The doctor disappears under the white tent. At first it is only a groan but then Elizabeth's protest turns to a wail and finally a scream as she twists herself backwards and away from him. His face appears, dishevelled and alarmed but he says only, "The head is not yet at the gate."

Mari is holding Elizabeth to her breast, humming to her and rocking her. Though intended to comfort, her actions are jerky and urgent, Elizabeth's damp face squashed to her chest, her hair matted with perspiration. Martha silently holds up the crumpled, blood-stained sheet in accusation.

The doctor holds his hand up in front of him as if to ward off a blow. "Yes, yes I know – the womb cleanses itself. Maybe the afterbirth is low…" His voice falters.

Elizabeth is mumbling to herself. On her lips is a litany of the names of the farms on the Powell estate. Mari stands back as Martha pours a goblet of caudle from the jug by the fire and goes to comfort her.

"What is that? We don't give spiced wine in the birthing room anymore! Get rid of it – in fact we'll drink it ourselves. She can have a few sips of good water." He rinses his hands in a bowl and wipes them on his britches. "Get me a man to meet me downstairs, will you," he orders Elin, as she puts the caudle in his outstretched hand.

As the doctor downs a large glass of port in the study, John looks on. "Where did you say your master is? Why are you still here?"

"Men have already gone after him, Sir. He could be anywhere from the salt marsh to the fish ponds!"

"Can't you get out and find him, man?"

John draws himself up to his full height. "I am in charge here. The master said I was to take charge of Nanteos – of the situation." The doctor snorts in derision. "I will send Jenkins after him, Sir," he continues quickly. "He was bred on the marshes. He will surely be able to tell where they would go."

"Get him in here. I myself will write what Powell must know."

John leaves and the doctor pulls his chair up to the fire. He presses his temples hard with his third finger and thumb, trying to relieve the pressure building there.

John comes in with Jenkins. The doctor appraises him for a moment. "You ride?"

"Not fast, but sure, Sir."

"You have children?" Jenkins nods. The doctor rubs at his forehead, irritated by the pain there. "Paper, pen," he snaps. John hurries out. "Her pains are stopping," he says suddenly, getting to his feet and going to the window where visibility is now no more than ten feet. "This baby is blocked. I can see only blood, fresh blood. I shouldn't be speaking about it, I... it is beyond my skill." Jenkins looks at him in horror. The doctor turns back into the room, clears his throat and continues. "You must go as fast as you can and find the Rev. Powell. Deliver my letter. Then send a younger man back with it."

"Sir... if I may?" Jenkins gestures to the door. "I must make ready."

"Of course, of course. I'll send John after you with the note in a moment."

Jenkins nods quickly and leaves.

Elizabeth doesn't react as Martha, Mari and Sarah quietly change the blood-sodden rags and cloths.

"Try and keep her awake, try and get her to drink," the doctor says. Martha gives him a scathing look as she pushes past with a bloody bundle. "I need to examine her again," he mumbles. "Her pains have stopped."

She confronts him. "It was after you examined her the last time that she started to bleed worse than a bacon pig!"

"Do what you're told, woman, or get back to the kitchen," he snaps.

Martha only shrugs at his rudeness and carries on. He examines Elizabeth again, no longer bothering with the modesty sheet. She writhes in pain.

One of the lead dogs comes back, wearing otter spraint like ambergris all across his shoulder and flank. The others crowd around him, brushing against him, trying to pick up some of the stink on their own coats. The frenzied cry goes up from the pack and is echoed by the men.

"A scent!"

Now the hounds gather together, excited and purposeful, noses to the ground. For a moment William stands completely still as the animals surge around him.

"Sir?" Roberts looks at him expectantly, but William seems not to have heard him. He calls again. "Reverend Powell, Sir?" But William still doesn't acknowledge him. Roberts looks round uneasily, but none of the other men has noticed anything amiss. He moves the animals aside and goes to stand by his master, asking in a low voice, "Sir, will I call the pack to order?"

William, his chin to his chest, shakes his head, as if ridding his wig of a wasp or a bee. For a moment Roberts goes to laugh at the sight, but William's expression is still vague, his eyes focused somewhere up ahead.

Johnes, flicking his whip to clear the dogs out of his path, joins them. "What are we waiting for, Powell? It begins!"

William pauses for a moment before looking down at his friend. "Yes." Again he makes that movement with his head and Roberts sees that he is crying.

Johnes looks at Roberts, but before he has a chance to speak, William has composed himself and turns to face the gathering. "Now. Now we will take him and Thomas will be avenged! My son..." His voice falters and Roberts brings the horn quickly to his lips. The low, repetitive echo of the pack latched onto a scent begins as they move inland, following the river.

Jenkins is passing the lake when he meets Cai returning home from the mine. Cai smiles at him in surprise – ordinarily Jenkins is reluctant to ride, though he is good enough with the horses in-hand. The older man stops, relief clearly written on his face, hoping for a chance to pass his errand to a more skilled rider.

Before he can speak himself, Cai asks, "Where are you going in such haste? How do you take a hunter for yourself, Jenkins?" Then suddenly, his voice urgent, he asks. "How does she do?" Jenkins just stares at him. "Mistress Elizabeth – how is she?"

"Very ill." The man looks down.

"But she has had others. She has never lost a child!"

"She bleeds; fresh blood the doctor says. I'm to fetch the master."

Cai looks in panic up at the house where a sickly yellow candle burns in the window of Elizabeth's bedroom. Lady, so close to home and her feed, frets and leans on the bit. He checks her roughly. "Who is with her? Tell me, man – who aids her?"

"The doctor from town. All is being done – but he says it is beyond his skill. Her pains have stopped."

For a moment Cai is unable to act. Torn between his instinct to go to her, snatch her from them and squeeze his strength into her, and his sense which tells him only Gruffydd can save her – he fights against himself. Tormented, he can only sit his mare as she restlessly turns circles on the drive. Then, "Give me your horse," he barks.

"I cannot! I must find the master!" Jenkins goes to gather up his reins and kick his gelding on but Cai is too quick for him and takes hold of the bridle.

"Get down – or I knock you down!"

Jenkins looks up at Cai in shock. The young man's face is desperate with fear. Now the old servant knows what he had only before suspected. Surprising even himself, he silently lets go of the reins and drops to the ground. He will turn back, stable Lady and find another mount for what he knows will be a fruitless journey to the salt marshes.

Cai thrusts himself across to the fresh horse and puts his crop to the startled animal's haunches. As he reaches the lodge the gates have been closed behind him so he backs up the hunter and takes the wall.

Inside Gruffydd's hut it is gloomy, although the low fog that plagues the valley does not come this far up. He makes hurried preparations as Cai paces, distracted.

"The blood is fresh, you say Cai? Red blood?"

"What other colour is there?"

"It's important – blood from an old bleed is brown. Haemorrhage or fever –"

"Then red. Please! Give it to me, I can take it so much faster."

"Calm yourself. Let me think… Is she fevered? Does her head ache?"

"I can take it!"

"You cannot! This is ergot – it could kill her, and the child. You should have followed the craft."

"For God's sake – now is not the time to lecture me! Can you save her?"

"I will try," he says, grimly. "I know what you've done

together, what this means." His eyes are the cool white-blue that give nothing away, the disorientating effect enhanced by his pale lashes.

"How? Who has told you?" Gruffydd shrugs. "Then why did you not try and stop it?"

"No one could."

"I must get back to them!" Cai slams out of the hut and pulls the tack onto Gruffydd's mule. The old man comes out with his satchel and fastens it to the saddle. "But please, won't you take my horse? I'll run cross-country." Gruffydd only shakes his head, turns and goes back inside.

He is banking up the fire with turf as Cai rounds on him again. "Come, I beg you – she's dying!"

"Just calm yourself, Cai. I'll ride my mule – I need to break and warm the ointment in my hands as I go. I need a steady mount. I cannot rush this."

"Then, move. For pity's sake!" Cai grabs at Gruffydd. The young man's hand is big and reaches right around the older man's arm, trying to shift him away from his task.

Gruffydd stops. He is still looking into the fire as he says quietly. "Let go."

"Elizabeth bleeds to death and you arrange your fire!"

"This fire must not go out." Cai has not moved. "Let go." This time his voice is even quieter, but he still does not look up. Though thin, Gruffydd's arm is rope-strong and Cai has to work hard to restrain him. "You are wasting what time she has left."

With a moan of despair Cai lets him go.

Catherine slides in, shutting the door quietly behind her. "Mama?" There is no answer. On silent feet she reaches the bed. Elizabeth's hand rests outside the sheet and the girl lifts it and squeezes it hard to her cheek. Elizabeth opens her eyes and a look of pain, that is nothing to do with her haemorrhaging body, passes across her face. She turns her hand so that it cups her daughter's jaw.

"Mama?" Catherine is crying now and Elizabeth bites her lip to stop her own tears.

"I am well, Catherine," she says. "What do you do here?" Catherine shakes her head. Her sobs are audible now and she has hiccups.

The child climbs onto the bed and snuggles under her mother's arm. For a moment or two they are still, the vibrations that wrack the young girl's body seeming to subside. "I want to help you," she says, her voice wobbly.

"Pardon, my darling. What did you say?"

Catherine sits up and holds her mother's hand. "Please, Mama. Don't send me away, please let me help you!" Her face is earnest, her eyes bright through the tears.

"Help me sit up a little then." As they struggle to prop Elizabeth up on her pillows she sees the primroses, still alive in the glass. "Ah! You *can* help me," she says. "These, these little flowers must go back. Take them back, Catherine, I don't want them to die here."

The girl nods solemnly and picks up the posy, soil and water dripping onto the sheet. "Oh!"

"No matter. Keep them in your bedroom tonight and at first light tomorrow, get John to take you to the tree on the ridge. Do you know the fine tree, the oak tree that I can see from this window?"

"That I drew? That I drew when you were not well before?"

"The same. Cai took them for me..." her voice falters.

The door opens and the doctor comes in followed by Martha and Mari, who holds William by the hand.

"There you are, child. Thank the good Lord you are not

lost! I've been searching the house for you! Come from here!" exclaims Martha.

"Children in the birthing room! Get her out!" The doctor turns to Martha.

"No!" Catherine is crying, scrambling across the bed. Martha and Mari go after her and pull her by the arms. She wails and kicks out.

"I've never seen her like this!" Martha cries, her cap knocked across her face.

"Stop this, now!" The doctor's face is red and he too helps to drag the girl from the room. She grabs onto the door frame and Martha has to prize her fingers, one by one, from the wood. In a panic, William begins to cry too and the doctor slaps him hard across his cheek. He gasps in shock and holds his breath. "Get them out!" the man shouts, exasperated. Without further ceremony he pushes the women and children out onto the landing and slams the door.

Catherine still holds the remains of the primroses tightly in her fist, though they are hardly recognisable. Only William is crying now, though he seems calmer with his face buried tight into Mari's shoulder. Martha bends down and takes Catherine's wrists in her hands. "I'm sorry..." The girl won't look at her. "Your Mama, she mustn't see you crying – it'll upset the baby and make her bleed." She waits for a response – there is none. "Do you understand me, Catherine? She must not be upset." Almost imperceptibly, the child nods. "What are these?" she asks, her voice kind.

Catherine gulps and when she speaks her voice is a whisper. "Tomorrow I must take them back and plant them by the tree up there." She gestures vaguely.

Martha and Mari exchange glances over her head. There's a pause. "Catherine, you must not go into this room again – for any reason, not until the baby is safely born. Do you understand me?" The girl is looking down, she shakes her by the shoulders, "Not for any reason! Oh, it won't be long now," she adds hastily as she sees Catherine beginning to cry again. "Mama needs to rest and she will want Mari with her. Will you go to Elin and help keep William company, like a good girl?"

Catherine nods. She is shaking slightly as she puts her free hand in Mari's outstretched palm. The three have gone out of sight before Martha opens the bedroom door again.

Inside, the doctor is collecting up his tools as quietly as possible. He hisses at Martha. "That did her no good at all! I've had to hold her down and force a hemlock tincture into her! Do you not know that a woman must be kept as calm as possible in the birthing room?"

Martha looks at him but says nothing. Finally he straightens up and snaps his bag shut. "Where is the man I met earlier – the valet?"

"John? He will be about no doubt. He never strays far from the house."

"Get him to meet us in the kitchens. I must act now."

Martha is frozen to spot. "What do you mean?"

"The labouring has stopped. It is like a sealed chamber with no windows – Powell's child is slowly suffocating to death."

"How would you… but what will you do?"

"There are ways and means. Don't stand there with your mouth slack – find him. We have no more time."

Mari, John, Martha and the doctor gather in the kitchen. Not one of them can bear to sit down.

The doctor begins. "I must speak to Powell. I need to know what he wants me to do. It's getting too late to act. There must be someone else we can send after him!"

"Everyone who can has gone, Sir," says John. His habitually neat hair is dishevelled now and his waistcoat undone. "Is there nothing we can do for her?"

"You can pray," the doctor says under his breath.

"I wish Cai were here! He would find the master. He rides with the wind." Martha's face is grey with strain.

"Oh where the hell is Powell?" The doctor punches the table in frustration and John looks at him in amazement. He rounds on him. "You – for pity's sake, you go and try and find him."

"But I… I don't really ride. I would not know where to look. I'm an inside servant."

"Get out there, man. Do something!"

John reluctantly leaves the room. The doctor turns to Mari. "Go to your mistress and stay with her. Keep her calm. Agree with her – pretend to understand what she says, she must be roused as little as possible before the… procedure."

Mari looks from one to the other. Martha's face has a doughy texture, all colour seeming to have drained into her neck which flares, red and blotchy. She nods briefly and Mari does as she's been asked.

Only Martha and the doctor are left in the kitchen. His sleeves are still rolled up and there is dried blood under his nails. His voice is expressionless as he says, "We must bring her downstairs. Prepare the table."

"But you can't! She'll die."

"She'll die if I don't… and the baby with her. I've heard of some who've survived."

"Oh God!" Martha's feet buckle underneath her and she reaches for the corner of the table for support. "I'll get the girl to take the children away. Far, as far as when a pig's slit," she says at last.

"Then scrub the table with vinegar and build up the fire." As he turns away he takes another deep draught from the bottle at his elbow.

Martha goes out into the hall. Mari is sitting on the bottom step, her face cradled in her hands. She looks up at the older woman but can only shake her head. Martha slumps to sit down beside her. "The children are to go away overnight, Mari. I'll tell Elin to take them to the lodge. If John hasn't gone already, I'll get rid of him there too; no point sending that fool out on the marsh."

Mari looks up, her face miserable with crying. "I know what it means." Martha is confused. "The table; the instruments in his bag. I know what he is to do. I have heard tell of it. It's not right!"

Martha doesn't answer but puts her arm around the girl's shoulders. She squeezes tight, so tight that it hurts, but Mari doesn't move away. "Go now, Mari," she whispers. "Do your job for our mistress." Her voice falters and she gets to her feet, leaning on her knees for support.

Elizabeth is watching Mari who stands at the bedroom window. Although it's only five in the afternoon it's already getting dark. She struggles to move her jewel box from under the bedclothes.

"You're awake!" cries Mari. "Oh please be well."

She climbs on the bed. Elizabeth winces.

"Where are your pains, Mistress? Doesn't the baby try to get out any more?"

"It is not as it should be. It is not as it was before," she sighs. "Where is Cai, Mari?"

"He... I don't know."

"Will you sing to me, Mari?"

The girl nods and comes to lie beside her. She sings softly, her voice faltering from time to time. Elizabeth seems to drift off. Then she says, her eyes still closed, "Where have you taken my children?"

Mari sits up sharply. "They are gone to the lodge with Elin. The doctor thought it better that they should go far away." She gets up and, keeping her face hidden from the older woman, busies herself with the fire. Elizabeth nods.

"Come back here, Mari." With a supreme effort of will, Elizabeth heaves herself into a sitting position, pulls back the bedclothes and gestures to the casket of jewels hidden there. "Lose it in water."

"What do you mean? Mistress?"

"I'm trusting it to you. Lose it in water."

"But what about the Reverend Powell, Mistress? What of Catherine?"

"Don't curse my daughter with it!"

There is the sound of commotion on the stairs and Mari hastily hides the box under the bed.

Martha, the doctor and Sarah come in, the women's faces tight with strain. He kneels by Elizabeth's bed, his voice strangely tender. He takes her hand and looks into her face. "We've come to take you down. We need to move you, I'm afraid. I think I can help you, but I'll need more room and other... tools."

"Where is William?" She is starting to cry.

They begin to move her, lifting her sheet and using it as a sling. She groans as they heave her up, slung like a deer carcass, between them.

"Oh where is Cai?" she whimpers in pain as they carry her down the stairs, her nightdress crimson. Metal instruments wait, gleaming by the fire as they enter the kitchen.

On the mountain, Gruffydd has left his mule and is gathering sphagnum moss. His voice can hardly be heard over the wind.

"Just wait, Cai! I'll rub the ergot into the moss as an enema to plug the bleeding."

The young man's horse snorts and paws the ground. "Hurry, I beg of you!"

"Wait! Be patient. There's nothing more you can do."

But Cai wheels his horse around and gallops away.

Mari stands in the hallway, holding a red-stained sheet bunched around the box. All activity is centred on the kitchen now. The door opens and Annie backs out, her hand held across her mouth. She does not even see Mari. The door opens again and Martha comes raging out, shouting, "Get back in here! We need you to help hold her down... and you'll be needed to clean up." Though she looks in Mari's direction, she doesn't seem to see her.

Annie keeps moving backwards and Martha has to come almost to the bottom of the stairs to get her, grabbing her dress at the neck. The girl whimpers and goes limp and Martha is able to turn her around. Shoving her hard between the shoulders, she forces Annie back into the kitchen.

For a few minutes Mari doesn't move. Disorientated, she stands, the bundle under one arm, her other hand twisting the cloth of her skirt into a ball. Then from the kitchen comes a scream – starting low, it builds to such a pitch that Mari runs from the house and, flinging the box onto the grass, falls to her knees, her hands clasped against her ears.

The party of men and dogs is concentrated on the river bank, moving purposefully. Even the noise of the hounds, random and chaotic before, has become uniform and rhythmic.

"Send the men with horses upstream and start to beat down towards us!" Powell bellows.

"Sir, I believe he must have his den near the weir… though we never did find it before."

"We'll find it today!"

As Cai appears at the gatehouse, mercilessly whipping the exhausted gelding, he sees Mari rowing the small boat into the centre of the lake. It wobbles dangerously as she pulls unevenly on the oars. For a moment he hesitates but, though she looks his way, she does not stop or call out to him. He focuses again on the house where the front door is wide open, Elizabeth's window dark now. For the last time he puts the whip to the horse's flank.

On the lake Mari stops rowing and drags the oars into the boat. It lurches as she heaves the bundle to one side, almost tipping over as she eases the weight out onto the water. With hardly a sound the jewel box sinks from sight.

Men and dogs are gathered at the weir.

"Don't let the hounds in there, Sir, they'll drown themselves!" shouts Roberts.

But William, triumphant at last, refuses to hear him. Eyes gleaming he shouts again and again. "He was right! Thomas was right. The devil's here, right under our noses all along!"

"Sir, don't go so near, you'll fall in!"

"Dig the bank away!"

One of the tenant farmers calls out, "He'll escape into the river as soon as he feels the spades!"

"Send in the dogs to head him off!" orders William.

"But sir, the current's too –"

"Get out of my way, Roberts –"

William grabs a long-handled spade and begins to dig. Johnes gestures to the men to loose the dogs and they hurtle into the river. All is chaos. Some of the hounds are fighting each other; others are carried downstream, men trying to get at them. Some of the men climb into the torrent, forming a human chain for safety and stretching out the otter nets under the water line. Desperately, they hold them taut against the ferocious current.

The river men have trapped the huge dog otter and struggle with it to the bank. It fights, claws and teeth trying to slash through the net, the powerful tail, pure muscle, thrashing, strong enough to knock a man down. Several try to get their spears into it, to hold it still for the final blow with the spade behind the head. Others struggle to keep the roaring, frustrated hounds at bay.

"What a beauty! Take care to preserve the head! Preserve the head, Powell!" screams Johnes.

"And the tail, Sir!" Roberts begs.

But with a strangled roar William snatches the spade. At first he uses the iron, bringing it flat down to bludgeon the writhing animal to death.

Gradually the men's shouts die away, silenced by the relentless, sickening thuds of the spade and one by one they turn from the sight of him, on his knees now, grunting with effort, the butt of the implement smashing the creature's skull to pulp.

At the house, Cai hurls himself from his horse. He pauses for a moment at the bottom of the stairs and calls out. A baby's scream makes him turn towards the kitchen.

At first he doesn't understand what he sees. Steam from the boiling water and candlelight bouncing off the coppers confuses the scene. As he comes further into the room, Annie, frozen, a handkerchief across her mouth, blocks his path. As he takes her by the shoulders and moves her aside she looks up at him, her eyes are white, but she makes no sound. There is a metallic smell in the room, like rain on hard earth.

He sees Martha by the fire, holding a wailing child to her bosom. But he cannot find Elizabeth. Next he focuses on the doctor who busies himself at the table, his arms red to the elbow. The table has been moved so that it sits against the iron roasting spit from which a length of rope hangs. Martha notices him, cries out, and suddenly he understands. The doctor straightens up, his face blotched and crumpled and at last he sees her hair, just visible beneath a sheet.

"No!"

As he crosses to the table the doctor tries to stop him but it is as if Cai moves through him. He groans and pushes the material away. Her face is soaking, yet from the chest upwards, she is herself – both arms still in the sleeves of her nightgown. But below this is another sheet, rucked up and covered in blood that is beginning to turn black. The scent of offal – warm and obscene, rises. A noise, hardly human, comes from him as he tries to gather her up but she is floppy and he cannot bear to disturb the mess below her waist. He fingers the rope tied to one of her arms, not making the connection. Bending across the table he lifts only her head in his hands and kisses her face.

"She's still breathing! She lives!" No one moves. "Sew her up; sew her up, you bastard!" he roars, grabbing the doctor by the throat. As he is forced back towards the table, the smaller man picks up a knife and holds it under Cai's jaw. There seems to be a noise from the table and Cai, distracted, lets him go. He holds his hand under Elizabeth's neck, bending his face towards her lips. There is no pulse. "No!" He climbs onto the table and lifts her torso to him, clutching it in a bear hug as her head lolls back and her arms hang loose like broken wings.

Gruffydd is cantering down the mountain road. Suddenly he pulls up and listens, his eyes closed. Under the gasps of the wind he hears a woman's scream of agony echo through the pass. Slowly he opens the bag of fresh moss. Piece by piece rolls out over the blasted grass and is carried away by the wind.

Also by the author:

the geometry of love

jane blank

"The funniest, sexiest novel I've read in a long time"
NORMAN SCHWENK

Fast-paced and darkly funny, *The Geometry of Love* is set in Sheffield in the 1980s where New Romantics vie with Northern Soulers for control of the clubs and the fashion scene. The miners are on strike, Thatcher is in power, but all this means nothing to two teenage girls looking for kicks, their one aim – to lose their virginity. In the wake of their fascination with Omar, a gorgeous French-Algerian, the action moves to France. The story, however, remains one of obsession: what happens when childhood friends refuse to let go and when East collides with West in a pre 9/11 world.

£7.95 (978 1 84771 039 0)

Reviews and quotes about *The Geometry of Love*

"The teenage sexual odyssey Jane Blank describes in *The Geometry of Love* is written with honesty, verve and humour. The author has a poet's eye for detail and the frankness of the young narrator's observations accurately reflects the obsessive nature of youth. As we follow the physical adventures of Susan and Miranda, it is touching to witness the ways in which these young women begin to form themselves. The resolution of the final section is both difficult and poignant. A book to transport the reader back to our pre-sexual – and yet most sexual – selves."

Hannah Vincent

"Blank's writing is suffused with tenderness and compassion, and her acute portrayal of the shifting emotions and unrepeatable intimacy of teenage girls is both touching and memorable."

Suzy Ceulan Hughes
(A review from www.gwales.com
with the permission of the Welsh Books Council.)

"A novel which explores clashes of culture in pre-9/11 Britain, *The Geometry of Love* deals with the fascination the West has with eastern culture and the Muslim religion. The influence a Muslim friend has on two young girls in their quest for the good things in life is revealing and is based on some true experiences."

Western Mail

"The funniest, sexiest book I've read in a long time."

Norman Schwenk

"Witty and saucy."

Bill Gallagher

Jane Blank's work has won prizes and awards and has been featured in numerous magazines and anthologies including *Planet, New Welsh Review, Poetry Wales, Poetry Quarterly Review, Western Mail, The Big Issue, Observer Magazine* and *The Independent.*

www.jane-blank.info